WITHIN THESE COUNTY LINES

Brian Zepka

Pennor Books

For Brooks and Graham.

It's never too late.

1

Warm blood trails down my forehead and into my eyes, turning the familiar emerald woods bordering my town into a copper-stained blur.

My breath comes fast and thin, each inhale barely filling my lungs. My heavy stomps crunch leaves and snap twigs beneath me like a chase scene straight out of a horror film. But the ache in my limbs, the tight pull of my muscles, keep reminding me this is real.

"Stetson, wait!" my ex-boyfriend, Murray, yells in a shrill voice as he runs after me.

He's my ex-boyfriend as of ten minutes ago.

I keep my back to him and quicken my pace.

His voice used to be my favorite sound. Its melody a line I blindly followed because wherever it took me felt like home.

Now it's an alarm, telling me to flee.

I wonder how something so familiar can become foreign, but then he calls out for me again and the pounding in my chest becomes the new beat I follow toward escape.

"I'm sorry!" he shouts. I gulp more air. "Please come back. We can get past this!"

The blood reaches my lips. I spit, but the taste of salt and metal lingers on my tongue. His shouts fade into the background as they're lost beneath the sound of my own ragged sobs.

I run until the sky melts into dusk, no destination in mind. The woods are familiar enough that I don't need a trail. My feet know the way, even if I don't. I only let up when I'm sure Murray is far behind, then force myself to silence the shaky breaths that might give me away.

Cross-country felt like a mistake when it led me to him sophomore year outside of the football stadium where he practiced. But now it's my salvation. My legs carry me far, fast, and away from our relationship once and for all.

When I finally stand still, my heart slams against my ribs as it slows. Colorful specks appear in my vision. I'm unsure if they're from the blood and sweat coating my face or the brain fog blooming in my head. I reach for the shifting circles, my fingers grasping at nothing, as if they can be squashed like bubbles. I want them to burst and disappear, along with the memory of their cause.

I get dizzy as I chase them, and before I know it, I hit the ground hard.

But I don't mind. The cool soil seeps into my skin. It's a welcome bit of relief after being on my feet since morning. This is the safest spot I've been all day, miles deep in the woods as the sun sets and the coyotes begin to howl.

When my awareness creeps back, I scrape my fingers through loose dirt, uncovering the top of a concrete sewer pipe buried like bone beneath the earth. My eyes follow its path until it emerges at a slope, where a thick, orange liquid drips from the rim, slow and syrupy. The entire opening is drowned in graffiti—neon yellow, green, pink, and orange clash against

2

the murky browns of the woods and the shadows of tangled leaves.

I drag myself toward softer ground, but my shoulder slams into a tree. Wincing, I tilt my head back. Carved hearts cover its bark, climbing skyward until they vanish into the canopy. The tree's roots stretch down the hill and twist around the pipe as if trying to crush it closed.

A long, slow sigh escapes me. I've been here before. I don't know how I didn't recognize it sooner, how I didn't realize where I was in these woods. Almost everyone in my hometown of Penango, Pennsylvania, has stood in this exact spot at least once.

This is the Ardor Tree.

Couples from Penango County's Stillwell Trail High School come here to carve their names into its trunk, believing it will bind them together forever. But I've come to learn that's far from true. Some promises are meant to break.

I push myself to my feet and take a slow, unsteady lap around the tree, trailing my fingers over the carved names. Then I reach the one I know best. My hand stills. My breath catches. And I pause.

Stetson + Murray.

I press my palm against our names, hard. The rough bark picks at my skin like tiny shards of glass. Heat rises in my neck, my blood simmering. This is what Murray always wanted—Penango County permanence. How was I ever supposed to move on from my relationship when it's carved into this town?

I wonder how the other names on this tree have fared, if they made it out of Penango, if their love stories had happier endings.

Michael and Alyssa sit right above us. Maybe they own a house outside of Pittsburgh with two kids in a quiet neighborhood. Below our heart, *Emily & Duncan* rest in the bark. I imagine they got married right after graduating from Stillwell Trail High but packed their bags for Chicago. They got out.

I search the tree for another heart like ours, two boys' names intertwined. But it's hard to tell. A heart a few steps over reads *Jesse 'n Mark*. It could be two guys. It could not be. But does it really matter? I don't want to be tied to Penango forever, stuck wondering about the lives of people who left their marks before me. That's how it goes around here. People worry about their neighbors until their own life has come and gone.

I roll my eyes before spitting at a rock half buried in the mud. We're raised to stay put. The world builds fake walls around us—county lines and carved hearts—to keep us trapped. If we leave, we're either abandoning our home or breaking someone's heart. We're told we need to start fresh or start over.

Why can't we just continue?

I pick up the rock, still slick with my bubbling saliva, and slam it against the *Stetson + Murray* engraving. The sharpest edge chips the *S* from my name after only a few swipes. My strength takes my breath away.

I don't want the next gay kid in Penango to stumble across the tree and mistake this heart for something it wasn't. This isn't the kind of love they should hope for.

Sometimes love doesn't last. And most of the time, it's better if it doesn't.

More chunks of bark fly from the tree as my fear hardens into anger. Every time the rock connects with the trunk, a sharp jolt of heat surges through my fingers. I squeeze my eyes shut and keep swinging.

Time passes. I'm not sure how many seconds or minutes. But when I finally stop, breathless, a fresh patch of pale bark stares back at me. I step aside, shoulders sinking as I take in the mess I've made. Now there's space for someone new. Maybe one day I'll bring another boy here to carve our names. But never someone from within these county lines.

The rock slips from my calloused hand, falls to the ground, and rolls a few feet down the hill. I wipe my dry lips before turning away from the Ardor Tree.

But the forest floor stops me from moving with a rumble. My feet falter.

"What the . . . ?" I ask aloud. I spread my arms for balance just as the ground settles. It's quiet, only for a few seconds, before the world shakes again.

This time, harder. Much harder.

I fall.

"Oh my gosh. Earthquake!" I yell out the warning as if I'm not alone. My knee slams into a thick root. I wince. "There's an earthquake!"

I've never experienced an earthquake before. How long do these last? I wonder if one of the nearby factories exploded. I search for smoke on the horizon but see something else.

The Ardor Tree's roots slither around me like a pit of snakes. They slink in and out of the ground, over rocks, up other trees, and through the sewer pipe. I rub my fists into my eyes, unsure if what I'm seeing is real or just a hallucination brought on by the hours of running through the woods.

I try to clear my vision, but no matter how many times I blink, the roots keep moving. The tree canopy above me sways, then the leaves fall in thick clusters. I shield my face from swirling debris.

This is not a normal earthquake—if it's even an earthquake at all.

"Help!" I scream, but no one is around. I've run too far. Safety in this county is just an illusion.

A deafening boom shakes the air behind me. I whip around just in time to see a massive branch swinging down from overhead like a wrecking ball. I throw myself to the side, barely avoiding its impact as it slams into the earth with a force that rattles my bones.

Another boom.

More branches descend, their offshoots twisting for my body. I can't dodge them all. One lashes my cheek, and my head nearly spins off my shoulders. I stagger, then collapse to the ground, too exhausted to get back up. My muscles are spent.

The roots wind around my limbs and slowly pull me into the earth.

I give in, staring at the endless navy sky. Tears slip past my temples as I mourn its possibilities that remain just out of reach.

The faint stars disappear with one fell swoop, like someone shoveling a final patch of dirt over my grave.

2

The next morning, I arrive at the Penango County Health Department at exactly eight thirty a.m. to begin my summer job as a pool inspector.

One earbud plays the *Stuff You Should Know* podcast in my left ear while my right takes in the squeak of shoes scraping against the linoleum.

The hosts are talking about the ocean currents, describing their force and unpredictability. The closest I've been to the ocean is staring at a screen saver in the school library. But the way they talk about its power tempts me to drive straight to the coast and throw myself in, just to be spit out somewhere new.

Yesterday was dark, to say the least. A complete crash out.

I woke on the forest floor beneath a star-filled sky, after the Ardor Tree's roots choked me until the world went black. The ground was still, and the branches calm, as though nothing had happened. A pair of squirrels scurried along the tree's limbs as if they were the safest path through the woods, probably just to humiliate me.

It all passed like an unexpected nightmare. I was sweaty and startled, but fine.

At home, Mom and Dad had no idea what I was talking about. They said they never felt an earthquake—had never heard of one happening in all Penango County history. Mom blamed it on my terrible sleep habits. Dad asked if I was drunk. I wasn't. And even if I was, my time with Murray would have sobered me up real fast.

In the bathroom mirror, my cheek, where the branch had whipped me, was smooth, untouched. No marks, no scars, nothing on my arms where those twisting branches should've left something behind.

The only proof that anything happened yesterday is the gash on my forehead. And I know exactly what caused that.

I'm glad the tree didn't leave my face even more busted before college, but it would've been nice to get some confirmation about yesterday's chain of events.

Maybe it was just stress. Maybe whatever panic knocked me to the ground before it all started had crawled into my brain and distorted my fears into something I could see instead of just feel.

Murray must be to blame. Another reason to stay away from him for the rest of summer. I can't risk another hallucination that makes me lose sight of my way out of Penango.

I'm hoping this morning will refresh my brain's algorithm and vanish yesterday into the dark web of my suppressed memories.

"What the hell happened to your head?" Whitley Wyomen, my best friend, asks by the health department's entrance doors, her eyes narrowed at my forehead.

8

Okay. Never mind. I forgot I need to turn off public comments if I want a true reset.

Her tone is light and breathy, and her accent a mix of Valley girl with some southern charm, like if you combined Paris Hilton's voice with Dolly Parton's. Because of this, people write her off as an airhead, but she's more determined and has got a wider range of interests than anyone I know. I can't think of another person who is first-chair clarinet in the all-county concert ensemble *and* strong enough to split enough wood each winter to heat every home south of Pittsburgh.

"I'm not ready to talk about it," I say, picking at my jet-black arm hair.

Mom and I share the same dark hair and pale skin. Dad jokes that we look like Morticia and Wednesday Addams. It's only funny to him because he has brown hair and olive skin that gets tan like Whitley's.

She raises her eyebrow. "What kind of answer is that? It looks bad. Should you get stitches?"

"It's clotting up," I say, stroking the wound with my thumb. "I didn't feel like driving an hour to the hospital."

"Well, how did the talk with Murray go yesterday?" Her dry blond hair falls off her shoulder as we move.

I swallow and crank up my podcast volume.

Mom is always yelling at me, "Take those damn things out of your ears." She claims there's no way I can pay attention to my surroundings while listening to music, podcasts, and books twenty-four seven. Her point is well taken. I've listened to podcasts that say you can't truly multitask. But I'm not convinced. After all, Murray managed to love me while hurting me at the same time.

Instead of answering her, I ask the front desk worker where the summer orientation is.

They point us past security and I step through the metal detector, pretending it's an airport TSA screening, something I've never actually experienced.

I've barely crossed the Pennsylvania state line. Once for a family reunion in Ohio, another time for a school field trip to Washington, DC.

I wonder what it's like to fly somewhere far away, out of reach of the hands that have harmed me.

The orientation room holds twelve people—thirteen if you count Victor, the environmental health specialist who interviewed us in the spring, now standing behind a podium. I always count crowds. It's a habit, something that comforts me when I arrive somewhere new. I even convinced the athletic department at school to let me run a *guess the attendance* contest at football games. It helps to know the proportion of strangers around me. I calculate friends and foes, entrances and exits. *React with evidence rather than emotion*—it's a favorite podcast quote of mine.

Victor starts the presentation, and a projector balanced on a tower of orange milk crates flicks on, casting a slide across the wall: *What do I do about solid stool in the pool?* Whitley snorts. I consider popping in my second earbud.

Nothing can describe the start of my summer better than stool graphs.

Our job is to inspect the pools across the county to make sure they're safe, clean of bacteria, and properly chlorinated. I'm not sure how good I'll be at it considering I can't even keep my own life from being a mess.

"I didn't know poop could be so serious," Whitley whispers.

The corner of my lip twitches. I cover my mouth to suppress a laugh. It's the first time I've smiled in two days.

That's the thing about Whitley: No matter how bad things get, she always finds a way to turn things around.

"Was your stool solid this morning?" she asks.

A gust of wind sends an overgrown tree branch scraping against the window. I jump, clutching my waist. No one else in the room flinches.

I up the podcast volume again, needing the distraction, unsure where my thoughts will lead or which trees they'll bring to life.

"You can find a list of sanitary fecal disposal methods on page three of your handouts," Victor drones.

I flip open my orientation folder, but I find myself scanning my own résumé where my eyes snag on one word right next to *University of Tennessee: (tentative)*.

My stomach twists.

My college enrollment still depends on financial aid, but at this point, I've filled out so many forms, I have no idea who I'm waiting on. Tennessee? Pennsylvania? The governor himself?

I emailed a help center last week, and all I got so far was an automated *thank you for your email* response. The thought of some machine scanning my application and deciding my future in seconds hardens my stomach even further.

Murray's voice creeps in too, the low, piercing tone he used all senior year to tell me I'm not cut out for college, that maybe Pennsylvania is as far as I'll ever get.

I grab my pencil and scratch out *(tentative)*. It's June, and college is two months away. I've made too many promises to myself to back down now. If I doubt myself, why wouldn't they? My future in Penango is tentative, not college.

I'll reset things the only official way I know how—with a No. 2 pencil, crossed fingers and toes, and a whole lot of delusion.

3

After the morning orientation, Whitley and I claim our desks upstairs before heading back down to the lobby to start our first pool inspections.

"Hello again," Victor says, waving as he takes a final sip from his drink. Ice rattles against the sides of the cup before he tosses it into the trash. A short woman stands next to him, wearing a visor so low over her eyes I can't tell where she's looking.

"This is Mary Jo," he says, gesturing to her. "She's also an environmental health specialist and will be your supervisor, Whitley." Mary Jo nods. "You'll be working with me, Stetson," he adds.

"Great," I say, forcing a smile.

I remove my left earbud, partly because it's harder to fake half-hearted listening in a one-on-one conversation, but mostly because the podcast just moved on to an episode called "Is Reality Real?" and it's hitting a little too close to the heart right now.

"Come on, Whitley," Mary Jo says. "You'll shadow me today so I can show you the ropes." She waves her along.

"Hopefully we don't have to shut down any pools today for low chlorine levels."

"Good luck," Whitley says, flashing me a peace sign before following Mary Jo out the door.

I turn back to Victor. "Should we get going too?"

He shakes his head. "The best way to learn is to get out there on your own." He claps a hand on my shoulder that sends a fit of coughs from my throat.

"You're not coming with me?"

I rub the tender patch of flesh on my head. The blood is dry and forms a fragile scab, like a thin layer of ice that could break at any moment.

Ignoring my question, Victor hands me a list of inspection sites, then taps on the paper so hard I almost drop the sheet. "I got a voicemail this morning about an old pool that's reopening and needs an inspection," he says. "I'd hit that one first. There's going to be a lot to look at. The address is on the back."

I flip the paper over. *Rainbow Valley Swim Club*.

"I've never heard of it."

Victor's eyes go wide. "That's surprising." He scratches the back of his head. "It has a colored history, you could say. Legendary almost. Like that old Ardor Tree."

My eyes go wider than his. How did I go from solving math equations in study hall to facing off against local legends in a matter of two weeks?

I know from my podcasts that the American school system is going to leave me unprepared for the real world, but dang, I didn't know it would be this bad.

Victor pulls a crumpled map from his back pocket and hands it to me confidently, as if I don't have live maps on my phone. "This will help you find your way. Good luck, kid." He turns and bolts down the hall as if he's afraid to talk about the pool any longer.

I stare at the coffee-stained mess of a map. The moment I spot the Penango River curving behind Murray's house, an ache creeps up my spine. I sigh and shove the wrinkled document into my pocket before memories of us jumping into the water from his tire swing flood in.

Like Victor, I'm scared to even think about this pool. Or the Ardor Tree. Or yesterday. Having some deep hometown lore seemed cool, until it started getting thrown back in my face. I don't want to solve it. I want to lie down.

But I need this job. More specifically, I need the money for college. So I leave on my own without asking anymore questions.

I pop both earbuds in for the drive. My old truck, handed down to me from my uncle, doesn't have Bluetooth, and I don't feel like messing with the adapter. I need loud music— something with enough drums to drown out my thoughts. The woods lining the health department seem to taunt me as I leave; their rigid branches rise like middle fingers in a crowded hallway. Dry leaves scrape across the pavement like stalking footsteps.

The swim club is twenty minutes south, just above the West Virginia border. My eyes flick between the road and my phone, waiting for an onslaught of texts from Murray. He hasn't reached out since I left yesterday.

That's what I wanted, so why does it feel so wrong?

"You've arrived," my phone announces as I pull up to a shaded driveway with no sign.

I double-check the address—it's right. But the internet calls this place *Pinehurst Swim Club, permanently closed.*

Rainbow Valley must be the new name. This is where having Victor by my side would actually come in handy.

I drive past a pile of moldy umbrellas and crumbling beach chairs, relics of a once-busy summer spot now left to rot. There are no crowds to count—just a lonely rectangular pool wedged between the trees like a piece in the game of Operation.

My jaw slackens once I get close. The water is a thick, murky green with garden snakes slithering across its surface. I gasp, glancing at nearby tree roots.

These snakes aren't hallucinations.

They're real.

"What the . . . ?" I stumble back over my own feet.

"Hello?" I shout, spinning around. "I'm from the county . . . here to inspect the pool." My voice echoes through the trees. It's silent.

I press my palms against my ears, rubbing at the cartilage to create a static that's better than the quiet.

Then, a slurping sound.

It startles me like a cold splash of water to the face.

I turn.

A shirtless boy suns himself on a lounge chair. He sips Coca-Cola through a yellow bendy straw and tosses a Skittle into his mouth between gulps.

I swear he wasn't there two seconds ago.

His skin is slick with sweat, pooling in the dips of his stomach muscles. He's tan as if he's already lived through an entire summer.

I want to say something, but I'd rather stare for a little bit longer.

He's around my age, lean and striking, like when I spot a lone, pink flower in a grassy field or catch a glimpse of a bald eagle diving from one of Penango's cliffs. His looks fill me with that same need to gasp at the rarity of the sight.

His funky, blue-lensed sunglasses and neon green earpieces add to his mystery.

If the pool's lore contains a hot boy like this, I might reconsider having a look. Heavy emphasis on *might*.

"Hello," I say, slowly approaching.

No response. Instead, he runs his hands through his curls. They bounce along with my heart.

"Do you work here?" I ask. "We got a report that this pool was reopening. You'll have to fill out a permit and undergo an inspection."

He pulls *The Dog Encyclopedia* from an orange backpack and rests it on his lap. Judging by his colorful getup, he might as well be the Rainbow Valley Swim Club mascot.

Still nothing.

I huff. His whole *too cool to acknowledge me* act is suddenly the biggest turnoff. Another boy from Penango who can't communicate. I shouldn't have expected anything different.

"Hello?" I try again. It almost comes out as a yell.

Finally, he glances up.

I wave.

He stares for a moment, expressionless. Then he looks behind him, as if I'm speaking to someone else.

"Yo!" This time I shout. "What is your problem? I'm talking to you."

He flinches.

For a split second, I feel guilty for snapping. His finger slowly lifts to his own chest.

"Are you . . ." He swallows. "Are you talking to me?"

"Who else would I be talking to?" I throw up my hands.

His expression changes. "You can see me?" His voice cracks.

"Obviously."

His back straightens. "What am I wearing?"

I squint. "Uh, a yellow bathing suit. Nothing else."

He screams, then holds up his book. "What am I reading?"

"An encyclopedia about dogs."

"You can see me!" This time it's not a question.

"Yeah? Why wouldn't I be able to see you?"

Without warning, he springs to his feet and hurls his book into the grass. The small wooden table beside him tips over and sends the Coca-Cola bottle crashing onto the concrete.

He lunges toward me. His body slams into mine with full force. I stumble, and my heel catches the pool's edge. His arms clamp around me, tightening like the Ardor Tree's roots. I twist, struggle, and claw at his grip—until his body begins to shake.

A choked sob escapes him, and slowly, his hold loosens.

My hands hover over his back, caught between my instinct to comfort him and the urge to run.

4

I search the area for whatever might have scared him. Maybe moving trees. Or Murray.

But there's nothing. Just the thick summer air and the sound of his heavy breaths against my chest. His tears soak through my shirt as he lets out a full-body tremor like he might shake apart.

The last time I saw someone full on sob like this was Whitley at her grandma's funeral. But this is something else entirely. It's panic, grief, exhaustion, something five times heavier. He's about to hyperventilate in my arms.

I grab his shoulders and push him back just enough to see his face.

"Hey." I lift his chin with two fingers. "Are you okay? What's wrong? What happened?"

He looks at me through tears, innocently searching my face as if I hold an answer he's been looking for forever. Snot trickles from his nose down and across his lips. He doesn't even wipe it away.

"You . . . can . . . see . . . me." He struggles to say each word, his voice wrecked.

I force a steady breath, keeping my expression neutral, careful not to let my confusion slip through and risk offending him in his unraveling state.

"I'm sorry," I say gently. "But I don't understand."

His breathing is quick, uneven. With a shaky hand, he reaches up and grazes my cheek. My muscles tense even though his touch is nothing like bark—it's softer, hesitant. His palm continues to drift up, threading through the waves of my hair. My pulse stutters. His other hand begins to trail down my forearm, then he picks at my arms like I'm a dandelion waiting to be wished upon.

I gasp, jerking away. "What the hell are you doing?" My voice cracks as I shove him back. "I don't even know you. You're freaking me out, dude."

"Wait!" he pleads. "Don't go. Please." He reaches for me.

I snatch my pool inspection kit off the ground and power walk to my truck.

"Why shouldn't I? You're not answering my questions."

"No one has been able to see me," he states, as if it's a totally normal thing to say. "I'm surprised you can, is all."

I freeze, halfway to my truck. "Like, see you in public?" I frown, glancing around at the abandoned swim club. "Are you on house arrest here or something? Is this even a public pool?"

He shakes his head. "No one has been able to see my body." He taps his stomach. "Like I'm invisible . . . or a . . . ghost." His voice drops to a whisper. "No one has been able to see me for nearly ten years."

We lock eyes. His Adam's apple bobs with a hard swallow as he waits for my response. Thoughts swirl in my head, but my mouth hangs open, useless. I'm like a fish yanked from the Penango River, gasping, floundering, and silent.

My body reacts before my brain can. I hurl my kit through my truck's open window and dive inside after it.

A second hallucination in two days? Maybe Murray did kill me after all.

I need this to stop.

The ground is still. I slap my cheek, testing reality—the pain is real too. My phone sits on the dash and the screen lights up with the title of my last played podcast: "Is Reality Real?"

Whatever their verdict is, I need to hear it because I'm asking myself the same damn question.

The engine roars to life just as the boy stumbles forward, his eyes wide with panic.

"Will you come back?" he yells. "I'm Xander. Please come back!"

I grip the steering wheel, unable to look at him. "I have to go!" I shout through the window. "I'm sorry! But I have to go." My voice cracks unexpectedly.

"Wait!" He lunges after me, hands outstretched, clawing at the air like he's drowning. My tires kick up dust as I reverse down the drive. The boy follows, chasing me through the haze.

Then a loose branch trips him. He tumbles into the mud. I expect him to get up and keep running, but he doesn't. He convulses on the ground, sobbing as I disappear around the bend.

I flip on the radio, letting the familiar DJ's voice ground me in something normal. Then I grab my phone and scroll through old texts—proof of things that I know happened, proof that I haven't lost my grip on reality.

But my mind keeps circling back to Xander. A cry catches in my throat.

First the tree, now this boy. What's next?

Whatever these visions are, I take them as a sign. Leaving Penango isn't just something I want—it's something I have to do.

5

I drive straight home after attempting, or failing, to inspect Rainbow Valley's pool. My hands tremble around the steering wheel, my grip unsteady. That was not what I signed up for this summer.

I'm mad at Victor for sending me there, at Murray for making me feel like my mind is unraveling, and at Xander for . . . appearing . . . existing the way he does. But mostly, I'm mad at myself for letting people into my life who have caused me to lose control.

When I get home, Whitley sits on my front stoop sniffing a flower. Her shoes are strewn across the front walkway, and her bare feet play with the overgrown grass. A stack of three pie boxes sits beside her.

"I got us some free leftover pies from the Bean for lunch," she says with a smile. "Figured I'd bribe you into a lunch break with our favorite diner food."

I grunt as I slam my truck door closed, then stalk toward my parents' brick rancher.

"What's got you so bothered?" she calls after me, frowning.

"This stupid new job."

She snorts like a horse, vibrating her lips. "We just started."

"Yeah? That doesn't mean it can't be stupid." I pause with my hand on the doorknob. "Have you ever heard of Rainbow Valley Swim Club?"

She shakes her head. "What's that?"

"Never mind. Forget it."

She rolls her eyes. "Well, you best not be thinking about quitting. We can't fund our Appalachian road trip with your complaints."

In August, we're supposed to drive from Penango to West Virginia, down through Kentucky, Virginia, North Carolina, and finally Tennessee. I'll stop in Knoxville. Whitley plans to continue onward to Florida where she'll attend the University of Florida in Gainesville.

We want to see more states in a couple weeks than we have in our whole lives.

That is, if there is life after Penango.

Instead of responding to her, I push through the front door and slam it behind me.

In the bathroom, Mom is tying her hair into a ponytail, wearing her blue scrubs for her hospital shift.

"You're home early," she says, catching my reflection in the mirror. "I thought this was a full-time job?"

"It is." I sigh. "But I had to take some personal time after unexpected events this morning."

She raises her eyebrows. "It doesn't look good to call out of a job in your first week, Stetson. This job is paying for your travel to Tennessee. If you get fired, you'll be walking to Penango College."

I nod stiffly. "I know, Mom. It's paying for a lot of things. Are you almost done? I have to pee."

"I need five more minutes, honey. I have work this afternoon. You can't change your schedule and expect everyone else to do the same."

I exhale. "Oh my god. Are you and Murray teaming up against me or something?"

She blinks. "I beg your pardon?"

I retreat to my room, thrust in my earbuds, and blast "Like a Prayer" from Miley Cyrus's live album at full volume.

I listen exclusively to live recordings. I've never been to a concert, but hearing a crowd of strangers from somewhere far away gives me hope that one day I'll be among them. And right now, a concert feels like the perfect place to scream my lungs out without anyone asking why.

Murray's smiling face stares down at me from the bulletin board above my desk. It's covered in movie ticket stubs, photos, and all the proof of our time together. The tiniest gap between his two front teeth is visible in every shot.

I yank the board from my wall and hurl it across the room. It crashes into my dresser with a thud that scatters the pictures, buttons, and thumbtacks like shrapnel.

I rip off my black shirt, still damp with Xander's tears, then collapse onto my bed, pulling my pillow over my face to scream.

Shortly after, the door flies open.

"Is there a damn exorcism happening in here?" Whitley asks. "What the hell is wrong with you?"

I sniff, hard. "Get those pies away from me!" I shout, pointing at the boxes in her arms.

The management at the Bean used to give Murray and me pies nearing their expiration date to deliver to old folks around the county. We'd always sneak one for ourselves, sharing sweet kisses laced with cherry, blueberry, or raspberry throughout the afternoons.

But now their sweetness makes me sick.

Whitley frowns and places the boxes on my dresser, then sits on the bottom of my mattress. I slowly pull my earbuds out.

"Okay, what is your deal?" she asks. "You've been so weird today. I know it's not our job." A few seconds of silence pass. "Are you going to tell me what happened with Murray or what?"

I rub my face. "I haven't told anyone about it," I admit. "I don't know if I want to yet."

"Did he cheat?" She leans in. "Because if he did, I will march over to his house and give him a piece of my mind."

"No . . . no." I sit up and rest my back against the wall. "He didn't cheat."

But he did something bad. Maybe worse than cheating. I'm still trying to figure out what can be forgiven and what can't. This was my first and only relationship. And like learning to swim, I didn't notice when I drifted too deep.

Whitley stares at me, hearing my unspoken words. "Okay. Do you want to talk about it?"

I shake my head. "I can't."

Her frown deepens. "Well, he does."

I blink. "Huh?"

"I got a ton of texts from Murray this morning. He wants to meet. He said you weren't answering him."

I jerk my head back, grabbing my phone. There are no new messages from him. Just the last text from yesterday before I went to his house.

"I haven't gotten anything," I say.

"Well, he wants to meet at the Bean sometime this week."

"What doesn't he get?" I mutter. "I told him we're done. I guess the seventh time isn't the charm."

"Maybe that's why he's using me as a mediator now. Clearly, something ain't right."

"Don't group me with him," I snap. "It's his reading comprehension skills that are the problem, not mine."

She raises an eyebrow. "I thought you were the math genius and he was the English literature star?"

I roll my eyes. "What's that got to do with anything?"

"Nothing." She shrugs. "But if you want to be a heartbreaker, you need to break the heart." She catches the air in front of my face and forms a tight fist.

If only she knew that I already broke the heart, multiple hearts—Murray's and the Ardor Tree's.

It's just that, somewhere in between, I broke too.

The next morning, I storm into the health department, marching straight for Victor's office as Queen's "We Will Rock You (Live)" blasts in my ears like I'm stomping into a wrestling match.

I need answers.

One hallucination is easy to dismiss. But two? That's harder to chalk up to coincidence.

Victor wasn't lying when he said this pool was like the Ardor Tree. Unlucky for me, because most adults in Penango are usually full of it.

I knock on his door, but more so as a warning, and enter before he gives me permission. He's reclined in his chair, watching a video of a man filleting a fish. His broad back muscles press into the chair's armrests.

"Oh, good morning, Stetson," he says, pausing the video.

"Morning," I say, crossing my arms. "So, I went to Rainbow Valley yesterday." I scratch my head.

"Oh, yeah?" he asks, stretching. "How'd it look?"

"Not great. That's why I'm here. The water was dark green. And there were snakes. I'm pretty sure someone would get really sick if they swam in it. What do we do when a pool looks that bad?"

He laughs.

I blink at him. "What?"

"Is that all?"

"Um." I narrow my eyes.

He rubs his chin before clasping his hands behind his head. "Listen, kid. One time, I went to a pool and found a dead deer floating in the deep end. Can you believe that? Its guts were spilled everywhere like little fishing bobs." He waves his arm across the desk. "The poor thing must've been shot by a hunter and ran into the water. Sad way to go." He sucks in a breath through his teeth, then holds up a finger. "Another time, I was inspecting a locker-room shower and guess what I found?"

"What?"

"Guess."

"Poop?" I cringe.

"A hoard of leeches." His eyes bug out of their sockets. "They were covering the walls. Anyone who showered in there would've been sucked near dry."

"Oh." I swallow, stepping back. "What did you do?"

"I called my buddy over at animal control. He took care of it pretty quick."

I shake off the mental image. "Well, is there anything we should do about the green pool?"

"Did you tell them to close it?"

"No one was there," I lie, trying not to think of Xander.

Victor throws up his hands with a laugh. "There's no point in stressing, then, kid. It's probably some coloring from mildew. A hefty dose of chlorine will do the trick."

I doubt that.

"I was thinking of going back today."

He huffs. "Dang, Stetson, do you actually care about this stuff? Most guys your age just want cash for booze and girls."

My face twitches. "Um, no. Not booze or girls," I say, my cheeks burning. Not boys anymore either, I'd like to think. "Honestly, I need the money for college. What happened at the pool that makes it so legendary?"

His shoulders tighten. "It's better if we don't discuss that."

I narrow my eyes. "Well, is there anywhere I can check the old inspection forms for this pool? I want to see why it closed in the first place."

If my financial aid would just come through already, I wouldn't have to care so much about this job—or keep bothering Victor, which I'm sure he'd prefer.

"There's a file cabinet beside your desk with last year's records. The older stuff is in the archives department in the basement."

"Is there anything on the computer?"

Victor shakes his head. "Oh, yeah . . . no. We don't have that."

Of course not. *Penango County Health Department: proudly stuck in the past since 1801.*

"Hey, kid," he continues. "Don't go digging too deep."

With no other way to learn more about Rainbow Valley, I press the *B* button and descend to the basement. The elevator shudders to a stop after a few beeps. The doors slide open and reveal a stark hallway—white walls, linoleum floors, and air so cold it feels like I've cracked open the garage after a January blizzard.

I step out, shivering.

At the first intersection, a pair of gray double doors stand propped open. Inside, an old man in a beige cardigan hunches over a book nearly the size of his desk, peering through a magnifying glass. Behind him, endless rows of metal shelves packed with cardboard boxes stretch to the ceiling.

I clear my throat. "Is this the archives department?" I ask. He looks up, bones cracking.

He's apparently from 1801 too.

"It is," he says, wincing. "What can I help you with?" Every word he mutters seems like it brings him pain.

"I'm from the health department. I'm looking for some old files for a pool site we inspect."

"This way." He waves me toward the shelves.

He taps his hearing aid as we walk. "You should lower the volume."

I lean forward. "I'm sorry, what?" I ask.

"Your music. I can hear it. You don't want to end up like me." He laughs.

My cheeks warm. "Oh. Thanks. I'll try." I remove my earbud and tuck it in my pocket.

After a few more steps, he stops. "These are the environmental health department files." He points to a shelf. "Sorted by year."

"By year?" My eyes go wide. "How can I find information on a certain pool?"

He coughs. "You'll have to look through each year's files for the specific pool information. What year would you like?" He claps his lips like he hasn't had a drink of water all day.

"I'm actually not sure." I grab one of the boxes and lift the dusty lid to peek inside. It's full of manila folders. "Are these in the computer?"

The man shakes his head. "No. We don't have that."

"Oh my gosh."

"Is there anything else I can help you with?"

I sigh. "No, thanks. I'll start looking."

The man returns to his desk while I sift through folders, unsure when the Pinehurst pool closed. With no clear starting point, I begin with the most recent records and work backward.

By the time I reach the 2020 box, my forearms ache from hauling dense files. Half an hour in and all I've discovered is that Pinehurst hasn't been open for over five years. I heave the next box, 2015, from the shelf. I'm determined to go back no further than 2010. If the pool wasn't around then, I'll inspect it without any background and make do.

Running my finger along the folder labels, I hit the *P* section.

Pinehurst.

"Aha!" I blurt, immediately clamping a hand over my mouth. The sound echoes through the cavernous room. As I pull the folder free, the box's lid crashes to the floor. My pulse spikes.

There are multiple Pinehurst folders.

I pry open the first one. It contains an old newspaper, but I quickly toss it aside, assuming it's irrelevant. The next folder stops me cold. Inside, there's a long, handwritten note. I lick my lips. Before I even start reading, a single word catches my eye.

Xander.

My heart slams against my ribs.

On site with police and fire departments. The pool is closed indefinitely due to the investigation of missing person, Xander Pomers. Pool patrons arrived this morning and found his car parked in the driveway. They discovered his keys on a chair, which prompted them to call authorities. I will follow up next week to assist with permanent closure.

My jaw drops. Hands shaking, I snatch up the newspaper I tossed aside seconds ago and scan the front page: *Authorities are asking for help in locating Penango teen, missing for nearly forty-eight hours.*

Below the headline, a smiling photo of Xander Pomers stares back at me—the same boy I saw at Rainbow Valley Swim Club.

My stomach lurches like I've just slammed on my truck brakes. Either Xander was a hallucination . . . or I spoke to a real boy who went missing ten years ago.

7

Outside, cicadas scream from the trees, their relentless buzz amplifying the anxiety knotted in my chest since reading about Xander's disappearance.

My earbuds sit in my ears, silent. They died an hour ago, but I haven't charged them. I'm too stunned to do anything, too overwhelmed to think.

Across the parking lot, Whitley's voice cuts through the noise. "Are you still driving me home for lunch?"

Yes. I need to get off this government campus. Out of town. And out of state. Her words spark an idea, one that just might be a solution to everything weird that's happened these past few days.

"Yeah, but what if it wasn't just for lunch?" I ask.

She tilts her head, smirking. "What do you have in mind?"

"Let's leave for our road trip now."

She rolls her eyes and stomps ahead of me.

I skip after her. "I mean, why wait? You know? We can leave just like your dad. Screw him. Screw Murray." Screw Xander and the Ardor Tree. "Let's leave everything behind."

She spins around on her heels so fast I nearly run into her.

"First of all, don't ever say *let's be like my dad* again." Her voice is sharp. "Second, we have a job that's going to make us a couple thousand dollars this summer. I'm not skipping out on that kind of money."

"But we've lived on less before."

"And we've lived in Penango for eighteen years. What's two more months?"

I huff. "You really don't want to?"

She crosses her arms. "Unless you have five grand in that pool inspection kit you're holding, then no."

I sigh.

"Plus, you know Bennie doesn't do well with sudden change, so I'm offended you would suggest that."

We reach Whitley's double-wide mobile home after about fifteen minutes, and her elder chocolate labrador, Bennie, stands behind a gate on the front porch, tail wagging like he's waited all day for her.

"Hey, Bennie!" Whitley yells from the passenger side window. She scrunches her nose. Bennie's tongue hangs from the side of his mouth, which is lined with gray fur, a reminder that he's been in her life longer than anyone.

"Good luck on your inspection," she says as she opens the truck door.

"Enjoy your lunch, or whatever it is you're about to do." I glance at Bennie. "Why don't you start getting him ready for the trip? He might want to leave early too. You never know."

She laughs and pats her thigh, beckoning Bennie to follow. "You're the mountain to my field," she says to me.

Her backyard stretches flat for a few yards before it quickly slopes upward into a steep mountainside. From Whitley's bedroom window, it looks like an ocean wave of trees surging skyward, towering over the house.

That's how most of Penango is—flat fields that eventually collide with rolling mountains. It's where our saying comes from: *the mountain to my field*. No matter how low we fall or how lost we get, there's always a mountain backing us up.

Whitley and Murray were my mountain range. But now I'm down a peak. Murray's mountain was a hidden volcano that erupted and slowly melted away everything in its path. The lava leaked into my field, turned my green to ash, and cut off my view of everything beyond Penango's grasslands.

Whitley is my highest peak. My strongest ridge. I'll do whatever it takes to protect her, including staying in Penango for two more months, even as its ghosts rise around me.

I call Rainbow Valley's number three times on my drive over—
no answer, as expected. But the moment I arrive, I know
something is different.

The driveway is clear. The pavement glistens under the
sun, wet as if it's been freshly hosed down. We haven't had
rain in the past day. Xander must've cleaned up the place. Or
someone else is here. Hopefully they're real this time.

I gulp and turn into the club's entrance.

Farther down, the old shed's doors are back on their
hinges, securely shut. The faded Pinehurst block lettering is
now covered by a vibrant sign: *Rainbow Valley Swim Club*.
The mildew-stained umbrellas and broken chairs are gone too.

A woman in her thirties or forties scrubs the pool deck
with a broom, her black Pittsburgh Steelers hat pulled low
over her face.

My tires crunch over the gravel as I come to a stop. She
straightens, gripping the broom, and narrows her eyes on me. I
tuck my clipboard under my arm, grab my inspection kit, and
step out of the truck, straight into a swarm of gnats. They
smack against my face, buzzing in protest.

Before I introduce myself, my gaze shifts to the lounge chairs beside the pool. Empty. No books, candy, or soda.

No sign of Xander Pomers.

"Can I help you?" the woman asks.

"Yes," I say, clearing my throat. "Hi. My name is Stetson Delancey and I'm from the Penango County Health Department. I've called a few times."

Her eyes go wide.

"It's nothing bad," I say, walking toward her. "I have to do a standard pool inspection before you can open . . . for safety and stuff. Although it looks like you've cleaned the place up a bit since the last time I was here."

She grins and throws her arms wide like she's expecting a hug. "You're the pool guy!"

Before I can respond, she tilts her head back and calls to the sky, "Honey! The pool guy is here."

I clutch my clipboard to my chest. When a Penango woman summons her *honey*, it's usually for the purposes of getting the worst man you've never met to do their dirty work. I prepare myself for a scolding, evil eye, or lecture on county government overreach.

From the woods, another woman appears, balancing a stack of orange plastic buckets in her arms. She's dressed in denim overalls and thick garden gloves.

"Hey there," she says, coolly. "We've been waiting for you."

A breath of relief escapes me. Oh. Honey as in . . . wife?

Finally—normal people.

"Sorry." I smile. "We got a call only the other day that you were opening."

"We're excited to get the pool ready for the kids," the woman with the overalls says, placing a hand on the other

38

woman's shoulder. "It's been for sale for a while. We're taking it over and making it a camp for queer kids from southwest Pennsylvania. The first busload of campers is set to come in early July."

It's ninety degrees, but a chill creeps over my skin, raising goosebumps. My mind loops through everything that happened here the night Xander went missing, back when this place was still called Pinehurst Swim Club. Or rather, everything I don't know about that night. The shadows beneath the trees seem to stretch into something darker. I steal a glance over my shoulder just to make sure my truck is still there.

"What do you think of the name?" the woman with the broom says. "I'm Sheryl, by the way. And this is Kim."

I shrug. "I like it. There's not much around here that is . . ."

"So gay," Kim finishes with a smirk.

I laugh. "Yeah, I guess. The more rainbow the better. I wish there was more when I was growing up."

They exchange a look, their lips parting slightly, like they're about to ask something obvious.

"I'm gay," I say, answering for them.

Kim's face softens. "That's great. We're together and grew up here too, so we know how hard it can be." She bends slightly, meeting my eyes. "You're very brave. Maybe you can hang out this summer when the campers arrive."

I blush. "Yeah, that could be fun. As long as everything checks out with my inspection."

They laugh, even though it wasn't a joke. But I'm not here to make friends. I just want to finish my job, make as much money as I can, and get out of this town without losing my mind.

Sheryl's expression shifts, her brow furrowing. "I don't know how much county history you know," she says.

I know some. I wish I didn't.

"But a while back, there was—"

"Xander," I blurt.

Her face twitches. "Yes. So, you do know. We're friends with his mom, Maggie. She gave us her blessing to turn this place into something meaningful. Swimming here at night used to bring Xander some comfort. We want to offer that same peace to other kids going through similar struggles."

I grind my shoe into the pavement. "And he was never found?"

Sheryl and Kim exchange a look, then shake their heads.

Kim bites her lip. "You try not to lose hope, but . . . it's hard."

Sherly rubs her nose. "His mother still struggles."

Kim clears her throat. "You should go ahead and do your inspection. I don't think we're quite ready yet, to be honest, but you can at least tell us what still needs fixing." Her voice is tight, her eyes glassy. She nods once before turning to Sheryl. "I'm going to get back to cleaning the campsites."

"Right, sure," I say. I gather my kit and make my way to the pool, eager to put distance between myself and this conversation.

But as soon as I peer over the pool's edge, my stomach drops. The water is still only halfway up. Its shade of green has darkened since yesterday, and the surface ripples with an oily film that shifts and twists like gasoline on pavement.

Their work was too good to be true. I wanted this place to be ready, so I could walk away and leave it behind—like I'm trying to do with Murray, Stillwell Trail, the Ardor Tree, and everything else in Penango.

40

"Nasty, isn't it?" A boy's voice cuts through the humid air.

I spin and come face-to-face with Xander Pomers. Our noses nearly touch. I stumble back.

"Do you want a Swedish Fish?" he asks, extending a crinkled yellow bag of candy. Tucked against his side is a thick book: *The History of the Dalmatian Dog Breed.*

"Xander," I whisper, pulse pounding. My gaze flicks to Sheryl. She's sweeping the pool deck, oblivious.

"Everyone's looking for you," I say, my voice climbing in pitch. "C'mon." I grip his shoulder. He stares at my hand like a kid watching a magic trick. "These people miss you . . . and your mom. She's going to be so excited to see you." My words rush out between ragged breaths. The thick air constricts around my chest like a tightening thread.

Xander shakes his head. "No, she won't. I told you—"

"Sheryl!" I yell. "Look!"

Her body quivers with alarm and the broom slips from her grip. She hurries toward us with a creased brow. "What's wrong with the pool?"

I look at Xander, then back to Sheryl. My shoulders sag. "It's . . . Can't you see?"

"See what?" She squints at the green water as Xander, or his ghost, stands directly beside her. "What am I looking for?"

I point. "He's right . . . here."

Sheryl shields her face from the sun, continuing to scan the pool deck. But she doesn't react.

I turn to Xander, my throat tightening. I lower my voice. "She really can't see you, can she?"

He shakes his head, eyes fixed on the ground.

"See what?" Sheryl presses.

I force myself to swallow. "It's nothing," I say. "I thought I saw a dead animal. But there's nothing here."

She lets out a long sigh, then pats my back. "You scared me there for a second." She picks up the broom and returns to the other side of the pool.

"Do you believe me yet?" Xander asks.

"No." I cross my arms. "Because what you're telling me is unbelievable."

"Yeah, it takes some time to understand." He chomps the head off a Swedish Fish with his teeth. "It took me a few months to come to terms with my invisibility."

"This is insane." I run my fingers through my hair. "Do you live in the pool? How do you look the same as you did in 2015? I don't get it."

"I'm frozen in time after what happened to me. Forever seventeen, I call it. I haven't aged a day. It's great for tanning since the sun doesn't shrivel me up. And I have a tree house I made in the woods for my home. I can show you—"

"Why can I see you, but Sheryl can't?"

He shrugs. "I have no clue. Which is why I think we got off on the wrong foot earlier this week. I'm as surprised as you are. Can we start over?"

"Start over with what?"

"Our friendship. I have zero friends. And I've never had a gay friend before."

I raise my eyebrows. "How do you know I'm gay?"

"I heard everything you said to Sheryl and Kim. It's one of the perks of being invisible."

I take a deep breath. "Listen, Xander. I don't know what you want from me, but I have a lot going on right now and this whole situation is really distracting. I don't want any new friends. I just want to inspect this pool and go home."

I step around him, but he moves to block me.

"But there must be a reason for this to be happening. You're the only person who has been able to see me in ten years." His voice cracks.

I hesitate. "What happened to you that night?" My tone is even. "What happened to you here?"

He studies the pool area like a deer caught in headlights. "I was swimming and then"—he snaps his fingers—"everything went black."

"Just black?"

"Oblivion."

My body shudders remembering the familiar feeling at the Ardor Tree.

"Then, who knows how long after that, I woke up on my lounge chair." He points to where we first met.

"Do you think you're—"

"Dead?" He nods. "I think so. Maybe I drowned without realizing. Or lightning struck the pool and I got shocked to death."

"But your body? What happened to it? It wouldn't just vanish."

"A bear got me. That's my best hypothesis. If you think Penango is rural now? Even just ten years ago there wasn't shit out here. Just trees." He licks his lips with a bright red tongue.

"So you're saying I see dead people?"

"Maybe." He shrugs. "You could be a medium and not realize it. I'm a firm believer in the afterlife now. But I haven't met any other ghosts yet." He taps his chin. "Unless you're also—"

"I'm not dead!" I yell.

He cowers.

"Who are you talking to over there?" Sheryl asks. "You need any help?"

I exhale, hard, and rub the back of my neck. My cheeks burn. "No. I'm fine. Almost done."

"I'm sorry," Xander says. "I didn't mean to freak you out."

"That's all you've been doing." I wipe my hand down my face. "It's wrong to suggest that I've died." My lips quiver. "I still have a lot to do with my life. I'm not dying here. In Penango."

"It's a scary thought, isn't it?"

I nod.

"I've carried that thought around for a decade," he continues.

We lock eyes.

"I'm not trying to make you feel the same way. I'd never want that for someone else. I just think you can help me. Could you help me? Help me figure out why I'm like this."

"Like what?"

His gaze drifts to the tree line and meets the sky. A lone crow caws.

"I guess we'll find out together."

The morning sun beats down on the health department's parking lot unhindered by clouds. It's Friday, and I'm wrapping up my first week as a pool inspector.

It's less of a joke than I expected. People take their pools seriously.

One apartment manager wouldn't let me leave until he finished a full demonstration of how he vacuums the pool floor. Another guy, who runs an assisted living facility, gave me an hour-long tour of the entire building as if I was considering moving in. The pool was part of the tour, but so were the cafeteria, nurse station, gym, and two fully furnished model apartments. It was a decent way to kill time until he led me into the men's locker room right before water aerobics. There were too many men over the age of eighty and not enough clothing.

Whitley shimmies between two parked cars to join me on my walk toward the building. I pause an episode of *Stuff You Should Know* called "Magic Eye Illusions" about those '90s pictures with hidden 3D images. It's comforting to pretend my current problem is just my brain being retro.

"Great news!" Whitley says with a smile. "Murray texted me back. He said he could meet you after work today. Maybe you can finally get through to him and wrap this relationship up."

I place my hand on her shoulder. "You're gaslighting me too now? I've been trying to get through to him all year. He doesn't listen."

"Maybe he doesn't want to ruin your last few months together."

"He already has."

"How? Can you tell me what he did to your head?"

My steps falter on the pavement. I can't tell her. Not yet. Our town is too small, our futures too fragile. One bad whisper and you're stuck in the mud on one of Penango's unpaved roads with no way out. I don't know if Murray deserves that. But I also don't know why I still care after what he did to me.

"Let's make a new pact now," I say, changing the subject.

Whitley raises her eyebrows. "As long as it doesn't replace our first one of moving as far away from Penango as possible."

I gulp. "Let's agree to never date another boy from Penango ever again." I extend my pinky finger.

She hooks her pinky finger with mine without hesitation. "That's easy, since I never wasted my time with one in the first place."

I laugh. "You've always been smarter than me."

Suddenly, Whitley gasps and grabs my arm, yanking me out of my spiral of destructive thoughts about Murray.

"What does he think he's doing?" she mutters, squinting ahead.

We both have clingers to shake this summer. Hers just happens to be her dad.

He stands in front of the health department's entrance, tapping his foot. I haven't seen him in two years, but he looks like he aged thirty. His muscles are gone, leaving him with Whitley's stick-figure frame. Angular cheekbones jut from beneath his eyes and cast shadows over his long, gaunt face.

He's a shell of the man who used to haunt Whitley's weekends.

My last run-in with him was supposed to be a quiet Friday night. I had just gotten the fire started in the pit out front of Whitley's house. Murray collected logs from the woods nearby while Whitley slid hot dogs onto metal skewers. Bennie sniffed curiously at Murray's gym bag full of sweaty football pads.

Just as the flames began to catch, headlights broke through the line of trees.

"Who is that?" Whitley asked, squinting toward the erratic lights.

Mr. Wyomen's truck barreled down the drive without slowing. Whitley groaned. "Oh no."

Our faces sank.

Whitley dropped the hot dogs onto the dirt and dragged Bennie toward the house. Murray grabbed my shoulders and yanked me back as Mr. Wyomen's truck crashed through our setup. The firepit toppled over, sending a burst of embers and flaming logs across the ground. Our chairs screeched and twisted beneath the truck's tires as he skidded to a stop.

"What the hell's the matter with you?" Whitley shouted. "You nearly killed us!"

"Serves you right," Mr. Wyomen slurred, stumbling out of the driver's seat and wiping his mouth with his sleeve. "Who set up all this junk in my drive?"

"We always set up the fire out here," Whitley said. "You're never home, so how would you know?"

"*Always* sounds like an exaggeration if you ask me," he said through a belch.

"Good thing nobody is asking you." She crossed her arms.

Mr. Wyomen shook his head and shuffled to the back of his truck, muttering curses.

Whitley rolled her eyes and pulled her sweatshirt sleeves over her hands before righting the firepit. She rearranged the surviving chairs and took a seat, crossing her legs.

Mr. Wyomen heaved a case of beer from his truck bed. "I got my crew coming over, so y'all need to disappear," he said, twirling his finger in the air.

"No way," Whitley said. "We just got set up. We have hot dogs and s'mores to roast." She shot me a look. "Sit down, Stetson."

The flames' light flickered across Mr. Wyomen's wrinkled face. Without warning, he stomped toward the firepit, gathered up the hot dogs, buns, and s'more supplies, and hurled them into the flames.

"There," he said with a twisted smirk. "Everything is roasted. Just like you wanted. You got five minutes to leave before I roast something else."

Now, in the health department parking lot, if Whitley hadn't spotted him first, I might have thought he was another fear-induced hallucination.

He waves, then starts walking toward us.

"Do not engage," Whitley hisses, dragging me toward the next aisle of parked cars.

"Whitley, wait!" he calls. "I've been looking for you." He breaks into a jog.

Mr. Wyomen has a new position at the department doing some kind of health research for the county. He got us these jobs through his connections last month when he returned, claiming sobriety and his first steps in a long-overdue apology.

I jumped at the opportunity. A full-time gig was the perfect excuse to avoid Murray all summer. Whitley, on the other hand, only took it for the fifteen-dollar-an-hour paycheck and the promise that her dad would help with her college tuition if she agreed.

She says he has a long way to go before coming close to making amends.

His second family, the one that came first in his heart as Whitley puts it, kept him in Pittsburgh for most of her childhood. And when her grandma died, Whitley spent the rest of her days alone with just her dog, Bennie.

Her dad is one of the reasons we're skipping town. She's tired of everyone leaving her behind. And now she figures there's no reason she can't do the same.

We run to a side door, breathless, and Whitley shoves it open with her hip. "Shouldn't we at least say hi?" I ask. "I don't want to make him mad."

"Do you think he ever stopped to think about all the things he should've done?" Whitley snaps. "No. He didn't."

"Well, do you want to talk about it?"

"Don't try that role reversal on me. You're the one who needs to fess up about your head." She jabs a finger in my face. "Did you learn that little conversational trick from one of your podcasts?"

"No." I laugh. "Well, maybe." I pause. "But have you seen him since he got back?"

"No." She folds her arms.

"Have you talked to him?"

"Just through email."

"Is he staying at your house?"

"Hell no." She wrinkles her nose. "Enough about him." She waves me off. "We dodged him for a reason."

"Are we being too harsh?"

"Harsh is direct and unforgiving," she says. "That's how you send a clear message. My dad sent one to me after he left home when I was eleven. That's why I know Murray, the eighteen-year-old star wide receiver of Stillwell Trail's football team, can handle one too."

10

After work, I arrive at the Bean to meet Murray—time and place set by Whitley.

We haven't spoken since Sunday, and I can't help but wonder what's left to say. For me, we're at the end of the phone call, just listening to silence, him waiting for me to hang up.

The diner isn't actually named the Bean, but that's what most people in town call it. It's an oversized silver Airstream van that's long since faded to brown. Trains rumble past on the railroad tracks beside it, kicking up dirt with every trip. Over time, the dust has settled onto the diner's outer shell, giving it a sandy coating that makes it look like a baked bean.

The management never bothers to clean it, so everyone in Penango leaves their mark, etching thoughts and messages into the dust with their fingers as they leave lunch. Most recently I've seen *STHS Seniors*, *dick*, *I'm dirty*, and *God Bless Penango*.

As soon as I park, I spot the side of Murray's blond head through the window, hovering above one of the red leather booths like a tall, yellow flower growing above its fence, but I know his pretty facade is fake and full of pests.

My earbuds die before the latest podcast finishes. I started a new one called *LGBTQ&A*, which interviews queer people from all over. I'm hoping to hear about someone who's gone through what I'm dealing with now. Maybe visions are part of the coming out process. Or maybe some of us are just superheroes. If it's the latter, I better have the ability to fly or make people disappear—both of which would help me get Murray out of my sight.

I toss my earbuds into the cupholder and rest my chin on the steering wheel, taking a few deep breaths. They don't stop my insides from quivering. I briefly consider reversing out of the lot before Murray spots me, but I know it'll only drag this misunderstanding on longer. I need to focus on work and getting to college. I want to. But Murray is in the way, and that's exactly what he wants.

I can't let him win.

As I head inside, I pass the word *love* carved into the dusty exterior wall of the Bean. It doesn't make me groan, laugh, or tear up. I just stare at it, indifferent—all it's meant this past year, all it was between me and Murray.

I try to slip into the Bean unnoticed, walking in with a family, but the second I step through the door, my eyes meet Murray's. He jumps to his feet. A smile spreads across his face, but my glare quickly shuts it down and pulls his lips into a frown.

He cracks his knuckles, a nervous habit of his that always stresses me out. I head to the booth and sit across from him without saying a word. He stands there for a beat, looking past me. Maybe he's searching for Whitley or checking if I brought backup. I haven't. But now that he notices, I kind of wish I had.

He finally sits, then folds his hands on the table.

Even though I'm trying to end things between us, my attraction to him hasn't faded—not even a little. I don't think it ever will. I'll give him that. His hazel eyes, framed by thick, dirty blond brows and dark, permanent circles beneath them, still make my legs weak, even as I sit. The blond hair on his muscular arms catches the sunlight streaming through the window, making it gleam.

"Hi," I say.

He rubs his head and looks everywhere but at me.

Running my hand through his freshly buzzed hair feels like petting a Labrador puppy. It's soft and comforting. Or at least, it used to be. It's definitely the softest hair in Pennsylvania, probably even the whole country, though I don't have much nationwide experience to back that up.

"How are you?" he asks.

I pick up one of the sugar packets next to the salt and pepper and slide it between my fingers. "To be honest . . . I'm confused why I'm here."

"No," he scoffs. "I don't want to start our conversation with that basic question."

I recoil from the table. "You asked? I feel like this should be about what I want after what happened on Sunday." The heat blooming in my head concentrates behind my forehead wound. I make sure it hasn't reopened with the faintest touch.

Ten seconds of silence pass.

"I'm really, really sorry," he says.

I swallow, hard, while tracing the veins around his knuckles with my eyes. "Is that all? We could've done this over the phone."

"I'm so, so sorry," he repeats. "Everything came to a head this past weekend and . . . I broke." He talks softly, which is unlike him, and the conversations drifting into our booth from nearby tables make it almost impossible to hear what he's saying. But I refuse to lean closer. "I want to talk about how we can get past this."

My eyes widen. "Murray, how many times do I have to tell you? We're not staying together."

A familiar waitress appears at our table. She places a basket of heavily peppered curly fries in front of me.

"Thanks," Murray says. "He'll like those."

I tap my foot.

"You need anything else?" the waitress asks. "We got the Penango Grits on special."

"This is good," Murray says.

I snarl my lip. Why did he want to talk with me if I'm not even allowed to speak?

Murray looks out the window, then taps his phone to check the time.

"Do you have somewhere else to be?" I ask.

He shakes his head and sighs.

"If you want to talk, let's talk," I say. "Here's a recap for you." I toss the sugar packet over my shoulder. "You've literally been whining about me leaving town for the past year when it's all I want. I asked you to stop and you didn't."

"I can't believe this is happening," he whispers. He looks out the window again and his eyes well with tears.

"It's not my fault you couldn't connect the dots of what would eventually happen this summer when I decided to leave, and you chose to stay. If you were nicer about the whole thing, I wouldn't have thought twice about being with you through college." The words come out quickly. Spit pools between the corners of my lips.

Murray doesn't respond. He just stares at me with blank, hollow eyes, the same ones from Sunday when his face turned into a stranger's. The spark that used to guide me has been swallowed up by a black hole.

Then his mouth twists, not into a frown or smile but a scowl.

"Damn it!" he shouts, standing up and lifting his arms.

I flinch, bracing myself. Without another word, he swipes the basket of fries from the table, and they scatter across the floor like the broken pieces of our relationship.

The waitress glares at us from behind the counter, her fingernails tapping its surface. "You still need to pay for those," she says.

"It doesn't look like he's coming, so they would've been wasted anyway," Murray mumbles.

"What?" I ask. "Just because this conversation isn't going how you want doesn't mean you can pretend that I never showed up."

Murray tosses some money on the counter. "If Stetson Delancey comes by here looking to talk, tell him I'm sorry."

"Murray, quit the shit!" I yell.

He doesn't respond again; rather he exits like he can't hear me. The bell above the door jingles as it swings open, an innocent sound that feels out of place, like wedding bells at a funeral.

"It appears he's ignoring you, honey," the waitress says with a frown.

"It wouldn't be the first time," I say, sighing.

I press my palms to my temples, feeling the pressure of Penango's last-ditch effort to hold on to me.

11

I climb into my truck with my head low. That didn't go well.

I tell myself not to be disappointed. I know he only invited me there to humiliate me. There was nothing I could have done to salvage the conversation. But it still stings. Murray has a way of making me feel everything in extremes—humiliation, love, and all emotions in between. He's always been good at making me feel special.

Like that night in October of our junior year during one of his football games. The scoreboard suddenly lit up with: *Stetson, will you go to junior prom with me? (Murray)*

I was so confused. Junior prom wasn't until April. Two hundred and fifteen people watched me descend an entire flight of stadium steps toward Murray, who stood waiting by the field's fence. I knew the exact number because the second my name flashed across the field, I panicked and counted them all.

"Is that for me?" I asked him.

"Of course," he said, grinning widely. "What other Stetson and Murray are there?"

My cheeks warmed, looking back at the sea of faces watching us. "Junior prom is so far away."

"Yeah, but I liked this idea. I didn't want anyone to steal it because I knew you deserved it the most."

Or when, not long after that promposal, the county paper ran an article about Murray being one of the few openly gay kids in town. The headline read: *Local High School Football Star Lives Out His Small-Town Dream*. When the journalist asked where he found the courage to live so openly, Murray said, "My boyfriend makes it easy."

He even refused to let them publish his story unless they gave me my own article too. So, in January, I ended up being featured in the *Penango County Spring Track and Field Preview*. It wasn't about me or my relationship with Murray. But I was quoted a couple times and Mom framed it and hung it in my bedroom.

But the following fall, after a football game, Murray used his talents against me—and I felt special in all the wrong ways.

Whitley and I walked into a barn party, the air thick with the smell of hay and cheap beer. The dim yellow barn light cast a mustard glow over the crowd. I did a quick head count—thirty of our classmates, all familiar faces. Most of them were wearing silver and black Stillwell Trail High gear.

My view went straight to Murray. He was perched on the second story, his long legs dangling over the edge. His jersey was still on, his cheeks flushed from the game. He held a red plastic cup in one hand, and the other was slung lazily around a teammate's shoulder. Bits of hay drifted down through the air every time they moved.

I waved. His glassy eyes landed on me, and for a second, I thought he'd wave back. But before he could, his teammate stood and shoved him aside.

"My people!" the guy bellowed with his arms outstretched. "Let's welcome Penango's smartest man to the party, Stetson Delancey! He's got bigger dreams than ours."

My heart slammed into my throat. Whitley's head snapped toward me. The barn fell silent, except for the low chuckles of the football team.

"We heard this town isn't good enough for you anymore," one called out.

"Yeah," another voice chimed in. "Are you sure you even want to be here? This might not be your scene."

Whitley grabbed my shoulder. "What's going on?" she asked. "This party sucks." My hands trembled, so I shoved them in my pockets.

My eyes locked on Murray. "Are you serious?" I shouted. My voice cracked with anger. He just stared at his feet.

I swallowed hard. "You're right!" I said, my voice sharper. "I don't want to be here." I spun on my heel and burst through the barn doors, letting the night swallow me before I said something I'd regret.

The most annoying thing about feelings is that the more I try to control them, the harder they bite back. I broke up with Murray because I thought it was the right thing to do to get space and grow on my own. But ever since then, I haven't stopped thinking about him.

And now, my chest tightens as I try to figure out how to balance Murray's needs and Xander's.

Freshman year, I would've been thrilled to have two boys obsessed with me. Like, what do you mean I'm in a love triangle with a jock and an edgy guy from the woods?

Just four years later, and the thought exhausts me. I'm on Do Not Disturb!

Then my phone lights up in the cupholder.

I sigh, already assuming it's Murray, and roll my eyes as the vibration rattles against the plastic. I ignore the call, letting it go to voicemail while I dig around for my earbuds, ready to tune out the world.

But my phone rings again. A jolt of frustration shoots down my arm as I snatch the phone from the console to silence it. Before I do, Whitley's face flashes on the screen. My eye twitches.

It's not Murray.

Without hesitating, I swipe to accept the call.

"Hey, Whitley," I say.

"Stetson!" she yells. She seems out of breath. I straighten my back as panic rips through my spine.

"What's wrong?" I ask.

"It's Bennie . . . He got attacked . . . Oh my gosh."

"Attacked? How? Is he okay?"

"I think so. But it's bad. I can't get him up." Her voice quivers. "I need your help."

"Hold on," I say. "I'm coming over. Where are you?"

"Behind my house. Along the river. Hurry!"

I tear down the winding roads so fast my truck nearly lifts off the ground over the shallow hills. Gravel spits from my tires as I slam to a stop in front of Whitley's house. I barely kill the engine before I'm out of the driver's seat, leaving the door wide open as I sprint into the woods.

The sound of rushing water grows louder with every stride.

Then I see her.

She's kneeling on the riverbank beside a motionless Bennie, her fishing rod and tackle box abandoned in the grass. The golden-hour sun catches her wide, panicked blue eyes—

and the deep gash splitting Bennie's right hind leg. Clumps of dried blood mat his short brown fur into dark, tangled patches.

"What the heck happened?" I ask.

"He got in a fight with a damn coyote," Whitley says. Tear marks line her cheeks. "I was casting my line and it came out of nowhere. It must've been rabid. There's no reason for it to be out at this time of day. The coyote ran away when I screamed, but it got Bennie . . . It got Bennie."

"It's okay, Whitley. I have my truck. We can take him to the animal hospital." I swallow, looking over Bennie's leg.

She shakes her head. "The hospital is an hour away and it'll probably cost a million dollars. I can take care of this at the house. But I need your help lifting him. C'mon."

I place my hand gently beneath Bennie's shoulders. Whitley wraps her arms around Bennie's hips, avoiding his back leg.

"One, two, three," I count before we hoist Bennie into the air. He lets out a series of high-pitched cries.

"It's okay, buddy," Whitley says through gritted teeth. "It's okay. We got you."

We crab walk through the woods with beet red faces. My forearms burn. Neither of us asks to take a break. I want to. Badly. Bennie is bleeding out in front of me and all I can think about is Murray's angry face as he ran away from me at the diner and Xander's sad eyes as he darted toward me at the pool. The images deflate me, weakening my muscles and dragging my feet like weights on a fishing line. This week is horrible. And it won't seem to end.

But Bennie holds no responsibility for it, so I keep on moving.

At the house, we lay Bennie on a rusty patio table. I step back, inhaling deeply, trying to steady myself. Whitley is inside for first aid supplies in seconds. I whisper softly into Bennie's ear, hoping to soothe him, but before my words can even settle, Whitley is back with bandages, scissors, and a bottle of alcohol.

"What can I do?" I ask.

She doesn't answer. Her fingers move with sharp precision, like they do when she plays her clarinet. She wraps Bennie's leg with such confidence she might as well be a first-chair EMT—if there were such a thing. Helpless, I run a hand over Bennie's head. His tail flops weakly, a tiny sign of relief.

With a final snip of the scissors, Whitley secures Bennie's bandage and stops the flow of blood. Then she claps the dust from her hands like she's applauding a job well done.

I exhale and fall back into one of the patio chairs.

"And what do you think you're doing?" Whitley asks. She stomps across the backyard and disappears into the shed.

I jump up from the chair. "Is there something else?"

She emerges from the shed with a rifle. "Have you ever been coyote hunting?" Her face is expressionless.

I laugh. "Are you serious?"

"Dead serious." She loads the gun.

"Whitley, there are probably hundreds of coyotes around your house."

"I know which one it is. It's been coming around here a lot lately." She looks through the scope. "It's missing the top chunk of its left ear, and its tail is all black . . . blacker than most other coyotes I've seen."

"But if it's rabid, it could be dangerous."

"Exactly," she says with added annunciation on the *t*. "This is why we need to go after Bennie's attempted killer while it's close. It will attack again if we don't."

"What if we just take this opportunity to leave town? This could be our sign. It's not safe for us here anymore!"

She loads the gun. "You coming or not?" she asks. "Bennie's attacker could be miles away after all this talk."

I bite my lip.

"If your aim is good enough, we won't have to get too close."

She raises her eyebrows, positioning the butt of the gun against her shoulder, and points it at a lone branch dangling from a nearby tree. She pulls the trigger. The bullet cuts through the knot and splits the branch from the trunk. It spins through the air like a boomerang before colliding with earth.

"I think it's pretty good," she says, smirking.

12

After locking Bennie inside, we return to the woods. Whitley leads the way. Her bushy hair collects dead leaves and bugs from the thickening tree canopy. Rays from the setting sun periodically bounce off her rifle butt and into my eyes.

As I grab a spider from her hair, she starts to hum, tracing her fingers gently along the trees bordering our path.

"*Way down in the valley, lies Stillwell High,*" she sings. It's the opening verse of our high school alma mater. "*Let us raise our voices for all to hear, over the hills and into the sky. Our ancestors came upon this land, a place of faith, honor, and tradition most grand.*" She stretches out her right arm, waving it over the ground.

"*We promise to serve and pledge our love,*" I continue. "*To always look out for thy neighbor and put Penango above.*" Twigs crunch under my shoes along to the melody of the song. "*For the lessons of life to us impart, knowledge to aid that can never be taken apart.*"

Whitley inhales, then takes over the next line. "*So adorn our hearts with the striking silver and black.*"

I clear my throat. *"For we have found victory here!"* My voice amplifies. *"And will live out the virtues to always give back."* I pump my fist into the sky.

"Wait!" she yells, and puts her hand over my mouth. "We should be quieter. We're going to scare away the coyotes. We can't let that sucker know we're close. Let's camp out here."

I nod, then lower my arm. "You're right," I say.

We sit beside a fallen tree. Silence settles over us like a midnight snowfall. We wait and search for any movements.

I tap my fingers along my knee, between flicking flies off my legs. My vision wanders from the coyote-absent horizon to the area around me. Whitley's phone rests on her lap. A notification banner showing eight missed calls from her dad flashes across the screen.

"You okay, Whitley?" I ask. She inspects the split ends of her blond hair.

"Yeah," she says. "What do you mean? We got to be patient. It hasn't been that long."

"I mean besides the coyote." I nod at her phone.

She swallows, then swipes away the notifications. "I'll be better once we get the coyote and Bennie is safe."

"If you ever want to—" I start, but Whitley holds up her hand to silence me.

"Shhh," she slurs. "Look."

A coyote stands in a clearing by the river. It's maybe fifty or so yards away. Its tail is black, but I can't tell if it's missing a chunk of its ear from this distance. Whitley slowly lifts her gun. She puts her eye to the scope.

"You going to take the shot?" I whisper.

"Yeah," she says, licking the corners of her mouth. "That's him. Ear is gone."

64

The coyote's head twitches in our direction. I freeze every muscle to avoid making noise.

"This one's for Bennie," Whitley mutters, then pulls the trigger.

The shot breaks the forest's stillness like a morning alarm. A flock of dormant crows erupts into the sky.

"I missed!" Whitley yells. She stands, then sprints toward the coyote.

"What?" I shout after her. "How do you know?"

"I saw him run away rather than drop dead. Come on!" She waves me along.

I follow Whitley's trail. We come to a screeching halt where the coyote stood. Our heads spin in search of its escape route. My chest heaves and Whitley's mouth is wide, sucking in air.

"I blew it," she groans.

"Yeah, I don't see it anywhere," I say, shielding my eyes from the sun with my forearm.

"Dang it." She kicks the dirt.

"It's okay, Whitley."

"It's not!" She huffs, then pulls her hair into a tight ponytail. "At least we scared it."

"We also have all summer to catch it, since you won't leave Penango any earlier than August." I force a sarcastic grin.

She shoots me a sidelong glance. "He better not stay free all dang sum—" She lifts her palm to my face. "Wait, do you see that?"

"Wha—"

"Paw prints! Come on!" She breaks into a sprint.

"Whitley, wait!"

I attempt to follow her but only complete a few strides before a set of familiar branches reaches above the next hilltop, then a line of neon words spray-painted across a cement pipe—the Ardor Tree.

"No . . . No . . . No," I whisper, dragging my feet to a stop.

I thought this summer would be a celebration. I just turned eighteen, got into college, and graduated high school. My teachers kept telling me to prepare for new opportunities, asking over and over how I was handling all the excitement. I should be running toward the horizon, not away from it.

But this summer just feels like it's going to be my last. Penango has other plans for me.

I turn to head back to Whitley's house but slam into something warm and sticky. Blinking, I take a step back and realize it's Xander's bare chest, slick with sweat. His defined pecs rise and fall with each deep breath, swelling like overinflated balloons. The contours are impressive. Too impressive. My fingers twitch with the impulse to trace them, but I lock my hands behind my back instead.

"She's quick," he says.

"Do you ever wear a shirt?" I step around him, trying to focus on literally anything else.

"Not when it's pushing one hundred degrees and humid. Usually, I don't wear anything at all. No one has been able to see me. But now that you can, I've been rotating through my favorite swim trunks."

My cheeks burn.

I wish he wasn't in his trunks. But I don't say that. I can't even believe I'm thinking it. I'm attracted to a ghost. My taste in boys is horrific—they're either emotionally dead or literally dead.

This is so sick and twisted.

"What do you think?" he asks.

I lick my lips. "Your body is hot, sure. Maybe I'll have time for your workout routine when I'm not being chased down in the woods by a ghost."

"Oh." His bushy eyebrows shoot up. "I meant what do you think of my swim trunks." He tugs at the purple waistband.

My face has to be just as purple at this point.

"But hey, if you think my body looks good, I'll take it. It's my first compliment in ten years. Another first with you!"

I nod. "You're welcome."

"Can I see yours?"

"My what?"

"Your body."

My jaw falls open. "Are you insane? Why are you here?"

He frowns. "Are you not happy to see me?"

A part of me is. I've never been this close to another boy's body besides Murray's. The other day at the pool, Xander's lips were as plump as his chest is now. I like how he just says what he feels instead of shooting looks, giving the silent treatment, or just flat-out ignoring me, like you-know-who. His expressions are more colorful than his swim trunks.

But the other part of me is terrified. The more I see him, the more I worry that these hauntings won't stop when I leave Penango. If Xander has nothing to do with Murray, then he has everything to do with me. And the more I run into him, the closer I get to facing what that really means.

"Let me back up," he continues. "I should probably tell you that I'm gay too . . . or was, depending on how we're thinking about things."

I cross my arms. "Is that a joke?"

He pouts his lips. "If it was, it wouldn't be a good one. Is there a problem?"

"No, not at all. I'm just . . . surprised by the chances. You're a gay teen ghost in Penango?"

He shrugs. "Gay for sure. I've thought about it for over ten years and am certain at this point. I am hypothetically a ghost. But ever since you showed up on the scene, I'm questioning that hypothetical. I came here so we could get started on solving this mystery. It'll be like queer Clue! What killed the gay kid at the queer camp with the—"

"Hold on," I say, waving my arms in front of him. "Why didn't you say anything the other day when you found out I was gay?"

He rubs the back of his neck. "It was on the tip of my tongue but . . . you're the first person I'm coming out to, so I got scared and swallowed it."

My eyes widen. "Oh no, really? My reaction sucked, then. I'm sorry. Congratulations."

"Thank you! Another first! What is that, number three or four?"

"Why didn't you come out in high school?"

He laughs. "Things were a little different in 2015. Someone needs a history lesson. But this isn't the time or place. Let's start talking about how you can bring me back to life this year."

"Fine. But I have a lesson for you. Telling someone to take their shirt off in the woods might work on some guys, but not me."

He laughs again. "Noted. But maybe that's something we can work on too. It would be much better than this boring, black polo shirt you're always wearing." He picks at my shirt's thick, cotton fabric.

"It's my work uniform. I'm usually just in a white tee."

"That's not much better."

He drapes his arm around my shoulder and starts walking, guiding me forward. My body tenses, but I don't pull away.

Instead, I let him lead, knowing I can't navigate this situation on my own any longer.

13

Xander and I sit in my truck parked in Whitley's driveway, the engine off.

Fireflies flicker over her front yard as the sun sinks behind the mountains. He tells me how in high school, coming out never even crossed his mind. He didn't have the words for what he was feeling. In such a small town, there were no examples to look to or adults to trust. I share my own coming out story, and how even years later with all the progress the world has made, it still didn't feel easy.

I came out to Whitley first. It wasn't by choice, but I wouldn't have had it any other way.

She caught me and Murray making out in my bathroom sophomore year.

Mom worked night shifts at the hospital and Dad took odd construction jobs in other parts of the state, leaving the house empty most evenings. No one was home when I brought Murray over. Or so I thought.

"Damn it, Stetson," she yelled, hands on her hips. "I told you years ago that if you were gay to just tell me. And here you are kissing in secret like this is some dang truck stop." She turned to Murray. "How long have you been together?"

I kicked Murray out of the house shortly after that. Then I collapsed in my room, crying in Whitley's lap.

She ran her fingers through my hair. "Oh, Stetson." She sighed. "Nothing will change. Times are different."

I nodded, smearing my tears across her thigh. "I'm afraid my parents will change."

"I'll make sure they won't," she promised. "When do you want to tell them?"

"We might as well just get it over with."

Mom was first. We planned on telling her the next day right before she left for work so I wouldn't have to deal with the aftermath for at least a few hours.

She was finishing up her ponytail in the bathroom when Whitley grabbed her shoulders and steered her to the living room.

"What in the hell are you doing to me, Whitley Wyomen?" Mom demanded.

Whitley plopped her onto the couch. "Your son has a declaration."

Mom checked her watch. "Better be a short one," she said. "You got thirty seconds." She crossed her arms, then her legs.

I sat in the armchair, yanking on the neckline of my white undershirt. "I . . ." My throat dried up.

I looked at Whitley.

Whitley raised her eyebrows.

Mom looked at Whitley.

Whitley looked at Mom.

Mom looked back at me.

I pulled so hard on my shirt that I ripped the crew neckline and turned it into a V-neck.

Mom stood. "It seems like the only thing Stetson is declaring is that he needs a new shirt. I have to get to work." She grabbed her keys from the kitchen and threw her purse over her shoulder.

"Stetson," Whitley whispered from the other side of the living room.

"I can't," I whispered back. "You do it." It was like I couldn't speak the language. I needed Whitley to be my translator.

"Mrs. Delancey," Whitley said, her voice firm. "Stetson is gay." The words hit me like a rockslide. Every boulder landed on my chest, cutting off oxygen and making it impossible to breathe. My toes gripped each thread of the beige carpet as I fought for air.

Mom froze beside the front door. Her hand slid off the doorknob. She turned slowly to look at me, her mouth slightly open.

"Oh, honey," she said, her voice much higher than usual. She walked over and kissed my forehead.

"Look at this thing." She grabbed my ripped shirt. "I'll pick up some new undershirts tomorrow. Do you like the V-neck? Because I can get you the V-neck if that's what you want." She checked her watch. "Oh Lord, I'm going to be late. There's still roast beef in the fridge. Stetson, heat that up for you two. And grab a bag of green beans from the freezer. You put that in the microwave."

She turned for the door.

"Do you think the neighbors will care?" I shouted, randomly. I was somehow able to get those words out but not the ones that actually mattered.

She snorted. "Like we give a damn!"

Then she was gone.

Whitley and I sat in stunned silence for a few seconds before we burst into laughter.

Dad was next. We planned it for the following Friday, when he got back from work and Mom was already at the hospital.

He barged inside, sweaty from the job site and grumbling about traffic.

It was D-Day—Dad Day or Death Day. Either worked for me because both outcomes were possible.

Whitley and I hid in my bedroom for an hour, trying to write a song on her clarinet. But his looming presence coerced us into the living room.

I sat in the same armchair, hoping for some good luck from when I—well, Whitley—told Mom I was gay.

Dad cracked open a beer before joining us. The sharp fizzing made my heart race like a runaway semitrailer.

"Mr. Delancey, can we talk to you?" Whitley asked.

Dad took a sip. "What's up?" he asked. "How is school?"

Whitley and I folded our hands. My toes pulled the carpet up from the subfloor.

Dad wore a fluorescent orange hoodie, the brightest and most fitting wardrobe piece for my coming out. He juggled the beer can between his thick hands, the way he always did. I watched it go back and forth until I made myself dizzy.

His hands were coarser than stone. Years of twisting electrical wires and gripping tool handles had singed, cracked, and calloused his skin. He could put out candles with his fingers, grab pans from the oven without gloves, and adjust the wood in the fireplace without a stick.

Whitley cleared her throat. "Stetson is—"

"Wait!" I lunged for her as if I could intercept the words coming off her lips like a football.

"—gay," she finished.

Dad took a sip of his beer and gulped, hard. He stared past us through the bay window, his expression resembling last spring's tornado, picking up every thought and reaction possible. I was just an onlooker, waiting to see what he'd spit out.

"That true?" he asked. He looked to the floor, but I assumed his question was for me.

"Yeah," I croaked. My armpits burned with sweat.

He stood, then walked across the living room, his arms swinging by his sides. I shivered. His hands could crush me in a second.

I closed my eyes.

A minute passed.

Nothing happened.

So I opened them.

Dad stood over me. Then he cupped my cheek. "Okay, son," he said.

I exhaled, long and slow, then leaned into his palm. In that moment, his hand was the most comfortable place I'd ever rested. Softer than any couch, any bed, and Murray's fluffy hair. But most of all, it was more affirming than any words he could have spoken.

"You got a boyfriend or something?" he asked.

"I do," I said.

"Well, bring him around here for dinner sometime." He gestured at the kitchen table.

And I did. I brought Murray around for dinner not just sometimes but most times. For three more years.

I let out a slow exhale once I finish my story. Xander places a hand on my knee as he watches me with a soft smile.

"That's amazing, Stetson," he says. "You're so lucky."

"You think?" I ask. I don't look back on high school and see luck.

"Yeah. You have supportive parents and an amazing best friend. Why do you want to leave again?"

"I've never done anything outside of Penango on my own." I poke the back of his hand resting on my leg. "I want to prove I can make it myself."

He shrugs. "What's there to prove on your own when the people who matter want to make life together?"

His words settle between us.

The truck cabin glows gold, bathed in the fading sunlight as if a campfire burns between us. The warmth and comfort from Xander's touch is quiet reassurance that everything I've been through has been worth it.

In a town where hearts are meant to break, it feels like a rare kind of privilege to sit beside a boy who is willing to help stitch mine back together.

14

Back home, I click between internet searches about Xander Pomers and the Penango County Police Department's public records.

But the results for Xander keep me locked in place. A few articles from the same southwestern Pennsylvania news source rehash the details of the day he went missing like a script.

He was seventeen years old.

A rising senior at Stillwell Trail High School.

The son of Margaret and Richard Pomers.

An animal lover and volunteer at the Four Paws Animal Hospital.

The veterinarian spoke with him as he left his volunteer shift at seven p.m.

He called his mom around seven thirty p.m. and said he was skipping dinner to go for a drive.

That was the last time anyone heard from him.

His black Honda Civic was found at Pinehurst Swim Club the following morning.

His car keys were found on a lounge chair.

The articles were updated every month until July 2016. Then the case went cold. Their last piece was titled: *What We*

Know on the One-Year Anniversary of Xander Pomers's Disappearance.

I skim it quickly, already knowing the answer.

They knew nothing.

But something about this article feels different. The wording of its final sentence isn't open-ended like the others. No more calls for tips, no new searches, no false hope. Just a flat statement:

Xander Pomers has never been found.

Every article uses the same yearbook photo. Xander wears an unbuttoned blue-checkered shirt over a white undershirt with a frayed neckline. Black stud earrings gleam from his ears. Three chains hang around his neck—one with a cross, another with a shark tooth, and the third with a pendant too worn to make out.

But it's his face that keeps pulling me closer to the screen.

Every feature is exactly as it is now. His sharp jawline, his fuzzy sideburns. It's all so defined it makes me self-conscious about my own baby-faced senior portraits.

I rub my smooth cheeks as I try to figure out the color of his eyes. Light brown would be an easy guess. But that would be a disservice. Hazel is too ordinary. Amber too dark. Orange too bright. I decide they're gold because, like the jewelry in a store window on Main Street, I can't look away.

He's the kind of boy who would build a thirsty following if he went missing today. And I'd probably be found at the police station raising awareness about his case in a custom T-shirt and waving a *Find Xander* poster.

But without me leading the charge, he was just forgotten.

I split my computer screen, snapping my internet search to the left and Xander's photo to the right. Scrolling through the third page of results, I stop. There's a different source. One I haven't seen before—*Philadelphia Gay News*.

The headline stops me cold:

A Missing Teen's LGBT Identity Might Hold Clues Related to Disappearance.

My fingers tremble as I click the link. A pdf file loads, revealing a scanned newspaper from 2016. The pages are crooked, their edges tinged yellow with time. I start reading.

A small community in southwest Pennsylvania continues its efforts to find Xander Pomers after he disappeared nearly a year ago on July 16, 2015. "The Penango County Police Department is still actively investigating his disappearance," according to the chief of police. "Detectives have followed a number of leads but have not determined what happened to Xander at that pool."

Nothing new. But then, a mention of his mom.

Xander's mother, Margaret, recently discovered personal items in Xander's room that might reveal he was struggling with his identity. Among them were drawings, books, and photos with LGBTQ themes. "I never knew anything about this," his mother said in an interview with PGN. "I want to hug him and let him know that whatever he needs to say, it will all be okay. If he's hiding because of this, or ran away, he doesn't need to. I want to share this story so other parents make sure their child knows they don't need to be afraid."

I clamp a hand over my mouth and stare at the wall as my eyes start to burn. I squeeze them shut but that only makes it worse when Xander's face flickers in the darkness behind my eyelids.

My life didn't really begin until I came out. No matter how well I scored on a calculus test or how fast I ran a cross-country meet, none of it felt like it mattered. On paper, I was doing everything right. But at home? I felt like a failure.

In middle school, I stood stiff with my hands clasped at my wrists, smile tight, and earbuds in to put as many layers as possible between me and the world. Letting people see the real me meant exposing the cracks, and I wasn't ready for that.

I've known I was gay since I was twelve. But I didn't know what it meant to live until I told the world. Xander never got that chance. Maybe that's why he keeps mentioning our "firsts." He vanished here in Penango's valley, trapped by hills too steep for him to climb.

Margaret Pomers asked that the following statement be provided on behalf of the family: "Xander's family and friends miss him very much and want nothing but his safe return home. Xander, if you are reading this, I love you and miss you dearly, just as you are. If you can reach out and contact us, please do. We want to make sure you are safe. Love, Mom."

All evidence points to Pinehurst Swim Club as Xander's last known location. And in a way he's still there, just not as the person he once was. So, what happened?

A lightning strike is possible. Accidental drowning is also possible. But if he died there, where did his body go? Even if a bear got him—like he claims—there would've been something left behind. Or pieces of it. Bones. Or blood. Unless Smokey Bear moonlights as a crime scene cleaner, there's no way an animal scrubbed the pool deck with bleach.

I've thought about running away from home every day for the past year, so it makes sense if Xander wanted to ditch his things at the pool and do the same. But he couldn't have gotten far without his car. There were no car shares, trains, or taxis to easily take him out of Penango.

None of it adds up. My brain goes haywire trying to make sense of it all. A dull ache creeps across my temples, and I press my fingers against them trying to force the pieces of his story to fit together.

Maybe it's time I start that Find Xander online community. Better late than never, just like coming out.

He didn't vanish into thin air.

Unless . . . he wasn't alone.

And if he wasn't alone, then maybe he didn't just die.

Maybe Xander was killed.

15

Early the next morning, my phone buzzes with Whitley's face flashing across the screen. I groan, already knowing that if I don't answer, she'll keep calling, relentless as a broken ceiling fan, churning and clicking until I'm fully awake.

I accept the call and put her on speaker, too drained to lift the phone to my ear.

"Mr. Delancey," she greets.

"Whitley." I sigh. "It's early."

"I just showered. I cut, like, one hundred pieces of wood this morning. We need to have a bonfire soon. Also, are you coming over to coyote hunt?"

I smack a hand to my forehead. "Right now?" My voice is groggy. "I don't know. I'm literally so tired from this week."

I wish I could tell her about Xander and the tree. She's working the same job as me so complaining seems lame when there's so much more to it. But I don't even know what I would say. How do I begin to explain that I see a dead person?

I decided overnight I can't start the online community for that exact reason. It comes across as less helpful and more desperate for attention.

"Ugh, Stetson. You're killing me. I need you."

So many people need me these days. Victor. Sheryl. Kim. Murray. Xander. Whitley.

I need a day for myself.

"Can I help you later this weekend?"

"No. Come now. We can't let the coyote escape our perimeter. Plus . . ." She trails off.

I sit up, suddenly more awake. "What?"

"I have some bad news."

"What?" I say again, sharper.

She exhales. "At first I didn't want to tell you because I didn't want to ruin your Saturday but—"

"Did Murray text you again?"

"Yeah." She sighs. "He's here now. He said he wanted to say goodbye to me or something before I leave for school. He just came over."

I roll my eyes. "That's such a lie. He wants to talk to you about me."

"I know. I'm not an idiot. But he wouldn't let up." Bennie barks in the background. "Has he texted you?"

"No. And he completely ignored me at the Bean."

"What? Why?"

"I don't know! And isn't it weird that he's only texting you?"

"Yeah." A silence stretches between us. Rustling wind comes through the speaker. "Are you mad he's here?"

The first word that comes to mind is *yes*. I don't want to see Murray. And I don't want my friends seeing him.

But I also know better than to act surprised when he finds his way back into my life through a call, friend, or uninvited memory. It's stupid to think he'd disappear just because I ended things. We share the same hometown. He still lives ten minutes down the road. Our parents shop at the same grocery

82

store. We swim in the same river. He's a part of my past, whether I like it or not.

But Penango County is just that—my past. It's where I am from but not where I'm meant to stay.

Less than two months. That's all that stands between me and crossing the county line and stopping history from repeating itself.

I wipe my hand down my face. "It's fine," I say. "You can see whoever you want."

"Okay, cool," she says "But now I need you to come over so I can get him out of here. I need a reason to tell him to leave."

I shrug. "You shouldn't need one."

"I know, but I do."

I press my fingers into my temples. I don't want to do this. But I know how this goes. If I don't go, he wins. He gets to linger.

"Fine. I'll be there soon. Make sure he's gone before I get there."

Later, as I pull into Whitley's driveway, the sharp crack of shattering glass cuts through the air. Thirty yards away, brown shards explode from the top of a tree stump. Whitley stands in the grass, rifle raised, wearing a bikini top and jean shorts. The sun glints off her back muscles, highlighting the peeling skin of a fresh sunburn. She fires another round, then swings the gun onto her shoulder and turns to face me.

"Took you long enough," she says.

"It's been a rough week," I say. "Do you want my help or not?"

She wrinkles her nose. "Well, it shows, cranky. You can give all your attitude to Murray since he's still here. He's using the bathroom."

"He is? I thought you were going to make him leave before I got here."

"I tried, but I think it just made him stay longer."

"Great." I run my hand through my hair.

Suddenly, the front door squeaks open. Murray saunters outside with a yawn, halfway through tying the drawstring on his shorts.

I've spent ninety percent of my weekends over the past three years with Murray, so whenever my life exists within the remaining ten percent, something always feels like it's missing. But that ten percent is going to be one hundred percent of the time now, so I need to learn how to make it seem whole.

I no longer wake up and ask, *What are we going to do today?* but *What am I going to do today?* And most of the time, I don't have a freaking clue.

My whole personality, my world, revolved around Murray. I wasn't just Stetson. I was *Stetson + Murray*, just like I carved into the Ardor Tree. I never thought it was a problem until he was gone and I was left standing on one side of the life we used to share like a seesaw, suddenly aware of how uneven everything had become.

"What are you shooting at?" Murray asks Whitley.

"I'm practicing for coyote hunting with Stetson," she says, nodding at me. "I told you I couldn't hang out that long because he didn't want to see you."

I sigh, then give her a look. She shrugs.

"I don't know how else to say it," Whitley explains. "Y'all's relationship is too complicated for me."

I huff.

"I'm leaving," Murray says. "Don't worry. I have football practice at Penango College this afternoon anyway." He reaches back inside the house, grabs his duffel bag, and slings it over his shoulder.

I should let him go. Let him keep walking. Let this moment pass without another word after how he treated me at the Bean. But then he moves by me and his scent hits, dry leaves and honey.

The pull on my heart is instant.

I hate it.

"Hey, Murray," I say before I can stop myself.

He ignores me. I stare at his hands. His knuckles are red and calloused. The sight makes me clench my fists.

He pauses at the end of the driveway. "Did you ask Stetson if he got my messages?" he asks Whitley.

Whitley looks at me, narrowing her eyes. "Yeahhh," she says slowly. "He said he didn't get any texts from you all week and that you ignored him at the Bean."

"He never showed up to the Bean." Murray scratches his head. "Could you ask him again? I know he's still waiting to hear on the money for Tennessee. But I just found out I can get us discount housing near Penango College since I'm on the football team. He could live with me there. It could still be something different for him. We . . . we could work on things. I just need to send in our info soon."

Whitley curls her lip. "I'm pretty sure he told you he doesn't want to do that. But why don't you ask him yourself?" She gestures at me.

"I tried! He's lying about the messages. I sent him an email too in case he blocked my phone number."

My arms cross tightly over my chest. "I'm not lying," I say. "And I didn't block you."

Whitley groans. "I did not wake up this morning wanting to be y'all's therapist."

Murray sighs. "Ask him."

"Stetson, do you want to live in an off-campus apartment at Penango College in the fall with Murray?" Whitley asks, her shoulders deflating.

I hesitate. If I tell him that I haven't gotten my financial aid yet, he'll never leave me alone. It'll be an opening, another chance for him to dig in and keep me stuck in this conversation.

Murray gives her a thumbs-up. "Yeah, you could say it direct like that. Holler when he responds."

"I'm not staying with you, Murray," I repeat.

He ignores me, again, and walks north toward town. "If he does say no," he calls over his shoulder, "I'd love to see him before he leaves for Tennessee. Just one more time."

Whitley plants her hand on her hip. "Murray Mifflin, are you drunk right now?"

He laughs. "I wish I was. It would make this whole breakup a hell of a lot easier."

She scoffs. "Stop being a baby and use your damn eyes. He's right here in the drive."

"Funny joke," he mutters.

Heat flares through me like a bomb detonating in my chest.

Does he really not see me? A horrible thought enters my head. Could I be invisible like Xander?

"Murray!" I shout, stepping forward. "Stop!"

But he doesn't stop. His ears don't twitch. His head doesn't turn. He keeps walking like I never spoke.

Like I don't exist.

I stand frozen, watching him disappear beyond the evergreen trees.

My voice shakes. "Whitley, am I standing in the driveway?" I ask.

"You sure are," she says. "And he just ignored the hell out of you."

Something sinks in my gut like I've jumped off a twenty-foot-high diving board. I lift my hands in front of my face, turning them slowly, inspecting every crease, scar, hair, and piece of me that suddenly doesn't feel like mine.

"Enough killing time," Whitley says, tossing me her rifle. Then she digs into her pocket and pulls out a box of ammo. "We have a coyote to kill. Load that up. I'm going to get my other gun."

She disappears inside the house and leaves me alone beneath the looming mountains. I press my shoes into the loose gravel, listening to the crackle of stone against concrete. The sound steadies me, my breath slows.

A truck rumbles past. The driver, a stranger, grips the steering wheel tightly. I hesitate, then lift a reluctant hand to wave. He nods in return, like he can see me. It lightens the tension in my muscles.

This purgatory started with Xander. Now Murray.

To one I exist. To the other, I don't.

If heartbreak is what killed me, then I must be on my way to hell.

16

After a string of failed coyote hunts with Whitley, it's time for real answers. I don't even think I was much help to her anyway because I was too distracted by one question.

Can Murray Mifflin still see me?

I reverse out of Whitley's driveway and head for Latitudes Avenue—Murray's home address. It's the oldest road in Penango, tucked just off Main Street. A mile in, the river appears through my passenger-side window, its slow-moving water a familiar backdrop.

Soon, stately homes emerge from between the trees. Most are white, but one is stone, another pale yellow. They all have too many windows to count. Their wraparound porches stretch like endless boardwalks, draped in hanging plants, American flags, and wind chimes like they're stuck in an eternal Fourth of July.

I pull up to 1109 and spot the dim glow of blue light seeping through the only arched window in the front of the house—Murray's room. I wait and watch for a silhouette to cross the light.

Nothing appears.

My gaze drifts downward to the front porch, a place I know far too well.

A key is hidden beneath an empty clay pot beside the door. The second porch step never had a tread. It's more awkward stepping down than up, but I got used to it. The third window to the right of the door doesn't lock. If the key ever goes missing, that's how we get inside.

Suddenly, the front door swings open, snapping my focus back. A bearded man stumbles onto the porch. The screen door slams into the aluminum siding with a crack, like a firework exploding too soon.

He plants one boot on the first step. I brace myself knowing the second step still has no tread. His other boot drops straight through the gap, and he crashes face-first onto the lawn. A burst of laughter rings out behind him from the doorway. Murray's mom steps outside, shaking her head.

I roll down my window farther to hear them better.

"Go on and get yourself home so we can do this again," Mrs. Mifflin says.

"You like this view?" the man asks, shaking his backside as he rolls in the grass.

Murray's mom smiles. She walks to the lawn, then gently kicks the man's side. "Get up, you dufus," she says. "You're going to wake Murray. He's taking a nap."

I sigh. If she only knew her son barely slept. I look back to Murray's bedroom window, and his black silhouette observes the scene below. I wonder if he's observing me too.

I exit my truck.

"Stetson?" his mom asks as I walk up the front pavers. "What are you doing here?" The bearded man scrambles to his feet. His face reddens.

"Hi, Mrs. Mifflin," I say, stopping a few yards in front of her. I'm not sure what Murray has told her about us. She used to love me. I wonder if those feelings have been lost too. "I'm here to see Murray."

She takes a deep breath. "Well, he'll certainly be happy to hear that."

I swallow.

"He's upstairs." She points inside the house. "Been a wreck this week."

I nod, then walk toward the door. Mrs. Mifflin grabs my arm as I pass. "If you ain't kind to him, you're going to regret coming in my house," she whispers.

The bearded man snickers.

"Understood," I say. "I won't be too long."

"Good. Because he needs his sleep." She releases me and I turn my walk into a jog.

I doubt Murray is taking a nap because I can't remember the last time he slept through the night. When we first started having sleepovers, I thought he was a psychopath plotting my murder like in one of my favorite true crime podcasts.

At two in the morning, I'd hear him cooking macaroni and cheese. At three, the shower would turn on. By five, he'd be playing video games like it was the middle of the afternoon. But it wasn't insomnia that kept him up. Murray never slept because he never knew who his mom had in their house.

After his parents split and his dad took a trucking job, a rotating cast of strangers filled his place. Murray told me about midnight bathroom run-ins with men he'd never seen before, about times they'd mistake his bedroom for his mom's and push open his door without warning.

But some nights, the imposter wasn't an imposter. It was his dad. And that kept Murray awake just as much as the

90

strangers. His dad never stayed for more than a day, but Murray made sure he was always awake to say hello.

I reach the top of the stairs just as Murray walks out of the bathroom. He's shirtless, wearing black Stillwell Trail Football shorts. He scratches his shoulder absentmindedly before disappearing inside his bedroom.

"Murray," I call out. He doesn't return to the hall.

I grab the banister and take a deep breath as I survey the familiar second floor. This hallway is where I first realized just how handsome Murray was.

It was the weekend before sophomore year homecoming.

"Should we coordinate our outfits for the dance?" I asked from his doorway.

"I don't have an outfit," Murray said.

His house once belonged to his grandparents, so that Thursday, we dug through his late grandfather's closet in search of something he could wear. What we found was a time capsule of suits from every era—long black waistcoats, pinstriped vests, checkered blazers, baby blue trousers, and even top hats.

"Fashion show! Fashion show!" I chanted, clapping my hands as Murray rifled through drawers, pulling out funky-colored socks and thick gold rings.

He tried on suit after suit and strutted across the upstairs hallway, as if his long legs were meant for the runway.

The first tan suit sagged at his ankles. He leaned against his mom's door and licked his lips, staring right through me. The dark circles under his eyes stood in sharp contrast to the bright fabric, making him look like a flamboyant British rock star at the height of his fame.

Next, he stepped out of his grandfather's room behind oversized sunglasses, slowly pulling forest green trousers up his leg. He teased his ankle, then his calf. He stopped at his thigh, then wagged a finger at me with a pout.

I laughed every time. And every time, I was stunned by how effortlessly he fit into each look. He was a man for every decade—classic like the '20s, smooth like the '50s, trendy like the '70s, and rebellious like the '80s. I wanted him forever, in perpetuity, the way those suits had stood the test of time. I thought, maybe we could too.

But looks only get you so far. And time made sure I learned that.

I knock on his open bedroom door. "Hey, Murray. It's Stetson." I turn inside and find him playing a video game at his desk.

"Murray?" I question.

He doesn't move or say anything.

I thrust my hands in my pockets. "Murray, can you please tell me if you're ignoring me or not? I have this weird thing going on and I really need you to say something." I grind my teeth. "Anything."

He grabs a pretzel and pops it into his mouth.

"Please." My voice cracks. "Can you see me?" I reach for him. My shaky hand hovers above his shoulder. Then the front door slams closed downstairs.

Murray pauses his game. "Who was that, Mom?" he asks, yelling into the hallway.

"Stetson," she says. "Didn't he come up there to say hi?"

Murray jumps to his feet. "Stetson! Where?"

He tosses his video game controller onto the desk and spins toward his mom's voice with a broad grin. His hazel eyes flicker, alive with something I've only seen a handful of times. Once after our first kiss. Another on the day he made the Penango College football team.

Next, he unexpectedly passes right through me as if I'm not even there. My skin detonates from the inside out and sends a cloud of dustlike particles bursting into the air. My breath catches as I watch tiny specs of my body shimmering in the blue light of his TV screen. A wave of dizziness crashes over me, leaving my limbs weightless.

Murray stomps down the stairs. "Where's Stetson?" he asks.

The shattered pieces of my body snap back together in an instant, like iron filings in science class drawn to a magnet, merging into something whole again. But even as my body reassembles, I feel hollow inside, and unsteady.

This must be what Xander has felt the past ten years. A decade of numbness.

The shock of what just happened knocks me off balance, and I collapse onto Murray's bed. A sob escapes before I can stop it.

My tears soak into his sheets. They're pale blue and covered in a repeating pattern of soccer balls, basketballs, baseballs, and footballs. They form perfect diamonds across the fabric that are easy to follow. I trace the pattern with my fingertips, tapping each ball in an even rhythm as my breath shudders out of me.

"Soccer ball, basketball, baseball, football," I whisper. "Soccer ball, basketball, baseball, football. Soccer ball, basketball, baseball, football."

The counting calms me and steadies my breathing. Below, I hear Murray muttering frustrations as he climbs the stairs. But I don't move from his bed. I don't even look up. What difference does it make? I got my answer.

He can no longer see me.

17

Later that night, beneath the full moon's glow, I return to Rainbow Valley Swim Club. Xander is sprawled out on his usual lounge chair, *Because of Winn-Dixie* open over his face, acting as a makeshift sleep mask. One hand is tucked behind his head, the other dangles over the side, swaying slightly in the night breeze, inches above the grass.

I tap his shoulder. His skin is damp—either from the humidity or a recent dip in the pool.

"Wake up," I say, my voice raw from all the tears I shed on the drive here.

He groans.

"Xander, it's Stetson. I need to talk to you."

He sits up. The book slips from his face and lands in his lap with a soft thud. He flinches as it hits his waist.

"Stetson?" he mumbles, rubbing his eyes. "What time is it?" A yawn stretches from the back of his throat.

"I don't know, and I don't care."

The sharpness in my voice slices through his grogginess like a defibrillator bringing someone back to life. He blinks, suddenly alert, then stands.

"What's wrong?" His eyeballs sweep over me from head to toe. "Why are you upset?"

"I'm like you," I say flatly.

He rests his hand on his hip. "Well, that's mean. I think I'm a fairly decent person."

I shake my head.

"Or is this about being gay?" he presses. "Because if so, I can help you work through that. I've had a lot of time to ruminate over the whole ordeal." He spins his hand through the air.

I grab his wrist, holding him steady. "It's not that. It's . . . people . . ." I swallow. He raises his eyebrows. ". . . People can't see me. Like how they can't see you."

His face goes pale, like he's just seen a ghost. And maybe that's because, for the first time, he has.

"Everyone?" he asks, stepping back only to trip over the lounge chair, landing hard.

"Only one person so far. My ex-boyfriend, Murray." My pulse pounds. "How did this happen?"

Xander pushes himself up, then locks his hands behind his head as he starts pacing.

Beside him, the pool looks full. Sherly and Kim must have been working nonstop over the past few days. But I can't tell if the water is blue or green. A dark gradient, somewhere between black and navy, spreads across the surface. Every slow-moving ripple catches the moonlight, silver glinting off the crest of each wave.

"Just one person?" he asks. "So everyone else can still see you?"

I nod. "That I know of."

"Then you're not like me."

"Murray just casually walked through my body like I was a damn lawn sprinkler!" I jab a finger into my chest. "I exploded into a million tiny pieces and landed on his freaking video game controller." My throat tightens. "I might not be exactly like you, but I am not who I used to be."

His eyes go wide. "Oh, shit. Yeah, that can happen."

He wraps an arm around my back and guides me down onto the lounge chair. I let myself fall against his warm, bare skin, my breathing shallow as I try to steady myself. His heart beats slowly beneath my ear. I focus on it and count each thud against his rib cage.

I make it to thirty-five before he speaks again.

"It's going to be all right," he murmurs as his fingers thread my hair. "We found each other for a reason. We'll get through this."

"I can't be dead," I say. "I was just getting out of here."

"You're not dead if some people can still see you. Did anything . . . happen recently? An accident?"

I exhale sharply. "So much has happened in the past couple weeks. I can barely keep it straight."

"Walk me through it. Quickly."

I suck in a deep breath. "I broke up with my boyfriend . . . then I started this new pool job . . . then I saw you . . . I went coyote hunting with my friend Whitley . . . then Murray lost his ability to see me . . . and now I'm here."

Xander's fingers go still against my scalp. The night air hums with cicadas and trilling toads. "Nothing else? I don't get why you can see me when no one else can."

"That list wasn't weird enough for you?" I tip my head back and catch the dark silhouettes of tree branches stretching across the gray sky. And then it hits me.

"Wait."

He stiffens. "What? Something else happened?"

I swallow. "I went to the Ardor Tree after I broke up with Murray. And it . . . it attacked me!" I've tried so hard to block out the memory I nearly forgot it.

His hand moves to my chin, pushing it up until our eyes meet. His expression is unreadable.

"You were at the Ardor Tree before this all happened?" he asks.

I nod. "Last Sunday."

His lips press together. His head tilts slightly like he's fitting a puzzle piece into place. "I was at the Ardor Tree right before I disappeared."

My heart skips a beat. "If we were both at the Tree . . . and I'm not dead . . ." My breath catches. "That might mean—"

Xander's mouth falls open. "Neither am I."

18

On Sunday, I curl up in Dad's armchair with my laptop, watching live music videos that the internet selects for me, too spent to change the queue. My week-long state of fear and confusion has exhausted me. I struggle to keep my eyelids open even as an up-tempo beat pulsates through my eardrums. Every time a scene changes and cuts to black, Xander's face flashes across the screen.

"Food!" Dad yells as he rushes through the front screen door. He grips two grease-covered brown bags in his left hand and a beer can in his right. He enters the kitchen and flicks on the pendant lamp hanging over the wooden table. The bags land on the counter with a crunch.

"What're you working on?" he questions, looking at my laptop.

"Who's working on what?" Mom asks as she walks into the living room from the bedroom hallway. "It's Sunday night. I don't want to hear about any type of work."

"Nothing. It's just music." I slam my laptop closed and take out my earbuds. "I couldn't possibly do another second of work. I don't think a full-time job is for me."

"Your first forty-hour work week will do that to you. Welcome to the real world."

"What happened to your head?" Dad asks as I waddle to the kitchen. It's the first time he's seeing me up close in a while.

"I fell at Whitley's house," I say.

"It looks like you didn't get the cream from the pharmacy like I told you to," Mom says. "The wound is slow to heal."

"It'll be fine."

Dad chomps on a fry, then mimics a fist punch, hitting me with a gaze sharp as a tack, seeing right through my lie.

Mom digs into the food bag and pulls out a salad. "What's this?" she asks, holding it out to Dad.

"Your salad." Dad's forehead wrinkles.

Mom sighs. "I said *I wanted a cheeseburger but should probably get a salad.*"

"Yeah. Then I asked which is it, and you said a salad."

"I said, *I guess a salad.* Which means you were supposed to treat me to a cheeseburger."

Dad scoffs. "And if I got you a burger, you'd be mad I didn't get a salad."

Mom ignores him and turns to me. "What'd you get, honey?"

One of the hardest things to understand about life is how sometimes, instead of just asking for what we want, we do the opposite, hoping it will somehow get us what we actually need.

It makes so little sense that even thinking about it feels like running in circles.

Like Mom with this salad. Or like when I wanted my family to know I was gay. Instead of telling them, being open, and making myself happy, I shut down, went silent, and made myself miserable hoping they'd notice and force me to tell them. Or like Whitley, when her dad left town. She wanted him to come back, but instead of saying that, she told him to kick rocks and never return, hoping he'd get mad and prove her wrong.

But feelings don't follow logic. That's why nothing about how we act makes sense. It's an equation that doesn't add up, something I can't count. Looking back, it's no surprise that when Murray wanted me to stay, he spent all his time pushing me away.

A chime from my laptop breaks my thoughts. An email.

I refresh my inbox on my phone, half expecting some long-winded hunting plan from Whitley.

Instead, buried between spam from shoe stores, I see it. Subject: *Financial Aid*.

A lump forms in my throat. I swallow a french fry too fast, coughing as it scrapes its way down. My thumb hovers over the email before I finally tap it.

I skim the words. My eyes move faster than my brain can process and I'm two paragraphs in before the first sentence actually sinks in.

I'm ineligible for aid.

The world tilts. My meal fades to black like a movie reel running out of film. My ears ring.

I see it in my mind—the word printed next to University of Tennessee on my résumé.

Tentative.

The future just changed from *tentative* to *certain* faster than I wanted, and not in the direction I was banking on.

My dream of leaving Penango was like a flashlight on its last flicker in a summer storm. Now the light is gone. I'm in the dark, unsure where to go next.

100

My mind races, searching for ways to undo this decision.
This job might be enough to cover my housing deposit in a few
weeks. But the rest? My paychecks won't even come close.
Nights and weekends are open for another position, but in a
town this small, every summer job is already taken.

My brain turns into a calculator, frantically adding,
subtracting, and multiplying work hours and tuition costs. But
the numbers aren't in my favor.

Murray won.

Checkmate.

I was supposed to be the first person in my family to leave for
college. The first to get a degree. Last fall, I never thought I'd
fit into Whitley's plan to go to school far from home.

Now it's clear that I don't.

At Stillwell Trail High, my first guidance counselor was a
seventy-year-old man I never met. He passed away at the end
of my freshman year, and the school struggled to replace him.

For two years, I assumed the position was still empty,
until one day I was called to the office. A young woman sat
behind the desk, flipping through a stack of SAT prep books. A
navy bandana held back her long brown hair, and her round
face was flushed like she'd been rushing around all morning. I
swore I'd seen her before, maybe in the halls, but I didn't
think she was a teacher, definitely not a counselor.

"Hi there," she said, barely looking up. "I'm the new
counselor for Stillwell." She exhaled, her shoulders slumping
like she was carrying the weight of the entire school. "How are
you?" Her voice was a little too fast and eager.

"I'm fine," I said. "I'm Stetson."

I sat across from her with my hands resting on my knees and earbuds still in from the walk over. This was during my Brandi Carlile phase when I had her live album with the Seattle Symphony on repeat after learning she was also queer.

"Do you mind removing your earbuds while we meet?"

She yanked open a file cabinet and slammed it shut, making me jump. I quickly pulled my earbuds out and shoved them into my pocket.

"I've only been here for a few days," she said, tossing a file onto the desk. "But, Stetson, you're one of the first students I wanted to talk to."

I shifted in my seat, picking at a loose thread on my jeans. "Why is that?"

"I was looking through your notes, and I wanted to see if what I was reading was accurate."

I laughed. "I hope so. I've been here my whole life. You'd think they have it all right by now."

She pulled a paper from the file and held it up. "You've had straight A's for all three years?"

I leaned over her desk to get a better look at the page. It was my academic transcript.

I nodded. "Aren't we supposed to?"

"And you run cross-country in the fall, play basketball in the winter, and run track in the spring?"

I shrugged. "Yeah. There's not much else to do around here. I'd be bored otherwise."

"And you lead mathletes—"

I crossed my arms. "Only because my calc teacher guilt-tripped me. They needed an extra person. It's easy, so I just jump in when I don't have games."

She ran her hand down the page. "Stetson, you should be proud of these accomplishments. And there's more."

I raised my eyebrows.

She smirked. "Have you applied to college yet? I know it's already your senior year, but I'm trying to catch up as quick as I can."

"No," I muttered, spinning my thumbs in my lap. "I'm going to go to the city first. Then I'll figure it out."

"What city?"

"Pittsburgh," I said. "Or maybe Cleveland. I have an uncle there." I pointed out the window as if the city was just beyond the tree line. "Anywhere outside of Penango, really."

Her expression softened. "That's great. I'm happy to hear you have a plan after high school. Have you thought about applying to schools in those cities?"

"Like where?" I asked. "My friend Whitley Wyomen wants to go somewhere crazy like Florida. You know her?"

She nods. "Whitley told me about that plan."

"I probably won't get accepted anywhere that my parents can actually afford, so it doesn't matter."

Her brows pinched. "I think you have an opportunity that a lot of students don't. And there are ways to make college more affordable."

"Yeah? I figure I'll work first to save up money. My parents get pissed whenever I mention anything other than community college—too expensive." I shook my head. "It's crazy that college isn't free like high school. And my boyfriend, Murray, wants me to stay close by too."

She leaned forward slightly. "Well, what does Stetson want?"

I frowned. "I just told you."

She shrugged, then slid me another paper across her desk. "Take a look at this." I skimmed the words. "It's a list of schools that might interest you. But no pressure. Do what's right for you."

I bit my pinky nail. "Thanks," I said, grabbing the paper and shoving it in my pocket, nearly crumpling it in the process. "I'll show Whitley."

Afterward, I went straight to Whitley's locker and told her I might actually join her grand escape plan.

Mom, however, was less enthused. She stared at me, unblinking, for a solid five minutes before finally saying, "When people tell you to pursue your dreams, they mean within reason."

"My counselor said this is within reason for me," I countered. "School might be good. You always said if I was going to spin my wheels, don't do it around here or I'd get into trouble like everyone else."

"You can apply," she said, voice clipped. "But only to state schools. We give the state half our money, the least they could do is provide you with an education."

So I wrote down the names of every state that didn't border Pennsylvania, tossed the slips of paper into a mason jar, and picked five. I could only afford five application fees.

This seemed as fair a way to choose as any.

By December, I had applied to the University of Kentucky, the University of Tennessee, and the University of Nevada.

California was my first draw, but I quickly learned their state schools barely accepted out-of-state students. I wasn't about to waste an application fee, so I pulled another.

I also drew Utah and Washington. But Murray made me miss the deadlines. Every time I submitted an application, he wouldn't speak to me for weeks. Two more rounds of silent treatment felt unbearable, so I just didn't apply.

When the acceptance letters came, I chose the University of Nevada because it was the farthest from Penango—mileage-wise—per my and Whitley's pact.

But then Mom found out it was in Las Vegas.

"You think I worked day and night my whole life to send my child to school in a city where people go to ruin their lives?" she scoffed.

"University of Tennessee it is," I said.

But now none of it matters.

I did a fine job of ruining my life on my own.

19

I wake up an hour before my alarm on Monday morning, my mind still buzzing from everything I learned this weekend—about Xander, about myself, and potentially about the Ardor Tree.

Something strange is happening in Penango County for the first time in its history, and somehow, I'm tangled up in it. This mystery has unearthed itself and wraps around my ankles like overgrown tree roots, tightening and twisting, keeping me trapped in this valley like everyone else who never made it past the mountains.

Xander and I agreed to visit the Ardor Tree later this week. He seems more eager to figure out what's happening to us than I do. I want answers, but I'm afraid of what they might mean, if this whole thing might be permanent.

He's spent years frozen in time, forever seventeen. But if that happens to me, if I'm trapped in this limbo with him, it means Whitley will grow old without me. My future friends at the University of Tennessee will move on, stepping into their twenties and adulthood while I stay behind, unable to even get into a bar.

Penango will be the only place I have left.

At work, Whitley chats about her plans to join the pep band at the University of Florida and rambles on about the dozens of beaches she's already mapped out. Every word flips my stomach. Every time she mentions Florida, I picture Tennessee and the image isn't as bright as it used to be.

I press a hand over my right ear and turn up my latest podcast, *Stories of Appalachia*. It's about folklore from the region. I listen closely, waiting to hear if Xander's case ever made it into an episode.

Whitley's voice quickly cuts through my thoughts. "Why are you being so quiet this morning?" she asks.

I blink. "What?" I fake confusion, swallowing hard. "I'm just trying to get organized for this week."

A lie.

I don't tell her about the financial aid. Or that I might be half ghost. Or that I'm communicating with a full ghost.

The pact we made earlier this year makes all of it worse. If I don't go to college, I'll be letting her down. I don't want to be another person who bails on her.

I wipe the sweat from my forehead and take a deep breath, forcing myself to swap out my negative attitude for something more productive.

Do they give bonuses here? Probably not. Getting zilch in financial aid must be karma for breaking up with my boyfriend before I even had a solid plan to leave town.

Fifteen dollars an hour seems like a lot when I'm buying burgers at the Bean and used vinyl records from the thrift store on Main. But now that I need money for . . . oh, I don't know . . . anything useful—it's a joke.

Whitley stares at me. I can't rely on her for everything. The universe must be telling me that if I want to get out of here, I have to start taking matters into my own hands.

"I'll be right back," I say. "I need to talk to Victor."

I enter his office and find him hunched over his desk playing solitaire on his computer.

"Morning, Victor," I say. "Can I ask you a question?"

He barely looks up. "You just did," he quips with a grin.

I clench my jaw, staring out the window and resisting the urge to roll my eyes.

For a split second, I wonder if this job is even worth it. Do I really want to spend what could be my last summer in Penango dealing with this? But maybe it's not the job I dislike. Maybe it's the place and the person. It makes me question if my frustration with Murray was actually about him. Or was I just tired of us being here? If we had met somewhere else, would things have worked out differently?

I shake off the thought.

No. It wouldn't. Not after what he did to me last week.

"Are there any open job positions left at the health department this summer?" I ask.

I also want to ask why he didn't tell me Rainbow Valley was a crime scene. But I swallow that question because I doubt the answer will be satisfying.

Victor shrugs. "I think we're pretty booked up. Who needs a job?"

"Me. I'm looking for something extra."

His frown deepens. "How do you expect to work two full-time jobs at once?"

"I was thinking nights or weekends."

He laughs. "Are you trying to kill yourself, kid?"

"No. I just really need the money."

He leans back in his chair. "You could always stay on in the fall if you do a good job this summer."

"I'm hoping to go to college in the fall."

He raises an eyebrow. "Well, I guess it's school or work, then. You can't always get everything you want."

I turn to leave, and this time, I don't fight the urge to roll my eyes. They roll so hard, the muscles behind them ache.

"How did you end up with Mary Jo as your supervisor while I got stuck with Victor?" I ask Whitley as I step back into our shared cubicle.

She polishes her clarinet's mouthpiece with a green cloth. "Mary Jo is such a boss," she says. "She shut down both pools we inspected last week. The second she puts on her visor, she turns into Erin Brockovich. I'm thinking about getting a visor too. It totally feels like my vibe."

"Can we get matching ones?"

"Only if you're on our level."

"I don't think Victor and I will ever match y'all's power."

"What did he do this time?"

"Nothing. It's what he doesn't do that's the problem."

Whitley shrugs. "It could be worse. At least he isn't hovering over your summer like Murray."

I sigh. "I guess."

"Speaking of that sorry boy—are you really not getting his texts?"

I frown. "Yeah. I wouldn't lie to you."

She studies me. "I don't know . . . You've been weird lately. When are you going to tell me what he did to your head? Or are you just going to let that gaping gash of secrets stare at me all summer?"

"Isn't it obvious?"

"I don't assume."

"Soon," I say, slamming my phone face down on my desk. "Anyway, I'm heading back to that strange pool I told you about."

"Oh, yeah?" She perks up. "What's up with that place again?"

"Dead animals. Green water. Middle of nowhere."

I still haven't mentioned Xander to her. The strangest part of all.

"That sounds amazing," she says. "Why are you complaining? I inspect hotels where everything is cleaner than a damn church. Are there any interesting people there?"

My body tenses. "What?" I laugh lightly, crossing my arms. "No. Who would I have seen there that's interesting?"

She narrows her eyes. "This is an example of you being weird."

"I'm not . . . It's just—"

She blows into her clarinet, cutting me off as she tests the freshly cleaned keys. "I'm heading into town after work for my first street performance," she says. "I got to make sure this baby sounds her best, so people throw me more than just dollar bills."

"Grease away."

She grins. "If I make enough money, I might be able to get us a few fancy hotel nights on our road trip this summer." She examines the shiny clarinet mouthpiece, then snaps on a new reed with a satisfied nod.

I scratch my neck. The reminder of my failed college plan sits heavier than ever.

Whitley keeps playing a slow, melancholy sound that fills our cubicle, the perfect score for a movie about my life's demise.

20

Light gray clouds churn across the sky as I drive south. They roll down the mountains and sink low over the trees like smoke from a snuffed-out flame. The first drop of rain splatters against my windshield just as I turn into Rainbow Valley's long driveway. My tires slosh through muddy puddles and send ripples across the murky brown water.

I park next to a new car I don't recognize.

At the top of a ladder, Kim brushes leaves off the old shed's roof.

"Hey, Stetson," she says as I step out of my truck.

"Hey, Kim." I give her a quick wave.

"These leaves have been here so long they're basically cemented on." She scrapes at them with her gloved hand, then glances up at the darkening sky. "I'm trying to clear them off before the rain." She jerks her chin toward the pool. "Sheryl is over there, if you're here for another inspection."

I nod and head down the drive.

Sheryl stands near the lounge chairs, deep in conversation with an unfamiliar woman. Xander isn't beside them. He has a habit of listening in on these conversations unseen, so I scan the trees and far end of the pool for where he might be hiding, but there's nothing.

A cool breeze hits my face, sending my hair swirling and raising goose bumps along my arms.

"Is the third time the charm?" Sheryl asks as I approach.

The other woman crosses her arms and gives me a once-over with a faint smile.

I grin. "Let's hope so."

Sheryl sucks in a breath through gritted teeth, rubbing her forehead. "Well, I hate to break it to you, but I'm about to kill that hope real quick."

At this point, I barely flinch. Hope isn't something I count on lately. I glance at the pool. It still looks like a Saint Patrick's Day–themed science experiment.

"We're thinking of draining the whole dang thing and starting fresh," Sheryl says, hands on her hip. "We tried shocking it with high levels of chlorine too, but that didn't do a thing."

"That could work," I say.

I hand her an informational packet on pool cleaning methods from the health department. "I'll check out the safety equipment while I'm here." I nod toward the bin of orange life jackets and the freshly constructed lifeguard stand.

It's strange to see something so new, so clean. Especially here, but really, anywhere in Penango. We're a town of hand-me-downs. We use old textbooks with scribbled notes from students long gone. Our rusted cars rattle down cracked back roads. And we wear our grandparents' hemmed clothes to homecoming dances. Just like the people, everything here is barely getting by. Keeping it all together takes up so much time, there's not a second to spare to even think about getting out.

I'm starting to understand how people get stuck.

"Before you do that, I want to introduce you to Maggie," Sheryl says, placing a hand on the other woman's shoulder. "Stetson, this is Maggie Pomers."

A cool rush of adrenaline floods my body. My breath catches. I yank out my earbud, suddenly needing to catch every single word of what she has to say.

"She's Xander's mother," Sheryl continues. "I'm giving her a tour of the grounds."

My throat tightens. "Hi, Mrs. Pomers," I say, my voice unsteady. "I'm Stetson Delancey—the local county pool inspector."

She extends her hand. "You can call me Maggie."

Her mouth moves exactly like Xander's when she speaks. Her hair is dark and curly like his too. The greeting is jarring—like hearing a friend's voice in a crowded room when I wasn't expecting them to be there.

And her eyes hold the same intensity, a deep, amber glow. But unlike Xander, the corners of her eyelids droop slightly, appearing like she's on the verge of tears even as she smiles.

"We're trying to recruit Stetson for camp," Sheryl says with a laugh. "Come to think of it . . ." She raises a finger in the air. "You should help chaperone our summer send-off dance. We just finalized the activity schedule."

I shrug. "What would I do?"

"Serve punch. Hang out. The kids would love having an older role model around."

Maggie swallows.

I shift my stance. "As long as the pool stays green, I'll be here." I force a small smile. "So . . . count me in."

Sheryl grins. "Then we'll have to keep it green all summer."

I stare at her.

"Kidding. Kidding." She lifts her hands in surrender.

"Xander would have loved this," Maggie says, pressing a hand to her heart. "I really appreciate everything you're doing here, Sheryl. It's beyond sweet."

"That's what it's all about," Sheryl says, nodding. "We have a page on our website dedicated to him. I'll have to show you later."

Maggie's cheeks flush pink.

"What made him come here?" I ask.

Maggie blinks and tightens her expression. "Excuse me?"

I clutch my clipboard to my chest. "I mean . . . why did he like swimming here at night?"

She exhales, rubbing her brow. "Right, sorry. My mind always goes elsewhere." Her hands move to her hips. "It was on the way home from the animal hospital. I think he liked stopping here to unwind after his shifts. It's quiet, you know? Peaceful. You could always hear the water lapping against the pool walls, especially back then. The trees, the birds . . . it was calming for him." She pauses. "Xander was a private person."

"That sounds nice," I say as I glance over my shoulder.

He's not there.

Maggie's gaze drifts to the side. She bites her thumbnail. "I do wonder if he came here because . . . he was afraid to go home. If he felt uncomfortable there, you know?"

Sheryl lets out a sigh. "Of course he didn't, Maggie." She squeezes her arm.

Maggie hums softly, but there's no conviction in it. Her hands slide from her hips into her back pockets. "It doesn't really matter what I think though. That was always my problem. I spent too much time in my own head. Never enough time in his."

114

A tear slips from her left eye. She catches it with the back of her hand.

Sheryl cringes. "It's okay, Maggie. Why don't we finish the tour and let Stetson get on with his inspection?" She nudges her gently forward.

Maggie nods. "Yes. Of course. Please excuse me. It's just—" She swallows, then forces a smile. "I'm just overwhelmed at how wonderful this place will be. It has me thinking about everything Xander is missing."

Her eyes meet mine.

"And everything he could've been."

21

The inspection wraps up without a sign of Xander.

I was hoping to see him, even though we hadn't made plans today. Lately, he feels like the only person who gets me. The only one who understands what it's like to live without hope that things will ever change.

I walk slowly down the drive, giving him time to sneak up on me, maybe drop down from a tree and shower me with Skittles.

But he never comes.

The passenger seat of my truck is empty.

Rainbow Valley's open shed holds nothing but a few stacked lounge chairs.

I replay our last conversation, when we were figuring out when we'd see each other again.

And then it hits me.

He's not here because he doesn't want to be.

All he talked about was the Ardor Tree. Any other plans were off the table.

His absence hits my heart differently than Murray's. With Murray, it's relief. With Xander, it's worry.

On my way to the Ardor Tree, the rain finally breaks free from the waterlogged clouds and falls at a steady pace. Deep puddles form along the road's shoulders, their surfaces rippling like a pool caught in a storm. Thunder rumbles before a streak of lightning splits the horizon.

I park along a muddy embankment near the trailhead and step out. My shoes slide on the slick grass as I lurch toward the woods, where the thick tree canopy shields me from the worst of the downpour.

Fog clings between the trees, dense and unmoving. Combined with the heavy green of summer leaves and the steel-gray sky, the familiar woods are cloaked in an unrecognizable darkness.

Then, at the edge of the obscured path, the neon graffiti on the sewer pipe begins to glow through the shadows. My breath catches.

Xander sits cross-legged in front of the Ardor Tree, shirtless, his head tilted up toward the carved hearts. He sucks on a blue slushy from the gas station. I grab my stomach as an unexpected drove of butterflies find their new home.

"What do you think this tree has to do with us?" Xander asks, his back still to me.

Raindrops roll from the soaked tips of his curls, trailing down his tanned shoulders and tracing the dips and rises of his arm muscles.

I sit beside him.

"Well," I say, clearing my throat. "It's the first commonality between us . . . in our journeys to ghostdom. So there's got to be something here. At least a place to start."

He turns to me, lips stained blue. My eyes flick to the chain around his neck, where the shark tooth rests against his collarbone.

"Commonality?" he repeats before taking another sip of his slushy. "That's a good SAT word. I sucked at those tests. Pre-vet schools were not kind to me because of it."

I swallow.

He leans sideways and nudges me with his shoulder. "Don't worry," he says. "I assume you did well on the SAT. You won't hurt my feelings if you say you got a perfect score. Own your shit. Life is too short."

A soft breeze chills the rainwater on my neck. "I did do well," I admit.

"There you go." He grins and drapes his arm over my shoulder. Heavy, dense warmth presses into me. "I bet I'd do better now. Guess how many books I read last year?"

A drop of water clings to the tip of his nose as he studies me.

"Twenty-four."

"Two a month?" he scoffs. "Insulting."

"Thirty?" I try. "I don't know. I give up."

"Sixty." He nods, satisfied. "The vocabulary section wouldn't stand a chance against me."

"It'd be an ignominious defeat."

He rolls his eyes with a smile. "Yeah, yeah. I'll leave this mystery for you to solve, then, smart guy."

Heat creeps up my neck.

"By the way," he adds, tone flat. "Your nipples are hard." Before I can react, he flicks my chest and stands.

I flinch, tugging at my soaked shirt, which has suctioned to my body. "So are yours," I mutter, scrambling to my feet.

His shoulders shake with laughter. "I know. I didn't say it was a bad thing." He winks. "Just observing."

I squirm for a response.

"Are you done yet?" he continues.

"Done what?" I ask, shifting my eyes upward from his chest.

His smirk deepens. "Observing me."

My face burns. "Let's focus on the tree, shall we?" I move toward the base of the trunk. The first carving I see is *Kelsey and Phil / Class of '97.*

"Where did you say your heart is?" Xander asks.

"Was." I correct him. "I smashed it off. Then the tree attacked me." I lead him to the spot where my original heart was carved. The white, inner wood of the tree has darkened since I last visited.

His eyebrows shoot up. "Oh, you really smashed it. I thought you meant you, like, threw a rock at it or something. I didn't know you went full Gimli on the poor thing and axed off a chunk. No wonder it fought back."

I exhale. "It was an emotional day."

"Screw that guy for making you so mad."

I shift the conversation before Murray becomes the focus. "The tree didn't attack you?" I ask.

Xander shakes his head. "Nope."

"What were you doing here?"

He smirks. "Carving a heart."

I raise an eyebrow. "With who?"

"Myself." His grin widens as he steps onto a low branch and starts climbing the damp trunk.

I follow.

"Here," he says, stopping about ten feet up. He points to a heart carved into the bark surrounding the words *Xander +* ________.

"Xander plus who?" I ask, catching my breath.

"Whoever I was meant to be with." His fingers trace his name in the bark, his voice barely above the sound of the rain.

"It was kind of a message to the future. That I'd find love one day. I didn't think it was fair that everyone else in town got to be on the tree, when I wasn't even allowed to be myself."

My pulse moves to my throat. "That's really sweet, Xander."

He huffs, then pushes past me and slides down the tree. His feet land with a splash in the mud below.

"Maybe so," he mutters. "But it backfired." He flicks a wet curl from his forehead. "I left here, went to the pool, and got killed. I guess I wasn't meant to be with anyone."

I drop to the ground beside him. "That's not true." I meet his gaze. "Remember, if I'm not dead, then you're not dead. We're going to fix this." A slow breath leaves his lips. "You're going to end up with a full heart."

"How?"

I roll my neck. "We get the tree to fight back. Maybe if it smacks me across the head again, I'll wake up from this nightmare."

"And me?"

"When it swings, jump in front of me so it hits you too."

His face lights up. "Yes! I've always wanted to do a rage room. I have a decade's worth of pent-up anger."

"A what?"

"Never mind." He shakes his head. "You have so much to learn, Stetson. How do we piss it off?"

I grab a rock and hurl it at the trunk. *Thud.* "Like that."

Xander grins and scoops up a handful of pebbles, pelting them against the bark like Pop Rocks candy.

I take a fallen branch from the ground and wind up like a batter at home plate. The first swing rattles my arms. The second splinters the wood. On the third, the branch snaps clean in half.

We continue our barrage of rocks, sticks, and glass bottles unearthed by Xander for several minutes. Xander even lands a few well-placed kicks against the trunk. Our breathing grows ragged. Still, the Ardor Tree stands unmoved. No shaking limbs or groaning roots. Just stiff, impenetrable silence.

Defeated, we collapse onto the soaked earth. Cool water seeps through my shirt, chilling my skin and sending the fine black hairs on my arms rising into the air. I press my arm against Xander's for warmth. His bare chest rises and falls in sync with my breath.

"I guess we're not as tough as we thought," Xander says.

"I'm just out of practice," I say. "I was a runner. Never got into the contact sports."

He sighs. "If only we could run away from this."

My ears perk up. "Have you tried? Like, if you leave Penango, are you still invisible?"

"I've been everywhere. The invisibility never changes."

"Everywhere?" I turn my head toward him.

He nods. "Name a place."

"Europe."

He chuckles. "A little more specific, please."

"Sorry. I've never left the country."

"Really?" He props his hand behind his head. "Well, then I have a lot to tell you." He taps his chin, thinking. "Let's see . . . Europe, Europe . . . Oh! One of my favorite places in Europe is Mont-Saint-Michel."

I frown. "I never heard of it."

"It's this castle in France that's built on a floating island. At low tide, you can reach it by land, but at high tide it's surrounded by water."

"That doesn't even sound real."

"You'd be surprised what's out there." He scooches closer to me. "Where do you want to go?"

The answer is instant. "Tennessee."

He smiles. "I like your confidence. What's in Tennessee?"

"College . . . hopefully."

His expression faulters.

"It would be in August," I clarify. "If I leave."

Xander doesn't say anything. He just closes his eyes and lets the rainwater wash over his face.

"I want to figure this . . . us . . . out first before I go. Don't worry."

We didn't solve anything today. But there are still two months left to try. I'm glad Whitley rejected my plan to leave town sooner. I need this time with Xander. And I think he needs me too. I can't imagine leaving him alone here.

"Why do you come back to Penango?" I ask. "When you could be anywhere."

"I always thought if something was going to change with my situation, it'd be here." He licks water from his lips. "And it turns out I was right."

I stare at the leaves, trying to decipher a code within their veins.

"Did you like meeting my mom?" he asks, eyes still closed.

My breath catches. "How did you know I met her?"

"I heard Sheryl and Kim talking about her visit earlier."

"She was nice. She really likes what they're doing with the pool." I pause. "Why weren't you there?"

"I left once she arrived."

"You didn't want to see her?"

"No."

"Oh." I hesitate. "Why . . . why not?"

122

His throat bobs. "When strangers can't see you, it's weird. But when your mom can't see you?" He exhales, shaking his head. "It's heartbreaking."

The heavy words settle between us.

"I'm sorry," I whisper.

"Don't be."

He rolls onto his side, finally opening his eyes. His hands tuck under his cheek and his shoulder sinks into the soft dirt.

"Thanks for trying to fix things," he says softly. His teeth clatter behind his lips. Without thinking, I slide closer until our waists touch, and we share warmth.

I could suggest other ways to solve this mystery. But right now, I just want to stare at his burning gold eyes and listen to the rain patter against the leaves.

If I had to be a ghost with anyone . . . I'm glad it's Xander Pomers.

22

The constant dread running through my body makes time fly. It's like everything in Penango has been rewired now that ghosts, the supernatural, spirits—or *whatever* Xander is—exist. Main Street holds a new thrill now I know some of its pedestrians might not even be alive. The trees no longer blur together like an old, shaggy carpet draped over town. Instead, they shimmer, alive with some unseen magic, their leaves glowing like green Christmas lights.

The first time I saw Xander, I thought I was hallucinating. I couldn't explain it. I blamed the Ardor Tree's weird energy and Murray's inability to see me on a brain fried by heartbreak. But on the second and third times Xander appeared? Those were proof. And yesterday, when he made the wet forest floor feel like home, he confirmed that he's real.

And I really need my best friend to help me make sense of this. Keeping a secret from someone you share everything with is a bit like trying split a dessert at the Bean—impossible.

"Hello?" Whitley's voice brings me out of my thoughts at the health department. She waves a hand in front of my face, then snaps her fingers.

"Earth to Stetson. What are you staring at?"

I blink rapidly, shifting in my chair.

"Hey, Whitley," I say. "Sorry. I was just thinking about something I need to tell you."

Her eyebrows shoot up. "Whoa. Do you have a little morning gossip?" She grins. "Is it good or bad?"

I lean forward. "That's the thing. I'm not entirely sure yet. I think I made a mistake." She tilts her head.

"This sounds serious." She holds up a finger. "But can I tell you my news first? It's good."

My stomach flips. "Oh, you have news too?"

"Yes!" she practically shouts. "I got a second job."

A wave of heat washes over me. My hands squeeze into fists so tight my knuckles crack, and I never do that, because that's what Murray does.

"You . . . what?" My voice wavers. "How? Where?"

"I'm going to be a research assistant for this graduate student's thesis project."

I blink. "How are you going to do that with our pool job?"

"The hours are, like, whenever I want. And it's kind of related to pools. She needs my help with . . . Hold on, I wrote it down." Whitley grabs her phone and scrolls. "Here we go— *a transitional adulthood study looking at the crossover in paths for the two role configurations of adolescence and adulthood.*"

I squint. "That doesn't even make sense. What do you actually do?"

"Get the names and contact information of the lifeguards at each pool so she can interview them about their lives."

"That's it? A bunch of Penango lifeguards? That's the most boring study I've ever heard of."

She waves me off. "I don't actually care about the study. This is about revenge."

I raise a brow.

"I want to show my dad that he's not the only supposed smart one in the family," she says. "He didn't have to ditch his daughter to go do stupid research in Pittsburgh like he says as an excuse. I'm doing it right here in Penango. Plus, she's paying me in cash."

I swallow hard, my mouth nearly watering. "Can I join?"

"I think she only needed one assistant, but I can ask."

I puff out my lips. Of course. Whitley's getting extra cash when she doesn't even need it. She has her dad's help. Meanwhile, I'm the one drowning. At this point, the universe isn't just against me, it's actively trying to flatten me. They should replace the icon on those *Falling Rock* warning signs along the Penango Freeway with my face. It'd be more accurate given the speed of my decline.

"I got to go," I say, standing abruptly. The backs of my legs shove my wheely chair into my desk with a loud bang.

Whitley grabs my arm before I can bolt. "Wait, I thought you had something to tell me?"

"Not anymore. I don't feel well. I need fresh air."

She pinches her lips. "You sure you weren't just about to admit how bad of a friend you've been lately?"

Her words snap something inside of me. Before I can stop myself, it comes tumbling out.

"I didn't get any financial aid for college, Whitley!" I shout.

This wasn't what I was going to tell her, but it's what I need to right now.

Her face falls. "Wait . . . what?"

"I didn't get the freaking aid." My ribs feel like they're caving in. "Murray won. He got what he wanted." My fist flies to my temple, pressing hard against the pounding behind my eyes.

"What are you talking about?" She glances around, lowering her voice. "Keep it down."

"What's it matter?" I throw my arms up. "I am so screwed. I'm never getting out of here. They can fire me if they want to! I don't care."

"How is this even possible?"

I let out a bitter laugh. "I have no idea. My parents must make too much money. Which is stupid, because I'm pretty sure college costs their entire salary."

"But I got some aid," she says, pacing our cubicle and shaking her head. "Why wouldn't you?"

"I probably applied too late or something. Money dried up."

The faces of students from my Tennessee class flash through my mind—the ones I've already connected with on social media, the ones who made me feel like I belonged somewhere else. They get to leave their hometowns. But me? I'm literally going to be a college dropout before I even set foot on campus.

No freshman fifteen. No flunking my finals. No toxic dorm romance to obsess over. Just a facepalm at the entrance gate.

"We need to do something about this," Whitley says.

I sigh. "Like what?"

"Go to that stuffy guidance counselor who helped you with your applications. Figure out what happened. There has to be another way."

"Oh, you're right! She's literally the only person who ever believed I'd get out of Penango."

Whitley smacks my shoulder. "And me. I came up with the pact, remember?"

I nod, but then reality punches me in the gut again. "Wait . . . it's summer. Will she even be around?"

"Email her. Or blow up her phone. We're working in the summer. This is her job. Hell, I have two jobs now."

Before I can agree, Whitley shoves me back into my chair, grabs my mouse, and clicks open my email.

"Now," she says, "let's get you out of here."

23

The feeling I had when I read Xander's missing person article in the archives reminded me a lot of the first time I realized my future with Murray might not play out the way I'd always imagined it.

It wasn't a passing thought, but a weekend of spiraling. My head spun while my body sank, like all my future plans were drifting away from me, a swimming tube lost in the river's current. In one moment, everything shifted.

It all started last fall, on a Friday afternoon in my counselor's office. It had been a couple of weeks since our first conversation about my grades and college prospects.

"I'd try to get these applications submitted as soon as you can," she said as she printed me out an application checklist.

My phone bounced on my knee as I tapped the screen, watching the seconds change. The only thing standing between my and Whitley's football pregame party with Murray was this meeting.

"I've already sent your transcripts and test scores to some of the schools," she added.

My spine stiffened. "Wait . . . really?" I held up my hand. "This is actually happening?"

She grinned. "As long as you do your part. This time next year you might be a far cry from Penango."

A squeal burst from my lips as I bolted from her office, down the hall, and toward Murray's locker.

He looked me up and down as I slid to a stop. "Was cross-country practice early or something?" he laughed.

I shook my head, panting. "Sorry. I just met with the guidance counselor again. I think I'm going to apply to college after all!"

"That's awesome, Stetson." He kissed my forehead. "You'll be the smartest guy at Penango College."

"Well, I don't think I'm going to apply to Penango College. I still don't want to go there."

His hands froze as he shoved a notebook into his bag. "UPitt?"

"No, somewhere outside of Pennsylvania." I unfolded the checklist and held it up. "She gave me this list of schools to apply to."

His face drained of color.

"What do you mean?" he asked softly. "You're going to live in Pittsburgh and I'm going to Penango College." His eyes scanned the paper. "These are all so far, Stetson."

"I never really thought I had a shot," I said. "And I told you I've been thinking about Ohio too. I want something new."

"What about what I want?" Murray wrinkled his brow. "How long have you been meeting with her about this?"

I took a step back. "It doesn't matter." I forced a laugh, trying to lighten the mood. "It's just an idea."

"I didn't know about this idea."

"It's not like it was a secret." My voice was sharper than intended. "I'm bringing it up now."

Murray licked his lips and nodded. "Okay, well . . . have fun in . . ." he glanced at the list. "Nevada." Then he slammed his locker shut and turned away from me.

"Wait—I wanted to talk about it," I said quickly. "Aren't we going to Whitley's house before the game?"

He spun back around, arms outstretched, his history textbook still clenched in his right hand. "Sorry, I have other plans for the game tonight."

"Since when?"

He shrugged. "It wasn't a secret. I'm just bringing it up for the first time."

An invisible fist punched me in the gut.

Now I'm standing in front of the same doors Murray walked through after the first crack in our relationship.

The guidance counselor emailed me back within an hour of my SOS message, telling me I could come by after work to figure something out.

I never thought I'd actually want to return to Stillwell Trail High School. I used to roll my eyes at alumni who returned to catch up with teachers on a random Tuesday afternoon. Wasn't four years enough?

But right now, it's the only place in town where I might find some hope.

Weeds creep up the sides of the school building, unchecked, like nature is reclaiming it after some long-forgotten apocalypse. I knock on the glass, and my counselor hurries toward the entrance juggling a large set of keys. The smile tucked between her plump cheeks sends me back to senior year, before everything changed, before Penango started feeling like a trap.

I take a sharp inhale as she pushes open the door.

"I'm sorry to hear about your aid application," she says as we head toward her office. "I can't imagine how stressful this must be."

"It hasn't been great," I say. "But thanks for meeting with me."

We sit. I stare at the floor, picking at the skin around my thumb. "Why did I get rejected?"

She purses her lips. "I wouldn't call it a rejection. It doesn't reflect your abilities as a student. You're just ineligible this year. You can always reapply."

I shrug. "Okay . . . but why am I ineligible this year?"

She lets out a slow breath. "It's a combination of factors . . . your family's income level, the number of students applying, when you submitted your application . . . You applied quite late." She tilts her head.

"So you're saying I'm screwed?"

She levels me with a stern look. "Do you really think I called you in here just to say you're screwed?" She leans forward, lowering her voice like she's about to tell me a secret. "At this point in the game, we do have one last shot."

My eyes widen.

"It's called the Keystone Rural Youth Mathematician Education Fund."

My ears perk up. "What do I have to do?"

"It's a bit of déjà vu for us." She takes a deep breath. "There are no set deadlines. Submissions are rolling. But we should move quickly. It's for students from rural Pennsylvania communities who demonstrate exceptional promise in math—which makes you a perfect candidate. They'll need your transcripts, which I can send over, a five-hundred-word essay on what you hope to achieve by studying mathematics, and

132

two letters of recommendation. I can write one. Do you know someone who could write your second?"

I nod before even thinking of a person.

"Great. Let's aim to submit everything by the end of July. Does that work for you?"

I spring out of my seat. "Yes! Thank you so much." My smile stretches so wide it hurts. "I might need therapy after this application, just to deal with the emotional roller coaster I've been on these past couple of weeks. But that can wait."

She laughs. "I'm here for whatever you need."

"Thank you, thank you."

Between my cheers, I spot an *STHS Class of 2015* banner above her desk. I pause.

"Whatever I need?" I ask, raising a brow.

She crosses her arms. "Don't push it."

I step forward. "Remember when you told me all that information about my grades and the activities I did?"

She nods. "Your high school record? Yes."

"Yeah. That. Would you be able to pull up someone else's record?"

She presses her brow. "Stetson . . ."

"A boy named Xander Pomers. Maybe?" I flash an innocent smile.

"No, Stetson. That's their private information."

I exhale. "I figured it was worth a shot."

"Stetson." Her voice drops to a more serious tone.

I grip the back of my chair. "Yeah?"

"Do not let another boy make you miss this deadline like the last one." She points at me. "I know more than you think."

I sigh. "I don't think this new boy could stop me . . . even if he wanted to." My nose wrinkles. "If that makes sense." She narrows her eyes. "No one can see . . . uhh . . . never mind." I grab my things before she can press me. "You have nothing to worry about."

Something shifts in my chest once I'm outside.

For the first time in days, the odds of getting out of Penango—of actually making it to college—feel possible again.

24

The first person I meet after seeing the guidance counselor is Xander.

I swear I won't let another boy make me miss out on a college application again. Lesson learned. July is nearly here, and August is creeping closer. But if I end up becoming invisible to more people than just Murray, if I freeze at the age of eighteen forever, then getting out of Penango won't mean a thing.

On my drive to the Bean, I think through my options for a letter of recommendation.

My cross-country coach and my mathletes advisor wrote the first ones for my college applications last fall, but I haven't spoken to either of them since December. Plus, every other applicant will probably use teachers or coaches. I need an edge. Someone whose letter will stand out.

Victor might not seem like the smartest person in Penango, but his credentials say otherwise. An environmental health specialist has a nice ring to it. I doubt most people have ever even met one. If he knows how to write, maybe impressing him wouldn't be a total waste of my time.

The Bean is mostly empty in its final hour before closing. Xander sits in a corner booth slurping a strawberry milkshake. He waves with a grin.

The waitress, the same one who witnessed my fight with Murray, nods at me from behind the counter as I make my way toward him.

"Seat yourself, I guess," she says.

I hesitate, unsure how to tell her that my friend already has a table. I pop in my earbuds so if anyone sees me talking to Xander—or myself, in their view—I can pretend I'm having a conversation on the phone. Although I doubt that will be convincing.

This whole situation has me acting more bizarre as the days stretch on.

Sliding into the booth, I glance at Xander. Something about him looks . . . different. Then I realize—he's wearing a shirt. Maybe for the first time ever. And not just any shirt. It says *STHS 2014 Mathletes*.

"Where did you get that shirt?" I ask.

"Hello to you too," he says. He slides me a second pink milkshake across the table.

I blush. "Sorry. I'm just surprised to see you clothed."

"I got you that shake. Hope you don't mind."

I eye the cup. "How did you order these?"

"I made them myself in the kitchen." He winks.

"Are we just doing dessert?"

"Who says dessert can't be dinner?"

I shrug, then take a sip. The second the liquid hits my tongue, my eyes water. I force a swallow, then break into a coughing fit.

"Oh my gosh, this is so sweet. What did you put in here?" I turn the cup in my hands.

136

"Oh, just triple the strawberry syrup and extra maraschino cherries."

I tap my chest, still recovering. "You're insane."

"It's good. I'll finish yours if you don't want it."

"No, I want it," I say, forcing another sip. "Back to your shirt."

He tugs at the fabric. "I got this from school. It's vintage, baby."

"You were in mathletes?" I tilt my head to the side. "I was too. I thought you weren't smart?"

He laughs. "I wasn't an idiot. I just wasn't at the top of my class. I was more like Cady Heron from *Mean Girls*. Cool, but still capable of solving for x and y."

I smirk. "You know *Mean Girls*?"

"Stetson, do I need to remind you that I'm not dead? I still experience life." He sips his milkshake. "Which clique were you a part of at school?"

I shrug. "We didn't really have cliques. There were only seventy people in my class. Everyone did sports. Everyone did theater. We were all Cady Heron."

He chokes on his shake. "Seventy people?" He wipes his mouth. "Wow. I read about Penango's population decline but didn't realize it was that bad. There were almost two hundred kids in my class."

"It was even worse before we merged with Hancock Valley High." I swirl my straw in my drink. "That's how I met Murray. He transferred in sophomore year."

The waitress appears at our table, her pen aimed at me like a weapon. "How did you get that shake?" Her voice is tight with suspicion. "Were you just in the kitchen? You can't go back there."

"I . . . um." My mouth goes dry.

"Tell her to look over there," Xander murmurs.

"What?"

"Just do it."

I gulp and point toward a framed photo on the other side of the diner. It captures Penango's Main Street in the early 1900s. "Wait, what's that over there?" I ask.

She scowls but glances over her shoulder. "What's what?" she asks.

In the split second that she's distracted, Xander snatches my milkshake.

I furrow my brow. What the hell is he doing?

When the waitress turns back, her face drains of color. "Wait—where did it go?" She blinks at the table. I still see the milkshake, but it must be gone for her now. "I swear there was just a strawberry milkshake sitting right here."

I press my lips together, struggling to hold back a laugh. Across from me, Xander grins, barely containing his own amusement.

"See? Just trust me," he whispers.

I clear my throat and morph my face into something resembling innocence. "I'm sorry," I tell the waitress, looking up at her with wide eyes. "I don't know what shake you're talking about. But a strawberry milkshake does sound nice. Could I order one?"

She studies me, then looks under the table for a final check. "Yes." She straightens. "But if I see that other shake, this will be the last one you get all summer."

I nod.

With a huff, she pushes through the red swinging doors into the kitchen.

Xander bursts into laughter once she's gone and slides my shake back across the table.

"How did you do that?" I ask, my pulse still racing.

"Turns out everything I touch goes invisible too. I guess that'll come in handy with you." He tilts his head to think. "My invisibility was depressing before, but now that I can interact with the real world, it's almost like a superpower."

"Everything?" I press.

"As long as it's not rooted to the ground . . . or a person. There are exceptions." He tosses the ketchup bottle between his hands. "I've been testing it since I met you. You just haven't noticed. No one usually does."

"What do you mean?"

He bounces his eyebrows and sticks out his tongue. "Watch this." He slides out of the booth and saunters to the counter. A second later, he returns with a napkin dispenser. "Need more napkins?" He smirks.

Just then, another waitress walks by the counter, pauses, and does a double take. "Hey, Brynn!" she calls out. "Can you grab napkins for the counter settings? I thought I already put some out."

I stifle a laugh.

"See." Xander shrugs. "People are too busy looking at their phones these days to notice anything weird."

He returns the dispenser back to its original place. The waitress walks by us again after helping a table and spots the napkins now that they're out of Xander's clutches. "Wow, thanks, Brynn." She taps the counter. "That was fast."

I narrow my eyes. "Okay, so you're definitely smarter than you let on."

His grin widens. "I'm glad you think so. But I won't be satisfied until I figure out how to break through the internet and cell signals to actually communicate with people. So far, every message I send just vanishes."

"What do you mean?"

"I've tried texting my mom. Emails too. But nothing ever delivers." He takes a long sip of his shake.

A chill spreads through my limbs. I lace my fingers together to keep them from trembling. "That's been happening to me."

His hand pauses around his cup. "How?"

I exhale sharply. "My ex . . . Murray. He was texting me, but I wasn't getting any of the messages. I thought he was lying. My friend Whitley had to set up our last meeting here and—oh my god."

Xander sits up straighter. "Are you okay?"

I push to my feet, spin in a circle, then collapse back into the booth. "I had a fight with Murray here. Just two tables over." I point at the spot. "But it wasn't a fight. He couldn't see or hear me. I was invisible."

My breath stutters as I replay the meeting in my mind. Murray kept checking the time, glancing at the door, waiting. He wasn't ignoring me. He thought I hadn't shown up.

"It happened after the Ardor Tree. I just didn't realize he couldn't see me at the time." I put my hands to the side of my head. "I've been like this longer than I've thought."

Xander nods. "Do you think we weren't killed . . . but cursed or something?"

"And that's why we can see each other. Because we share the same curse."

"We have to figure out what's going on with that tree."

I bite my nail, then turn toward the faded photo of Penango's Main Street hanging on the wall.

"I've been listening to this podcast about Appalachian folklore. Every mystery or curse in these mountains has an origin story."

140

"Right."

"We need to find ours." I point to the photo again, this time on purpose. "The Ardor Tree is part of Penango's history. We just have to dig deep enough."

Xander exhales. "I have been looking, you know."

I arch an eyebrow. "But I bet you haven't gone through the county archives at the government building."

His grin returns. "I certainly haven't. You've been keeping this from me? What do they even have there?"

He slides out of the booth and stands. The snug sleeves of his T-shirt stretch over his shoulders. His sharp jawline cuts through the neon diner lights.

His presence is magnetic, and before I even think about it, I'm standing too.

"I can take you there," I say, my voice softer than intended. I catch his next breath in my mouth.

He leans in just slightly. "Then let's get out of here."

But before we can make a break for it, the kitchen door swings open.

"Hey!" The waitress stomps toward us, balancing a fresh pink milkshake on her tray. "I just made this. Where do you think you are going? You need to pay!"

Xander grabs my wrist, his eyes twinkling with mischief.

I don't second-guess what happens next. I just run with him.

I trip over his heels as we dart toward the exit. My palms press his back, urging him to move faster. At the door, he fumbles with the handle, his focus flickering between me and the furious waitress gaining on us.

She can't see him, so he's not running from anyone, but I can tell he's enjoying pretending to live again.

25

Xander doesn't let go of my hand as we leave the Bean. He moves me through the parking lot as yellow streetlamps flash on and cast buttery spotlights along empty sidewalks.

His gaze stays fixed ahead while mine studies the dark hairs and freckles scattered across his tan arm. Our fingers are laced in a way that still feels unfamiliar, like shiny hubcaps on an old tire. It's nothing like the grip I've known for the last three years that pulled me in all the wrong directions.

"I think we're in the clear," I say through a laugh. I stop myself and drop his hold because, regardless of what I'm feeling, to anyone else it looks like I'm getting dragged through town by an invisible dog.

Xander turns and his eyes go wide. He points over my shoulder. "Think again!" he shouts. "Apparently the waitress is a better track star than you and she's got a pie with your name on it."

"What?" I choke out.

Before I can even look back, Xander grabs my shoulders and pushes me past the post office and down a hill that slopes into the Penango River.

We crouch on the damp dirt, just where the water glides over smooth rocks and seeps into the soles of my shoes. I peek up at the street, half hidden behind Xander's arms, waiting for the menacing, pie-wielding waitress to run past our escape route, but no one comes. The streetlamps buzz. The road is empty.

Xander falls back, laughing. "You look so scared," he says.

I narrow my eyes. "Did you just make that up?" I ask.

He nods, one hand clutching his shaking stomach.

I exhale. "Why would you do that?"

"It's fun getting chased."

My body tenses. There was a time recently when being chased didn't feel fun at all.

Xander notices my expression change and swallows his laughter. He grabs my hand, then puts it on his chest. "Do you feel that?" His heart beats quickly beneath my palm. "I haven't felt that too much over the past ten years. Now with you, I'm feeling it almost every day."

I look down and swallow hard.

"Don't worry, Stetson," he continues. "I would've intercepted the pie if the waitress was actually after you."

I finally crack a smile. "You're like my invisible bodyguard."

"Hopefully I'm more than that." He winks.

Then he stands, peels off his shirt, and tosses it over my head before wading into the river. "Let's swim!"

I slowly drag his shirt off my face and over my nose, taking in the scents of sweat and pine clinging to the cotton. The water curls around Xander's calves like a cat greeting its owner. He glances back, smiles brightly, and waves me in.

But my feet stay planted on the cool stones along the shoreline. I dig my toes into the earth.

"What's wrong?" Xander asks. "Was it the prank? I'm sorry. I didn't mean to freak you out." He crawls toward me in the shallow river.

I shake my head. "It's not that. My stomach is just off from the milkshake."

He arches a brow.

I look left, then right. Across the water, the tire swing behind Murray's house sways gently in the breeze.

My stomach doesn't hurt. It's my heart. And it's not ready to let the river carry me somewhere new when it still remembers who used to bring me in.

During Murray's junior year football season, his coach told him he needed to improve his receptions. He was great at catching long balls—legendary even. Sophomore year, he won two games by snagging fourth-quarter Hail Mary touchdowns, making him the school's hero for a week.

But short catches were his weakness. Screen passes, quick slants: He'd drop anything tossed to him from five feet away. I'd wince with every fumble. By the third drop, I'd start preparing for his postgame spiral. If he had a rough night, he wouldn't want to do anything afterward but sulk and relive every missed throw.

It never made sense to me how he could catch a fifty-yard bomb but not a soft toss. It didn't make sense to him either. He never struggled like that before.

"Help me train," he said.

I nodded so hard I probably looked like a bobblehead.

After every game, we huddled over my phone and replayed each catch and drop in slow motion.

144

As soon as the weather got nice again, we started with slow and lazy tosses back and forth in his backyard. But after a few weeks of staring at the tire swing hanging above the river, he got an idea.

Soon, I was hurling footballs through a moving tire toward Murray jumping through the air, his body slick with river water, chest bare and glistening, arms outstretched.

Thud. The football hit his chest.

Giggle. His arms tightened around the ball.

Splash. He disappeared beneath the water.

Thud, giggle, splash.

Thud, giggle, splash.

Over and over.

It was the soundtrack of my junior year summer.

At day's end when we were exhausted from practicing, we'd float side by side down the Penango River, letting the current carry us past the county line. But we quickly swam home at the first sign of sunset, afraid we'd ventured too far.

I became so good at throwing a football that I considered quitting cross-county and trying out for quarterback. I didn't. And Murray fell into his coach's good graces again fall of senior year when he caught nearly every pass that came his way.

As the season wore on, and the air turned cold, Murray changed too. He stopped looking for me in the bleachers after each catch. I lost his thumbs-ups, waves, and smiles. Eventually, he ran off the field without a glance.

I sat there every Friday night for him, clapping less, crying more. We spent a whole summer building something in the river. I thought it would carry us forward. But it turns out, it washed away just as fast.

Xander splashes me. "Hey, zombie-boy," he says, grinning. "Don't let this beautiful night go to waste."

I wipe the grainy river water from my brow, blinking against the softening light. Suddenly, I don't want to waste anything anymore.

I wasted three years on a boy who made me small. I might have wasted my time applying to college. I'm wasting my summer checking chlorine levels at pools no one swims in. Worst of all, I've wasted too much time listing reasons not to try. Not to feel what's in front of me.

I want to move on from the memories of Murray. Maybe I do that by diving into this dream with Xander.

He is here. And he's nice. And funny. And smart. And . . . hot. And most importantly, he sees me and wants to help.

That would be reason enough for most people. It's more than enough for me to just get in the damn water.

I take off my shirt and walk into the river, stepping carefully over slick stones.

Xander gives me a once-over. "Okay, you might have the best T-shirt tan line I have ever seen," he says.

I glance down, laughing. My shoulders and stomach are ghostly compared to my arms. "Shut up. I haven't been sunbathing for ten years straight like you. Skin cancer was still a threat up until, like, two weeks ago."

He spits water. "Yeah, well, now you can."

"Not for long though," I counter. "We're fixing that, remember?"

But he doesn't answer the question. Instead, he waves me closer. I step forward. He stands once I'm beside him and our eyes meet in the knee-deep, cool water. He takes my hand and places it on his chest again. His heart thuds.

A new soundtrack.

I swallow. "Does this mean you're having fun?" I ask. My skin breaks into goose bumps.

His lips part, then he places his hand on my chest in return. "It feels like you are too," he says.

I breathe out. "I'm feeling a lot of things."

He brushes a loose hair off my forehead. "I can be everything for you."

"Only good feelings, please."

His smile tilts. "Can I tackle you?"

I laugh. "What?"

"Can I tackle you?" he asks again, more serious.

"You could've just walloped me. It might have been more fun that way," I tease.

"Yeah, but by asking I want you to know that you can feel everything with me but fear. No surprises."

My mouth goes dry. "Okay." I nod. "You can tackle me." I look over my shoulder to make sure there are no pointy rocks. "Just watch my head."

Thud. His shoulder hits my chest.

Giggle. I grab him as I fall.

Splash. We disappear beneath the water.

26

At work the next morning, I keep my attention on the department door, tracking each coworker as they stroll in. My fingers drum against my desk, hoping Victor arrives early so I can get this recommendation letter business off my mind and return to fantasizing about Xander's hands all over me, like they were in the river.

I kind of wish I drew the University of Massachusetts from my mason jar since New England kids just get to think about boys all summer. And beaches. And debutante balls. And lemonade. Or at least it seems like they do. I doubt Cape Cod's swim club is an abandoned, mildew-infested drainage ditch.

Whitley shows up and I relax my gaze. "Hey, Whitley," I say, offering her a smile.

I texted her an apology last night after things went well with the counselor.

"Hello," she says. "Any other secrets to share this morning, now that you realize how helpful I can be?"

I force a sarcastic laugh. "No."

Technically, it's not a lie. I still need to tell her about my invisibility . . . and Xander. But not this morning. Xander and I are meeting in the archives department at three p.m. to investigate the Ardor Tree, and I'd rather have evidence before I unload everything on her.

"Who is going to write your second letter?" she asks, stirring an iced coffee. "You should ask Murray as a joke. I bet he's desperate enough to do anything to win you back."

I roll my eyes. "That's not even worth the trouble."

She smirks. "So who then?"

"I'm thinking Victor."

Whitley chokes on her drink. "Victor? That might be even more trouble."

"Yeah, well, options are limited." I sigh. "Did you get in touch with any lifeguards for your research study yesterday?"

She sips her coffee again before answering. "Not yet. But I cannot wait to start. I ran into my dad as I was leaving yesterday and casually mentioned my research to him." She grins. "He stuttered, like, ten times, then said, *I didn't know you were interested in that type of thing*. It was perfect. I wanted to say, *Yeah, well, you don't know a lot of things about me*, but I didn't want to extend the interaction."

I tap my fingers against my chin. If Victor turns me down, Whitley will absolutely force her dad to write a letter for me out of spite. I should probably stay out of that family drama . . . but desperate times, desperate measures.

"Have you talked to Murray since Saturday?" Whitley continues. "I still can't believe he was ignoring you at my house after spending all year complaining about you ignoring him. Is this the kind of crap he pulled that made you break up with him?"

Before I can even open my mouth, two heads appear over the ledge of our cubicle. Whitley and I straighten our backs.

"Dad?" she asks, voice flat.

Mr. Wyomen leans against the cubicle wall, arms crossed; strands of his thin, wispy hair shift under the HVAC vent. His collar looks two sizes too big for his skinny neck.

And standing next to him, like a jump scare, is Victor. How did he sneak in without me noticing? I lick my lips, suddenly on edge.

Mr. Wyomen slides off his rectangular glasses. "Whitley," he says. "Good morning." Then nods at me. "Stetson, how are you?"

"I'm fine," I answer stiffly.

A few awkward seconds pass.

Victor clears his throat. "So, Stetson, how's that green pool of yours coming along? Did you find the files you were looking for?"

I swallow. "Um, kind of. I'm still working on it."

"Well, don't let me down." He points at me with a lopsided grin. "Mary Jo says Whitley is doing great work, so I trust you'll do the same."

Great. Another person to potentially disappoint.

Whitley narrows her eyes. "Can we help you?" she asks.

Mr. Wyomen huffs, his face reddening as he scratches his eyebrow.

Victor chuckles. "Ah, the joys of working with the family," he says.

"I wanted to tell Victor about your research," Mr. Wyomen finally says.

Whitley's jaw tightens. She presses her lips together, then forces a strained smile before scooting her chair toward them. "Okay."

Victor perks up. "Research? We love hearing about student projects in the department. What's the topic?"

Whitley folds her hands. "Well, it's not exactly for the department. I'm assisting a graduate student at the University of Pittsburgh with a study about, um, transitional adulthood. We're interviewing lifeguards in Penango about their experiences growing up."

Victor nods, lips pursed. "Very impressive. Feel free to stop by my office if you ever need any advice. Not that I know anything about adulthood. I'm still figuring it out myself." He bursts into a wheezy laugh that rattles the cubicle walls.

Whitley blushes. "Will do."

"Smart kid you got here." Victor claps Mr. Wyomen's back too hard, causing him to cough.

After a moment, Mr. Wyomen catches his breath. "Well, I think we all have some work to do. Thanks for checking in with us, Whitley." He waves before walking off with Victor.

Whitley watches him leave, then shoots me a look.

"Checking in," she mutters. "He doesn't get it. I'm his daughter, not his secretary."

I shrug. "I mean, he probably wants to keep things professional at work—"

"Don't." Whitley glares. "Or you won't get a dime of my research money."

I hold up my hands in surrender. "You're right. He's *suchhh* a dick," I say, laying on thick sarcasm.

"Better," she says, finally cracking a smile.

"I'll be right back," I say, holding up a finger. Victor's words just handed me the perfect opportunity to ask for my letter of recommendation—if he really does want to help students.

I hurry after him and catch up by the mail bin. He's flipping through a stack of envelopes, tucking them under his arm when I approach.

"Oh, hello, Stetson," he says, barely looking up.

"Hi, Victor," I say, slightly out of breath. I scratch the back of my head as I try to find the right words.

He raises his eyebrows. "You got something else you want to talk about?"

I nod. "Yeah, actually. Sorry if this is too forward, but after hearing you say you like to help students . . ." I shift my weight. "I was wondering if you could help me."

He cocks his head back. "Depends. What's the ask?"

I swallow. "Well, I am applying to this scholarship for school with a tight deadline. As in, due in two weeks. And I need a letter of recommendation."

"No shit?"

My face twitches. "Yeah. It's stressful."

He rips an envelope clean in half. "I've always wanted to do one of those things."

I blink. "Really?"

He smirks. "Yeah, it sounds so official."

"So you'd do it for me?"

He pauses, tapping his chin. My shoulders sag. A nearby printer spits out pages in rapid succession, but it still can't keep up with my heart rate.

"Tell you what," he says. "If you can get that green pool under control, I'll write you a letter."

I stare at the carpet.

"I think that's a fair deal," he continues, shrugging. "Since you've only been here a couple weeks, you have to show your worth." He laughs like this is a joke.

"Sure . . . yeah," I say, rubbing my neck. "You have a deal."

"Good." He steps forward and jabs his index finger into my shoulder—hard. I stumble back, pain radiating from his point of contact.

"I don't want to have to go to that spooky pool myself." He giggles more. "It gives me the creeps."

His grin is wide, but something about it unsettles me. I retreat farther until my back presses against the wall. I don't know what I was expecting, but I didn't think I'd have to bargain for a recommendation letter. He already has my résumé, academic transcript, and references from my job interview. What else does he need? He's the least serious adult I know but is the only one who takes writing a recommendation letter seriously. Go figure.

I want to scream. Just drop to my knees in the middle of this office and let out the frustration tightening my chest. But that won't help my situation.

Instead, I shove this letter into the *tentative* folder in my brain, right next to going to college, leaving Penango, remaining visible, and my general future's well-being.

27

I get to the elevator at 2:25 p.m. Xander appears at 2:59 p.m.

He wears a red ringer T-shirt, jean shorts that cut high above his knees, and dirty Converse sneakers. A white lollipop stick juts out from between his blue-shaded lips. My stomach flutters. I squash my hand against my abdomen, trying to calm the unexpected commotion inside me.

"In all my ten years of invisibility, I never thought to sneak into government buildings," he says, inspecting the ceiling. "Another first for us. If we don't solve our problems this summer, I should totally break into Area 51 in the fall."

I huff out a laugh, but it comes out breathier than I intend. His voice, his smirk, his jokes. It's unfair. He doesn't even have to try to be cool.

He taps the side of his head. "Also, why do you always wear those things in your ears?"

I rub my fingers over my buds, then shrug. "I listen to live music."

"By who?"

"Anyone. Loud stuff. I like when the crowds chant."

"Why?" He bites his lollipop.

"It makes me feel like I'm somewhere other than Penango."

"You know, I've been on stage at the Coachella and Lollapalooza music festivals."

"No way." I gasp. "Being invisible has its perks. I bet that was amazing."

"It would've been even better with someone else." He flicks the lollipop stick into the trash. "What's been your favorite concert?"

I press the elevator button. "I've never gone to one."

"What?" He drops his chin. "We need to change that." His eyes float to the ceiling, mulling over a thought.

We do. But there are other things we need to change first.

When we reach the archives department, the same old man in the same beige cardigan leans over the same gigantic book. I wonder if he's even turned the page since my last visit.

He looks up from his magnifying glass. "Hello again, young man," he says with a faint smile.

"Hi," I say. "You remember me?"

He nods. "Of course. Not many people pay a visit to the archives department. Especially during the summer months. It can get rather lonely down here in the basement."

"Well, I'm glad we're here, then."

"What can I help you with today? Another pool?"

"No, actually. My friend and I are interested in a tree. The Ardor Tree, to be specific. Do you know about it?"

He winks. "Everyone in Penango does. My wife and I are on there—Stillwell Trail High School class of 1973."

"Great!" I nearly shout. "Can you take us to those files?"

"Yes, it would be under the parks and preservation department." He points to his left. "But would you like me to wait until your friend arrives to show you?"

The blood drains from my face.

I turn to Xander. His eyes are fixed on the floor, his jaw tight as he crunches down on a fingernail. My heart aches. I just reminded him, again, that he's nobody to the rest of the world. This must never feel good, even after a decade.

"I'm sorry," I whisper, barely audible.

He forces a small smile that doesn't reach his eyes. "Don't worry about it," he says softly.

But I don't believe him.

I turn back to the old man, fumbling for my phone as an excuse. "Actually, uh, he just texted me and said I can do this on my own." I clear my throat. "You can take me back now."

The man nods. "Right this way."

As I follow him, my shoes squeak against the floor, the familiar metal shelves groaning beside us. Xander trails just behind, his presence a shadow.

"What has you interested in the Tree?" the old man asks.

I shrug. "I just want to know more about why people write their names on it." I glance at Xander.

"Ah, yes. Love. An eternal question." The old man sighs. "Let me know if you find the answer." He grips a shelf for balance. "Have you fixed yourself on there with a nice young lady?"

A deep laugh escapes the back of my throat before I can stop it. "Uh—no, not really."

"One day," he muses. "One day."

"I wonder who the lucky young lady will be," Xander whispers. He clutches his hands behind his back as he walks.

I wrinkle my nose. "Shut up." I nudge him with my elbow. "At least I put my name on there with another person."

He gasps dramatically, clutching his chest. "Damn, Stetson. I was joking. But low blow."

"Sorry, stress." I put a hand on his shoulder, squeezing. "This is a big moment."

His hot breath tickles my ear as he leans in. "It doesn't seem like you handle stress well." A shiver shoots down my spine.

I open my mouth to respond, but the old man interrupts us. Or me.

"Now, the Ardor Tree is just a nickname, you know that, right?" he asks.

I nod, refocusing.

"So, I'm not sure what you'll find specifically on the tree itself, but it sits on the Thaddeus Gregor Preserve. That land was a grant from William Penn to the Gregor family sometime around 1700."

I make for the boxes on a shelf labeled *Parks and Preservation*. My mouth goes sour. "Please don't tell me these are sorted by year." I stare at him with my jaw slack.

He chuckles, then coughs into his fist. "No, no. Fortunately all the Gregor Preserve records are in one spot. They're on the fourth shelf down."

Relief washes over me. "Awesome. I'll let you know if we have questions."

He starts to walk away but pauses, lifting a finger. "Oh, and, son. We close in an hour, so you'll need to finish by three forty-five."

As he disappears down the aisle, Xander lets out a groan. "He's kidding, right? We have to dig through three hundred years of Penango history in forty-five minutes?"

"Apparently." I exhale. "Let's not waste another minute talking. I'll start with the left side of the shelf. You take the right."

We get to work, pulling boxes from the shelves. Dust coats my fingertips almost instantly as I lift the cardboard lids and sift through brittle manila folders.

The first box is completely unlabeled. I fish out a slip of paper and skim its contents:

The 200-acre Gregor Preserve contains meadows, uplands, and mature woods, and provides passive recreation and over eight miles of mown and wooded natural surface trails.

I smirk and shake my head.

I'm a rational person. Or at least, I used to be, before I ended up in a basement with my invisible friend searching for the origins of a moving tree.

Math has always been my thing because it makes sense. The numbers add up the same way no matter who does the calculations. Unlike English class, feelings, or this entire summer.

If Murray and I worked through the same math problem and came up with different answers, one of us would be right and the other wrong—it's simple. But if we read the same story in English class, wrote about completely different themes, and turned in wildly different essays, we'd both get an A.

We lived through the same senior year of high school, but somehow, we feel completely different about what happened during it.

That's why the financial aid rejection stings so badly. It was supposed to be based on metrics, a formula, a system that made logical sense. But something else must've been tossed into the mix, something unpredictable or subjective like feelings or human error.

And that's exactly what this summer has been. An unsolvable equation. A problem I never saw coming.

"What exactly are we looking for?" Xander asks, stretching onto his tiptoes to grab a box from the shelf.

"Something suspicious looking," I half answer, flipping through a document about event permits for the preserve. At this rate, I won't even get through one file before this place closes.

Xander pulls out a photo. "Here's a picture of a horse farm," he says, holding it up. He squints at one of the horses. "This brown one is definitely giving some serious side-eye. It's up to no good . . . Could be our guy."

I snort. "Yeah, we found our culprit. Mystery solved." Then I sigh, glancing at the long row of shelves. "Honestly, just take pictures of everything. There's no way we can read through all of this here. We'll go through them later."

"Ohhh," Xander hums. "Here's a picture of Thaddy Daddy."

I frown. "Thaddy what?"

"Thaddy Daddy," he repeats with a smirk. "Thaddeus Gregor. Keeper of the preserve."

I shake my head. "Let's not call him daddy when he could be responsible for our demise." I scoot to Xander's side and take the picture from his hands. It's a detailed sketch of a colonial man with long hair, a black top hat, and sharp stare. "Okay, your side of the shelf is way more interesting than mine. They must be hiding the good stuff over here."

"Then dig faster," he instructs.

We tear through his box, quickly forming a system. He pulls out documents, I snap pictures with my phone. Words and images blur together in my mind like a cash-grab machine at a carnival, except instead of snatching dollar bills, I'm trying to grab onto clues.

It's the handwritten captions beneath the illustrations that stand out the most:

Thaddeus Gregor, born in 1631, was a soldier in the parliamentary army during England's Civil Wars.

Thaddeus Gregor, a "First Purchaser" of Pennsylvania after receiving one of William Penn's Fall 1681 plots.

Thaddeus Gregor and his four children, leaders of the Quaker migration to Pennsylvania.

"Hold up," I say, sitting up straighter. A caption stops me in my tracks. Something's different.

A number.

"What?" Xander slides closer on his reddened knees. "Did you find the Ardor Tree?"

"No. But look at this picture."

Xander sighs. "It's just Thaddy Daddy and his kids again."

"Yeah, but look—it says his three kids. Henry, Albert, and Agnes. Every other picture says four."

His brows knit together. "Whoa. Who's missing?"

I scroll back through my photos. "There were always two men and two women before. This time, one of the girls is gone. It looks like her name was Louise." A dozen more pictures from the box show her missing.

Xander's mouth tightens. "Maybe she died?"

"Or maybe she went invisible?"

His throat bobs as he swallows. "Or she just wasn't in the mood for a family portrait."

I shake my head. "These are drawings, not photos. She didn't get caught in traffic. Someone intentionally left her out."

Suddenly, my phone alarm blares through the silent archive.

Xander jumps. "Ah," he yelps. "Why did you set an alarm?"

I groan. "Crap. We need to clean up before Grandpa locks us in here."

I snap a few more pictures while Xander hurries to restack boxes. Just as he slides the first one onto the shelf, the lights snap off.

A door slams somewhere in the distance. The sound echoes like a closing prison cell. It settles in fast that the archives department has no windows.

It's black, darker than midnight.

"Uhhh, did he forget about us?" Xander asks.

"He must have," I say, gripping a stack of papers.

"We have enough info for now. Let's get out of here."

I nod, even though he can't see me, and take a cautious step forward. Immediately, my hip collides with the edge of a steel shelf. A pained whimper slips from my lips.

"Stetson?" Xander's voice shifts.

"I'm fine," I mumble, gripping my side. I reach for my phone, fingers fumbling in my back pocket ready to use its flashlight. But I stop when Xander's hand settles on my shoulder.

Slowly, his palm glides down my arm. His fingertips trace a quiet path over my skin until he links his fingers with mine. The warmth of his hand spreads through me like fire over dry leaves.

"Here," he murmurs. "Let me help you."

I swallow. Hard.

"Okay," I say. It's barely more than a whisper.

My phone stays in my pocket. If he doesn't need the light, neither do I.

We move together through the pitch-black aisles with our fingers entwined. Every few seconds, Xander gives my hand a gentle squeeze, reassuring his lead. I squeeze back, letting him know I trust the path he's chosen for us.

The darkness doesn't feel so suffocating anymore. If anything, it feels like we're the only two people left in the world.

28

At home, I grab my family's laptop from the kitchen table and lead Xander to my room. He follows close behind, quiet but observant, taking in everything.

My face warms as I watch him. "Sorry, my house is small," I say.

"It's the same size as mine was," he replies, staring at photos in the hall.

A few steps later, I plop onto my bed, the plaid sheets still wrinkled from the night before, and rest the laptop on my thighs. Xander mirrors me exactly, until our knees touch.

"Let's see what we got," he says, rubbing his hands together.

"Hold on," I say, fishing out a USB cord from under my pillow. "I need to hook up my phone."

Xander groans. "This can't just sync to the cloud?"

I shoot him a sidelong glance. "Not all of us can steal MacBooks whenever we want."

"I'll get one for you. What color do you like?"

I tap my chin. "I don't know how I feel about that."

Without another word, Xander suddenly springs up from the mattress and wanders toward my bulletin board on the floor where the pile of pictures is scattered like fallen leaves, left untouched since my meltdown a couple weeks ago. He crouches and lifts up a photo from the mess.

"Is this your ex-boyfriend?" he asks.

My fingertips go slick with sweat against the laptop keys. No one else has ever referred to Murray like that before, out loud. Xander's words hit me like a slow-building breeze.

I swallow. "It is," I say, scratching my throat.

He studies the picture of Murray and me petting a goat at the Penango County Fall Festival. His lips press into a thin line.

"Why do you still have these?" He sifts through more of my Murraycentric photo collection. "I thought he was mean to you. Are you two back together?"

"No." I sigh. "I've just had other things to worry about."

"Sure," he says, thick with sarcasm. He tosses the photo back on the floor.

I cross my arms. "We're not together."

"But you still like him?"

"I want nothing to do with him."

"Then what's that?" He gestures toward my closet doorknob, where a Christmas ornament dangles. It's two ceramic snowmen, labeled as *Stetson* and *Murray*, cuddling between tiny Christmas trees.

I exhale. "I forgot that was there."

"You forgot about the bright white, red, and green thing hanging from a door you open every day?"

I grunt. "It's been there for years. It's just . . . I don't know, a routine thing. I don't think about it." My eyes flick toward the stuffed animals Murray won for me at the fall festival, piled in the corner of my room like relics of another life.

164

"Why don't you?" Xander's voice is quiet.

"Like I said, it's just the way my room has always been."

He returns to my bed. But this time he sits on its edge. His back is stiff while he twirls his thumbs in his lap.

"What's wrong?" I ask.

He clears his throat. "I care because . . . because if you let things stay the way they've always been, life stretches into one, long period of grief. You mourn the person you should've been in the past, and you feel sorry for yourself because you'll never be the person you want to be in the future. What's the point of living if you never let yourself change?"

My stomach tightens. "Well, when you put it like that . . ." I force a shrug. "I just figured there was no rush. I have all summer."

"I wish I didn't." His voice drops. "I wish I didn't have forever. Forever is meaningless when nothing changes. I'd rather only have a week left on earth if it meant I got to experience something new."

"Aren't I new for you?"

He turns his head slightly, just enough for me to catch the flicker of something intense burning in his amber eyes. "Yeah. And that's why I—" He stops, bites his lip, and whips his gaze toward the wall.

"That's why you what?"

"Nothing."

"Why you what? Tell me." I scooch closer to him, my heart pounding.

He stands. "Forget I said anything."

But I won't forget. And I don't think I can pretend I wasn't imagining certain words leaving his lips either.

With the Fourth of July around the corner, summer suddenly feels like it's slipping away. And here I am, still surrounded by pictures of my ex-boyfriend who I broke up with weeks ago. I only have one and a half teenage summers left. Why waste the best season surrounded by the worst person?

I push the laptop aside and stand. I scoop the photos from the floor, their glossy edges crumpling beneath my grip, and dump them into the trash can beside my desk. Flares of color—Murray's tuxedo vests, our matching ties, the bright lights from school dances—flash before me like a shattered kaleidoscope.

"There," I say. "Change can be quick."

Xander watches me, his lips curving into the faintest smile.

"You want more?"

I crisscross my room, searching for anything else with Murray's fingerprints on it. My corsage from senior prom sits on my nightstand, its once-white petals now dry and shriveled. I bring it to my nose before launching it into the can like a basketball.

Next, I slide open the top drawer of my dresser and remove a thick stack of birthday, Valentine's, and Christmas cards. Murray's sloppy handwriting is scrawled across each one. They land in the trash pile.

Then I make for the stuffed animals.

"Goodbye, Pink Teddy," I say, grabbing the bear's squishy bicep and tossing it into the closet. The impact rattles the hangers against the metal rod.

"So long, Rainbow Dolphin. Later, Pointless Pikachu. Bye, Simba. See ya, Mr. Caterpillar. I always thought you were creepy anyway."

Xander giggles.

I clap my hands and slam the closet door closed. "Consider him gone."

Xander exhales. "I didn't mean to make you upset."

"I'm not upset at all." I roll my shoulders back. "I feel great, actually. You were right."

Xander kneels beside my bulletin board and runs his fingers along the empty cork. "You should bring this with you to Tennessee. Cover it with pictures of us."

I raise an eyebrow. "We need pictures of us first."

He grins. "We can change that too."

The laptop dings as the photos from the archives finish uploading. We both turn toward the sound. The glow from the screen becomes the only light source in the room as a late afternoon storm darkens the sky outside.

"Should we look at these first?" I ask, nodding at the laptop. "And have our photo shoot another time?"

"Deal," Xander says, twisting a curl between his fingers before pointing toward the window. "The electricity in the atmosphere is making my hair static anyway."

I want to run my hand through his curls, to feel their charge, but instead, I climb onto my bed and keep my hands busy at the keyboard. Xander follows, just like last time. But he's closer. This time, it's not just our knees bumping, but our arms, hips, thighs, and calves. Even our toes nearly touch. He catches me glancing down at the small gap and, without a word, tilts his foot sideways until his baby toe brushes mine.

He doesn't speak, just exhales softly, the warmth of his breath landing on the side of my neck.

Outside, the wind picks up, cracking my plastic blinds against the wooden sill.

I try to focus on the laptop screen, but my hands are shaky as I open the downloaded folder. Dozens of files appear.

Xander's long, tan finger moves across the screen as he counts them. He sighs. "We have enough documents to write an entire history book on Thaddy Daddy."

"Hopefully chapter one has all the answers."

I double-click the first image. It's the same illustration of Thaddeus Gregor and his four adult children. They look like any other colonial family from a high school textbook. I press the arrow key to flip through the files at rapid speed.

"Wait," Xander says, nudging me. "You're going too fast. Go back. I read a lot, but I can't read that fast."

"I'm looking for a drawing without the other girl so we can see when she disappeared," I explain, licking my lips as I continue clicking. "We need to figure out the order of events. Once we have the date we can—"

"But you already skipped something important." Xander pushes my hand aside and smacks the left arrow key so hard my thighs vibrate from the force. "It's not always about numbers, Stetson. Look past the obvious."

I blink at the screen. It's a rough black-and-white sketch of an old woman hunched under the weight of a pile of sticks, or hay, or firewood. Her shadow stretches across an open field.

"I don't recognize her from the family pictures," I say. I read the caption:

Abigail Mattson upon the Gregor Preserve after fleeing her home in Ridley Township, now Delaware County, Pennsylvania.

Xander's fingers tighten around my arm just as rain starts to patter against the window.

"What?" I glance down at his grip. My phone is an inch from his face. His breathing suddenly goes uneven.

He scratches his neck before flipping the screen toward me. "I think I know why Louise disappeared."

I scan a list of internet search results he pulled up for Abigail Mattson.

Abigail Mattson, a Puritan minister's daughter, was one of two Pennsylvania women tried for witchcraft in 1683, nine years before the Salem Witch Trials. The other, Louise Gregor, was the daughter of a well-known Quaker leader. Accusations included bewitching, cursing, and killing livestock and plants, and appearing to townspeople in spectral form. Both were exiled from local communities.

My body stiffens. A bolt of lightning escapes from the clouds and illuminates Xander's horrified face. Rain hits the window in heavy, tapping bursts like fingers drumming to be let inside.

A five-pointed star enclosed within a circle is all over the internet image results. "What's this picture?" I ask, pointing to the screen with a shaky finger.

"It's a pentacle," Xander answers. "It says it's a popular symbol among witches used in magical evocation."

"So we were right. We're not dead but . . . cursed."

He drops my phone, then swallows. "Do you think we could get those stuffed animals from the closet?" His lips tremble. "I need to squeeze something."

I nod, unable to blink.

He tosses me Pikachu. I hand him Simba. Without asking, he slides under my comforter. I set the laptop aside, ending our investigation for the night, and slip under the covers beside him. The screen locks, plunging the room into blackness.

In any other moment like this, I'd be reaching for my earbuds to leave my house and escape into someone else's story. But I've lost track of them like a loose balloon at the park. And right now, I don't care to find them. Not when Xander is inches away. His soft breaths are like comforting baby coos.

More lightning flashes, just enough for me to see his wide eyes staring back at me.

Neither of us says anything.

Neither of us looks away.

29

Whitley and I sit at the dinette booth in what used to be her grandma's kitchen.

Now, technically, it's just Whitley's kitchen. But she won't call it that, too disrespectful toward the woman who raised her when no one else would. Since her grandma passed in the spring, Whitley's been riding out her remaining time in Penango here, refusing to move or even discuss it.

With witches and curses tied to Xander's disappearance, I need another force of good on my team. And recruiting Whitley is like adding ten people instead of one. She can literally wield an axe.

If there's anyone who knows how to push through a bad situation, it's her.

The navy fabric covering the booth cushions is torn in multiple places, where fluffy, white stuffing spills out through the ripped seems like marshmallows oozing from an overstuffed s'more. A deer's head is mounted on the wall behind her, killed by her grandfather decades ago, its antlers thick with dust and cobwebs.

"How is Bennie?" I ask, picking at the skin around my thumbs.

Whitley pushes her hair back and calls out, "Bennie!" She makes a series of kissing noises.

A moment later, Bennie limps in from the hallway, his head swallowed by a giant, white plastic cone that makes him look like a space dog.

"Good . . . Well, actually . . . not so good," she admits. "He kept trying to eat the bandages on his legs. I had to get this cone from the store." She knocks on it with her fist. "And I've been pulling him around in a wagon for our walks to keep the weight off his back legs. I think he likes it though. He's always been a little lazy."

"Aw, Bennie," I say, frowning. "He's bruised but not broken."

"Nothing can break Bennie. Isn't that right, Bennie?" She pats his head. "Say hello to Uncle Stetson."

"Hi, Bennie."

He whimpers.

"There it is." Whitley grins. "Good boy, Bennie."

I take a deep breath. "Sorry I took the past few days off from coyote hunting. There's been so much going on. Did you catch the beast?"

"It's cool." Whitley gets up and grabs a soda from the fridge. "I haven't been out to the woods either. I'm too busy playing veterinarian. But if you're free soon, we should hunt again." She cracks open the can and retakes her seat. "We're letting that killer get too comfortable."

I salute her. "But if I keep helping with hunting, will you help me with something too?"

"Yes." She takes a long sip. "But only if you start sharing what's been going on with you lately."

I tug at my neckline. "That's kind of why I'm here."

She lifts a finger. "Wait, actually, I rescind my commitment."

My body deflates. "What?"

She sighs. "If this has anything to do with Murray, I can't help you. I've never been in a long-term relationship like that. I have no advice."

I smile. "I wouldn't put you through that. It's not about him."

"Oh, heck yeah. I'm recommitted." She leans forward, placing her elbows on the table.

I tap my finger against my chin. "Wait, actually, I rescind that response."

Her eyes roll.

"It does have a little to do with him. But it's mostly about a missing person."

She tilts her head. "Are you trying to make Murray go missing?" she whispers.

I shake my head. "I'm trying to make sure *I* don't go missing."

Her smirk disappears. "What the hell does that mean?"

I take another deep breath and tell her everything.

Halfway through my story, she lifts her soda and dumps it on my head.

"Are you for real, Stetson?" she asks.

"Ugh," I grunt, licking soda from my lips.

She stalks off, grabbing Bennie's food bowl and rinsing it in the sink. "I have more important things to do than listen to this baloney."

"I'm serious, Whitley," I say, shuffling toward the counter in search of a paper towel as the soda drips from my nose. Bennie tries to lick it up, but his cone stops him.

"Murray was just ignoring you that day to prove a point. You weren't freakin' invisible. That's the serious answer here."

"I'm not done the story," I snap, and yank a towel from the roll. "I knew you wouldn't believe me right away. That's why I needed time to get evidence."

"What evidence could possibly support you saying you've been hanging out with a teenage boy who's frozen in time? Are we in Forks, Washington, now?"

"The presence of a witch."

She snorts. "Now we're in Salem?" I grab her arm before she can walk away.

"Actually, yeah. Kind of. Pennsylvania had its own witch trial before the one in Salem, Massachusetts. Louise Gregor was accused, and her family owned the land where the Ardor Tree sits. Xander and I think she might've cursed it. And then we got cursed when we messed with the tree."

"Who is Xander?"

"The boy only I can see."

"Oh, right, the ghost." She taps her forehead. "I wasn't listening before."

"Okay." I huff. "He's not a ghost. Now you're being rude. I'm trying to open up here."

Whitley folds her arms. "You really think a witch cursed that tree?"

"I know how it sounds. But I didn't tell you before because it sounds ridiculous—"

"It is ridiculous," she hisses. "But . . . it makes you and Murray look less crazy."

"And you already had your dad and a wild coyote to worry about. I didn't want to add curses to the mix. I put some thought behind this . . . even if you don't believe me."

174

"I'm coming around." She nods. "I know you're too smart to make up something this dumb."

"So, will you help me?"

She shrugs. "What can I do?"

"There must be a way to reverse what's happened to Xander and me. We just don't know why he disappeared at the pool, and I disappeared at the tree."

She squints. "Who hacks at the Ardor Tree? That's a mortal sin in this town. No wonder you're half dead. What the hell were you thinking?"

I sigh. "I wasn't. My emotions got the best of me."

Whitley steps forward and wraps me in a hug. My body slumps against her, letting myself lean into the warmth radiating from her body. Sunlight filters through the window and we sway lightly like trees in a soft summer wind when the woods are at peace.

"I need more time to process this whole curse thing," she says, her voice calmer. "But I'll do what I can to help."

"I knew you would," I whisper. "I don't want to deal with this alone anymore."

"You never had to." She pulls back, then rips another paper towel from the roll and dabs at my cheek. "I'm glad you finally get that," she says.

I sigh as my shoulders sag.

"I've been here the whole dang time, Stetson. Stop keeping secrets." She pushes my wet hair from my face. "We're almost out of this town. Don't break our pact now by putting a wedge between us."

"I won't. I promise."

"So, what's my first mission?"

"Can you see if the lifeguards you're interviewing for your research know anything about Rainbow Valley Swim Club? Or when it used to be Pinehurst?"

She nods.

"Maybe it's, like, an urban legend among the lifeguards."

"I wouldn't be surprised." She grabs her phone. "What were those witches' names again? I need to look this up."

"You sure? The story is freaky."

Whitley scoffs. "I ain't scared of witches." She snarls. "I hope this Xander boy is nice. Coyotes aren't the only thing I can hunt."

30

It's ninety-nine degrees on the Fourth of July. I sit on my bed in just my boxers with my face inches from the pedestal fan, humming into its spinning blades while debating what to wear.

Whitley, in all her persuasive glory, scored us an invite to a lifeguard party. She asked one of them about Pinehurst Swim Club, and after their face went ashen, they said they could help her out. But only at the party. They didn't want to discuss what they knew at work.

And by *us*, I mean Xander, Whitley, and me. I'm bringing the group together for the first time.

Suddenly, there's a single knock on my door. Then it flies open.

"Hi, Stetson," Xander says, stepping in. Starburst wrappers fall to the floor around him like tiny toy parachutes. "Quit lying around and put some clothes on. We have a mystery to solve."

"Hey!" I shout, scrambling from my bed and covering my crotch with my arms. "How did you get in my house?"

"Oh, relax." He unwraps an orange Starburst and pops it into his mouth. "We just saw each other half naked in the river the other day."

My face burns. I grab a pair of wrinkled khaki shorts from the floor and slide them on, then walk to my closet and sift through the five tops I have to choose from.

I look Xander up and down. He wears a baby blue Hawaiian shirt covered in navy and white palm leaves, cutoff jean shorts, and dirty Converses. "Is this party a luau?" I ask.

"Don't hate on my style." He gestures to his feet. "I was going for a classy red, white, and blue look. I got red socks. See?" He flashes his legs. "I haven't been to a party where I could talk to someone in decades." He grins. "Dress to impress, they say."

"They do say that," I affirm.

"Say what?" Whitley asks, walking through the doorway, wearing denim shorts, a white tank top, and a red bandana holding her hair back.

Xander retreats to a corner. My eyes bounce between them.

"About dressing nice," I say, clearing my throat.

"Who's dressing nice? Because it certainly isn't you." She plops a plastic bag holding three forty-ounce beer bottles onto my desk.

"Xander," I mumble.

Whitley freezes, midway through opening one of the bottles. "The ghost is here? Where?" she asks in a whisper. "Oh my god."

"She doesn't have to whisper," Xander says. "And I'd prefer it if she didn't call me a ghost."

"You don't have to whisper," I relay. "And he'd prefer it if you didn't call him a ghost. He's in the corner by my dresser."

178

Whitley stares at him, or rather that part of my room, with her fingers touching her parted lips. "I thought it was supposed to be cold when there's a ghost around."

Xander sighs. "There she goes again."

"That's because he's not a ghost," I say. "He's just cursed. Like me. Remember the witches?"

"Yeah . . . Yeah. The witches." She waves a hand. "I've been looking them up all week. I'm only partly convinced." I glare. "I got us invited to the party, didn't I?"

"Yes." I throw up my hands in surrender.

"Can I . . . say hi to the ghost—I mean him?" she asks.

I nod. She inches toward the dresser, arms outstretched like she's feeling for an invisible doorway.

"Hello, Whitley," Xander says as she gets closer.

"He says hello," I repeat.

Whitley flinches. "He does?" Her poking hands turn into swats.

"You're getting close." I scratch my neck. "You're going to hit him."

"Can he feel it?"

I shrug. "I don't know. But it's still rude even if he can't."

Xander's back presses against the wall as Whitley's arm sweeps right through his stomach. Blue and white particles swirl in the air like sand caught in the wind.

"It doesn't hurt," Xander says, looking down with a grimace. "But it definitely doesn't feel good."

"Whitley, stop!" I lunge forward and yank her back by the shoulders.

She gasps, cradling her arm against her chest. "I felt nothing."

"You wouldn't," I say.

"Is he mad?"

Xander laughs and shakes his head. The loose dust
particles from his shirt zoom back into their original place.

"No," I say.

She lets out a long exhale. "Okay, so, if he's going to the
party, how do we talk to him?"

"Through Stetson," Xander says. "Our designated
medium."

"I'll tell you when you need to know something," I add.

"Okay," Whitley says slowly, narrowing her eyes. "Don't
talk shit about me behind my back."

"I think Xander has more important things to worry
about."

"I don't know about that." Xander taps his chin. "I've
been alone for so long, a gossip session sounds fun. What's
Whitley's dirtiest secret?"

I laugh.

"Don't laugh at me," Whitley says. "I was setting ground
rules. You didn't say if he was a friendly ghost."

I smack my forehead. "That wasn't at you. That was for
Xander."

Whitley gasps. "Did he say something nasty?"

"Oh my god." I throw my arms up. "This is stressing me
out. Let's just get to the party."

"We're waiting on you." She opens a beer bottle. "Does he
drink?"

Xander nods.

"Yes," I say as I pull on a shirt.

Whitley hands me the bottle. "Then here, pass this to
him."

I do. He takes a swig.

Whitley screams.

I jump. "What's wrong?"

"The bottle," she says. Her voice trembles. "It just . . . It vanished in the air."

Xander wipes his upper lip with the back of his hand. "The bottle's a part of me now."

"Um," I begin, scratching my head. "Yeah, that can happen. I told you I wasn't making this up."

Whitley runs a hand through her hair. "I can't believe this."

"Well, at least you have two more bottles."

"Thankfully." She picks up one of the remaining beers and chugs half of it. "I'm going to need them."

I swipe my keys from my bedside table. "You guys ready?"

"Wait," Xander says, touching my forearm. "Can Whitley take a picture of us? We need to start your collection for Tennessee. So you can remember me."

"Good call. Whitley, can you take our picture?" I toss her my phone.

Her head flinches back. "Of you and Xander?" I nod. "Suuure."

Xander presses against my side and nuzzles his shoulder into mine. He wraps his arm around my back, then his hand squeezes my hip. His warmth seeps into my skin and unravels the tension in my muscles like when a sip of hot tea slides into my stomach.

"Is he ready?" Whitley raises the phone.

"Yes," Xander and I say in unison. We laugh through our posed smiles.

Whitley snaps a few shots. "I took a bunch."

I grab my phone from her, eager to see our first photo.

"Oh," I say, turning to Xander as my face falls.

Xander leans in, looking over my shoulder. "What's wrong?" he asks.

The picture is only of me. My arm is wrapped around nothing.

His smile sags into a frown. "Yeah . . . that makes sense." He exhales. "I don't know what I was expecting." A beat of silence passes, then, forcing a grin, he takes a sip of beer. "You'll just have to remember me from this summer, then."

He pats my back, then walks out with his eyes on the floor.

The warmth of his touch lingers, but soon, it just feels cold.

The party house sits directly across the street from Penango College. *Register now for fall classes!* flashes on a big LED sign at the campus entrance, which is a row of identical three-story brick buildings standing lifeless on a bed of dead, yellow grass.

Three girls perch on the front porch steps of the house. They wave us over with arms covered in blue star stickers and smeared fake tattoos. We follow their call, stepping over smashed beer cans and crushed red plastic cups littering the lawn like the aftermath of a country music concert tailgate.

"That's the girl who said she could help us out," Whitley whispers in my ear.

"Which one?" I ask.

Before she can answer, one of the girls struggles to her feet, gripping the splintered banister for balance. Her half-lidded eyes don't match the energy of her glittery hair ribbons and glossy nails.

"You made it!" she calls out, her voice sluggish from alcohol.

"Yeah, thanks for inviting us," Whitley says. "This is Stetson and—" She glances at me, then bites her lip. "Um, it's just Stetson."

"I'm Amanda. This is Amy and Julie," Amanda says, tapping the other girls on their heads. Amy is asleep. Julie blows us a kiss. Her face is badly sunburned, and her French braids are moments away from unraveling.

Whitley leans closer to my ear. "Amanda is the girl who knows about Pinehurst," she says. I nod subtly.

"They want to do the interviews too," Amanda says. "I hope my answers for that were okay. I never really thought so much about becoming an adult." She grins. "It felt like therapy or something."

Whitley touches her shoulder. "Oh, no. Don't think like that. You were good. There weren't any right answers, to be honest. We're looking for personal stories about growing up."

Amanda nods. "Right on. That's cool. So, do you want to come inside?"

We follow her in. The house is livelier than the front yard, though it reeks of warm beer, sweat, and something sour like a mix of my oldest cross-country shoes, Murray's football pads at the end of the day, and Bennie's accidents when Whitley forgets to clean them up.

A pulsing speaker in the living room spits out a country song; its flashing purple light serves as the backdrop for two girls snapping selfies in its glow.

Xander grabs my shoulders from behind and coughs into my ear. "What is this place? This isn't the kind of party I was hoping for."

A few of the windows are open, but with it pushing a hundred degrees outside, they might as well be closed. The heat swirls through the house like steam trapped in a pressure cooker. In the kitchen, five people lounge on the counter, shouting over each other. Another group plays flip cup at the table, chugging beer and howling like wild animals. Everyone glistens with sweat.

Xander points to a tray of soggy hot dogs swarmed by flies, then sticks his finger in his throat. "I no longer miss the presence of other humans," he says.

Whitley winces. "Don't tell my dad these are the participants in my study," she says. "He'll never think I'm legit. Better yet, don't mention this party to anybody."

She tugs at the bracelets around her wrist, but my attention shifts past her, out through the sliding glass door. On the back deck, gripping a beer so strongly the can caves under his fingers, stands Murray. My chest tightens like he's squeezing me too.

Amanda laughs, oblivious to my spiraling. "We started drinking at ten this morning, so it's been a gradual decline in decency," she says. "But we're doing fireworks later and there's still beer outside. Have at it."

"Where should we start?" Whitley asks.

I fixate on Murray.

She follows my gaze, then lets out a heavy sigh. "Oh. Oh, no."

Xander leans in. "That's him. From the pictures. It's your ex."

I exhale. "Yeah. Unfortunately, it is."

"Relax," Whitley says. "According to your story, it's not like he can see you."

"I know," I say, inhaling sharply. "But the sight of him is bad enough."

She groans. "For the hundredth time, if you told me what he did, I could actually understand your feelings."

184

Xander gasps. "Was he a cheater?" he asks.

"No." I drag a hand down my face. Why didn't I think about the possibility of him being here? He's starting in the fall.

"Let's get what we need and get the hell on out of here," Whitley proclaims.

She's right. A Penango College party with my ex isn't where I want to spend my night. None of the couples here know that in a year's time their boyfriend might be a gaslighter, their girlfriend might resent them for wanting something more, or their perfect person might do what Murray did to me earlier this summer.

I step around her.

"Hey, Amanda?" I ask.

She raises her eyebrows.

"Before we grab drinks . . . Whitley said you knew something about Pinehurst Swim Club."

Her expression changes. Her back stiffens. She glances over both shoulders before pressing a finger to her lips. "Don't be so loud," she whispers. "That's sensitive stuff."

I shift on my feet. "Oh. Uh. Sorry."

She nods toward the flip cup table. "You can ask Robbie about it."

"The guy in the tank top?"

"Mm-hmm." She swirls her half-empty cup. "His stepsister was the one who went missing there."

"Went what?!" Xander, Whitley, and I shout in unison.

For the first time all night, Amanda isn't laughing.

31

"There's another one of us!" Xander yells.

"We don't know that for sure," I say, my pulse hammering in my ears.

"Know what?" Whitley asks.

I pause and wait for Amanda to leave the kitchen before speaking again. "Did you know his stepsister went missing?" I ask, nodding at Robbie across the room. "Because that's a hell of a detail to leave out."

She shakes her head. "Amanda told me her friend's sister worked at Pinehurst. She said they might have a story for me. That's it."

I don't hesitate. "Wait here." I chug the rest of my beer, set the empty bottle on the counter, and push through the crowd toward the flip cup table.

Xander follows close behind, silent as a shadow.

Robbie stands at the edge of the table. His lanky arms are nearly as long as his legs. A sunburn spreads across his freckled shoulders beneath an American flag tank top.

"Hey, are you Robbie?" I ask, wiping the foam from my mouth with the back of my arm.

"Yeah, man," he says, barely looking at me. "What's up?" He pours a tiny amount of beer into a plastic cup as he prepares for the next round of the game.

"I'm Stetson."

"Cool."

His disinterest tightens my jaw. I begin counting the players to calm myself. Across the table, a guy with a mullet gives me a thumbs-up. "Yo, Murray!" he shouts. "You in?"

My body goes rigid. The hair on the back of my neck prickles before I even turn.

Murray is right next to me.

His overgrown buzz cut is longer than I remember. I shift my counting from players to his strands of hair, but my brain stalls like I'm looking at a math equation I can't solve. He stares straight ahead, right through me as if I'm some nameless freshman in a crowded hallway.

I tell myself it's not his fault. He doesn't know I'm here. But somehow, the humiliation still swallows me whole.

"You want me to mess with him?" Xander asks. "I can tie his shoelaces together. Or put hot sauce in his drink."

A grin tugs at my mouth. "I appreciate the offer," I say. "But we need to stay focused."

"I didn't offer you anything," Robbie says, his expression darkening. "Do we have a problem?"

Someone switches the music from country to rap and ups the volume by several notches. The bass shakes the floor and forces me to lean in to hear Robbie over the noise.

I rake a hand through my hair. "Your friend Amanda . . . she said I could ask you about Pinehurst . . . about your stepsister."

Murray's voice is too close behind me. He laughs about another drinking game, and his hot breath collides with the nape of my neck, weakening my knees.

Robbie's head jerks back. His bloodshot eyes drag over me. He sighs, and the scent of beer and barbeque chips lingers between us.

I step back. "Do you know the Pomers?" I press. "They're family friends of mine. Their son went missing at Pinehurst." My heart pounds as I pick my next words carefully. They could send this conversation in any direction. "I'm trying to help reopen his case."

"Nice," Xander says. "Play the sympathy card. Make him feel bad!"

I shoot him a side-eye.

"I've heard of them," Robbie says as he stacks cups on the table.

"Oh, good. So—"

"So, what?"

"Well, I was hoping—"

"You want to talk about this right now?" Robbie scoffs.

I pick at my cuticles. "If you don't mind. Pinehurst is reopening. Have you heard? It's been hard for Mrs. Pomers. If you could share anything, it'd help us. Big time."

"Okay, let's not blame this Robbie ambush all on my family," Xander cuts in. "You're missing too, kind of. Isn't your mom also upset?"

"What's in this for me?" Robbie asks, crossing his arms.

My mouth falls open. "Umm, uh," I stammer.

Behind me, Murray keeps talking, his voice needling into my skull like an alarm I can't turn off.

"Anything I uncover could help your family find your stepsister."

188

Robbie shrugs. "I never really knew my stepsister."

Xander grabs my wrist. "Don't lose him," he says. "He doesn't seem like an emotional guy. Ditch the family angle."

The music gets noisier. Murray talks louder. My ears start to ring. I lick pooling sweat from my top lip.

Robbie tips back his beer can and chugs the rest. Desperate, I blurt, "I have a few more forty-ounce beers in my truck." I lift an empty bottle to his face. "I'll give them to you for free if you tell me what happened to your stepsister."

Robbie laughs and slaps a hand on my shoulder. "Damn, dude, okay. Now you're talking. I got you." He nods toward the hall. "Let's go upstairs though. There are too many people down here. I'm not technically allowed to talk about this."

A chill prickles down my spine. We have to go to a secret location for this conversation. He must have the answer to why Xander went . . . and I am going . . . missing.

"Yo, Murray," Robbie says, clapping him on the arm. "I'll be right back. Hold my spot at the table."

"For sure," Murray says. His eyes bounce over my shoulder, then go wide. "Whitley?"

He takes a step forward and immediately trips and falls. He lunges for a chair to catch himself, but instead, he drags it down with a crash.

The entire party erupts. "Ohhhhhh!"

Murray groans as he pushes himself up and reaches for his feet. His shoelaces are tied together in triple knots.

Xander snickers beside me as he admires his handiwork. "Success," he says. I drag my hand down my face. "Oh, come on. It's funny. If he really hurt you as bad as Whitley says, then he deserves it."

A few of Murray's new friends haul him to his feet. I wait for him to say something to Whitley, anything, but a sharp whistle cuts through the noise and pulls my focus in the opposite direction.

At the entrance of the kitchen, Robbie nods toward the hall like I'm his dog.

Whitley scampers over from the other side of the kitchen island. "Where are you going?" she asks, folding her arms tight across her stomach.

"Robbie's bedroom," I say. "He knows something."

"Should I come?"

I shake my head. "Just Xander and me."

She wrinkles her nose. "Oh, so I have to stay down here with Murray. Why does Xander get to go?"

"He's invisible."

"Ha ha." Xander laughs.

Her eyes narrow. "Are you sure it's safe up there? What if Robbie kidnapped his stepsister? What if he knows who killed Xander? They always say family members are most likely to commit the murder."

I freeze.

"I'm not dead!" Xander shouts. "Tell her we already determined that. It's just a curse from those witches. I have a chance to come back. Tell her!"

I swallow. "Xander wasn't killed," I say. "We were cursed. And the answer to breaking the curse could be upstairs."

"And so could trouble." Her bottom lip trembles. "All I'm saying is, be careful. Xander can't help you. No offense." She looks behind me even though Xander stands next to her. Xander sticks out his tongue, then mouths *no offense*, mocking her words.

"Cute boys tend to make you unaware of your surroundings," she continues.

190

I groan. "Whitley—"

"I'm just saying . . ." She lifts her hands. "You brought me into this situation for a reason. Holler if you need help. I'll wait down here, still dealing with your ex, like I have been all summer." She flops onto the living room couch, next to a couple making out, and crosses her legs.

Xander turns to me with a mischievous grin. "Am I the cute boy she's referring to?" he asks.

"What?"

"She said cute boys trip you up."

"Forget about it." I swipe at the air.

"You're a cute boy," he says. His golden eyes flicker toward the floor like he's not sure he should've said that out loud.

I sigh. "Xander . . . it's not the time. Look." I point to the staircase. "We're losing Robbie."

He's already made it to the landing and nearly slips out of sight. I jog after him, my pulse hammering louder than the bass rattling the floor.

The stairs creak with every step, the hardwood splintering beneath my weight. My hand trails along the railing and sends chipped white paint fluttering through the air like brittle snowflakes. At the top of the stairs, Robbie shoves open his bedroom door, but I hesitate before following him inside.

The stench hits first. It's worse than the stale beer and sweat choking the downstairs air. It's a mix of dusty laundry, cigarette smoke, and something sour that sends my head spinning. Wrinkled clothes are strewn across the stained carpet, and the only window is covered by a damp bath towel instead of blinds, barely hanging on by two plastic clothespins. I avoid looking at his bed, fearful of what's on those sheets.

Whitley's warnings echo in my mind.

Stay aware. He could be dangerous.

"I really wish my sense of smell was gone too," Xander says, pinching his nose. I try to breathe through my mouth.

"Are you sure you've never heard of Robbie before?" I ask Xander in the hall.

"Yeah. He would've been, like, ten years old when I was at Stillwell Trail. If a kid did something to me at Pinehurst, maybe I deserve to be dead." He forces a laugh, but I don't. An unease settles in my chest.

I step inside, knowing Whitley is only one call away.

Robbie slinks around us and shuts the door. The sharp click of the lock sends a hot wave of anxiety through me.

"I get all your beer?" he asks. He maneuvers through the mess with ease, avoiding the piles of clothes like they're obstacles in a game only he knows how to play.

Xander nudges me forward. I stumble over a shoe that used to be white. "Uh, sure."

He extends his hand. "Shake on it." Dirt cakes the creases of his palm. His fingers waver in the thick air.

I glance at the door. "Is that necessary?" I ask.

Robbie's lip curls. "What I'm about to tell you is going to make no freaking sense. So, yeah. It is necessary because I can't have you back out of the deal."

The room suddenly feels smaller. My mouth dries out from the stale air. But I force myself to lean in and shake his hand.

"We have a deal," Robbie says, voice low.

"Yeah," I say, shoving him off me. "Now tell me what happened."

He snickers. "Why do you care so much about Ra-Ra?"

"Ra-Ra?"

"That's a nickname. My bad. Her real name is Dara. My stepsister." He moves toward his dresser.

Xander and I exchange a look. "When did she go missing?"

Robbie shrugs. "It depends on who you ask. I think she just ran off." He opens the top drawer and rummages inside. "Long story short is that she ruined my family. My dad married my stepmom when I was a kid. That's how Dara became my stepsister. She was way older, but kind of chill, I guess."

He puts a cigarette between his lips, then flicks a lighter. The flame sparks against his shadowed face. "But then she ran away. My stepmom lost her damn mind over it. She kept saying weird crap—like Dara was in the living room when she wasn't there. Or she'd stare at the kitchen table and swear Dara was eating dinner with us. But the chairs were empty." He taps his temple. "Crazy, right?"

My pulse thrums in my ears. "Where do you think Dara went?" I ask.

"Hell if I know." He exhales a thick cloud of smoke. "I haven't seen her since. And my dad kicked my stepmom out when she started blaming us for ignoring Dara. She said only men couldn't see her."

Xander tugs at my wrist. "Stetson, it's like you," he says. "Only certain people can't see her. Just like how only a certain person can't see you. She must be cursed like us."

The muscles in my throat tighten. I take a step back, tripping over a mound of sweatpants.

"And what does her disappearance have to do with Pinehurst?" My voice shakes.

Robbie slams the drawer shut. "She worked there as a lifeguard," he says like it's nothing. "But I don't think that had anything to do with her running away. Now go get me my beer." He grabs my shoulder and pushes me toward the door.

I dig my heels into the carpet. "Wait. Where is your stepmom now? Can we talk to her?"

He scoffs. "I don't know. You're asking too many questions. Don't mention this to anyone. If this isn't what you're after, then I can't help you." He swings open the door.

"But—"

Robbie's face reddens. He stabs out his cigarette against the wall, smearing a black streak of ash across the paint.

"Come on," Xander says, seizing my arm. "He's drunk. I don't want you getting hurt over this. We have enough to work with."

I nod.

Xander grips my hand, steady and firm, just like at the archives.

We bolt.

Robbie thinks his stepsister's story makes no sense. But for me, it's all too clear.

Our feet hit the stairs in rapid thuds. We take the last three in a single leap and land with a loud smack against the living room floor. Whitley jumps from the couch, startled. Murray stands across from her.

"What's wrong?" Murray asks. "Are you finally going to tell me if you've talked to Stetson?"

"I said I did, but he hasn't responded," Whitley says.

"Try again." His jaw tightens. "I want to see him before summer ends."

Whitley glares. "Maybe if you weren't such a jerk at the beginning of summer, he'd talk to you himself."

Murray grabs her arm. "Wait . . . he told you about that?"

Whitley shakes him off like a bug crawling on her skin. She falls in step beside Xander and me heading straight for the door.

We don't stop or say goodbye. I have no intention of returning the bottles of beer we promised Robbie, mostly because they don't exist.

Behind us, confused, Murray watches Whitley leave alone like she's running from no one.

But me? I'm running from everyone.

32

We flee the party like we just committed a crime.

The wind roars through the truck's open windows, whipping against our skin, carrying the scents of freshly cut grass and distant bonfire smoke. It takes everything in me to shout loud enough over the rush of air for Whitley to hear the recap from Robbie's room. Xander sits in the back and occasionally pokes his head between the seats to add any details I leave out.

Whitley wants to keep the investigation rolling tonight. But with it being the Fourth of July, the chances of finding Robbie's parents at home, or sober, are slim. And if we do get into trouble, the cops will be too busy policing fireworks to care about three kids playing detective.

I can't keep going tonight anyway. Seeing Murray again made me sick, the kind of sickness that lingers, twisting in my stomach as if I just stepped off the Gravitron at the county fair. The blurry vision. Unsteady feet. The weight in my gut. None of it is useful for what we need to do next.

I drop Whitley off at her house with a fist bump.

When she's gone, Xander wastes no time climbing into the passenger seat to fill the empty space beside me. I inhale slowly, pressing my forehead to the steering wheel, taking in the stillness after all the noise.

Without Whitley asking questions, we fall into silence. It settles thick and heavy between us. I put on Kacey Musgraves's live album from New York to ease the tension. Her soft coos float from the speakers. I drop my phone into the center console and grip the steering wheel, but before I can shift into drive, Xander flicks the music off.

"Hey," I say. "Why did you do that?"

He doesn't answer, just reaches into the back seat and pulls a plastic bag full of candy root-beer barrels onto his lap.

I raise my eyebrows. "When did you get that?"

"I put them in your truck before I came over your house earlier." He pulls a barrel from the bag and pops it into his mouth.

My face twists. "How did you get into my truck?"

He shrugs. "It was open."

"Oh."

He nods with the candy bulging through his cheek. "Yeah. You shouldn't be so trusting in a town where multiple kids have gone missing."

I sigh and reach to turn on the music, but he smacks my hand down.

"No," he says. "We don't need that. I like all the other sounds."

"What other sounds?"

"Listen."

He leans back. His arm rests on the center console, inching closer to mine every few moments.

At first, all I hear is the quiet shift of my own breath. But then, once I relax, the world outside sharpens. A shrill, rhythmic wail of cicadas vibrates in the air. Fireworks crackle in the distance, their echoes stretching over the hills. Red shadows flicker across Xander's face. Then blue. Then gold. His Hawaiian shirt is half unbuttoned, revealing his sweaty, tan chest.

"I don't like how you get when you see or talk about him," he says.

"Who?"

He cocks his head slightly, letting the glow of the fireworks catch in his amber eyes as he finally looks at me.

"Murray?" I ask.

He nods, rolling the root-beer barrel between his teeth before biting down. "He makes you, like . . . jumpy."

I don't respond, rather, tap my fingers against the steering wheel and watch gold sparks rain down over the fields.

"Why are you scared of him, Stetson?"

My pulse stutters. I whip my head toward him, and he's watching me, waiting.

"What did he do?" His voice drops.

I swallow.

I haven't told anyone. Not my friends. Not my family.

Because telling them means changing the way they see Murray. Right now, he still exists in their memories as something good, something hopeful. The boy I loved. The boy who, for a time, loved me back and made me the happiest person in Penango. We beat the odds. If they knew, if they saw him the way I do now, that image would disappear. I don't want to be the reason it does.

He made a mistake. And he lost me over it. But does he need to lose other people too? Why change Murray for them? Why make him another bad example from Penango?

But Xander? He doesn't have memories of Murray. He doesn't carry the weight of who Murray used to be—or what we used to be. To him, Murray is already nothing.

Maybe if I say it out loud, Murray will become nothing to me too.

"Do you have time for a story?" I ask.

He shrugs. "You're the one driving." He licks his teeth. "I'm free for as long as the road takes us."

I glance at the clock. 10:13 p.m.

"Okay," I say. "Well, the last few months with him were terrible. I'm leaving Penango in the fall, or at least, I am trying to leave. He didn't want me to and resented me for it."

"I figured that part out."

"Just wait. I'm not done."

Xander drags his thumb across his lips. "Go on, then."

The first time I really noticed Murray change, when the melody I trusted went off-key, was right after the barn party, when he singled me out in front of the football team.

I tried to make things right after that.

A couple of weeks before Thanksgiving, I planned a celebration just for us. I didn't know how to cook, so while he was at football practice, I went to Boston Market and bought everything for dinner—roasted turkey, mashed potatoes, mac and cheese, sweet corn, and corn bread. I let myself into his house with the spare key under the clay pot by the door, set the dining table, transferred all the food into ceramic dishes, and even lit a cinnamon-scented candle.

It was supposed to be perfect.

Murray walked in no more than ten minutes later. His cheeks were flushed from practice and his pants streaked with mud. He slung his gym bag against the wall, then rounded the corner into the dining room.

"What the—" His jaw fell slack.

"Happy Thanksgiving!" I raised my arms like I had just pulled off a magic trick.

His face softened. "Did you make all this?"

I shook my head. "I had some help."

He laughed and plopped into his seat across from me, shoveling mac and cheese onto his plate without hesitation. "Thanksgiving isn't for two more weeks."

"Yeah, well, remember how you asked me to junior prom early? I thought I could be early with Thanksgiving, since you're going to your aunt's house in West Virginia."

He nodded. "Yeah, I guess this is something I should get used to since you'll be gone for the next four years." He twirled his fork in his mashed potatoes. "You won't come home for Thanksgiving break if you're in Tennessee."

My fingers tightened around my fork. "I don't know what my plans will be."

"I think I know."

I rolled my eyes. He was too busy tearing through his turkey to notice.

I forced a smile. "Should we start dinner by saying what we're thankful for?"

"Yeah, sure," he said.

"You first," I instructed.

"Hmm." He tapped his chin, pretending to be thoughtful. "I am thankful I get to spend a few more months with my boyfriend before he moves away and breaks up with me."

My nostrils flared. "Is that supposed to be funny? Because it's not."

He shoveled another bite into his mouth. "I'm just saying what's true."

"I'm trying to make this work."

"Whatever you say." He shrugged. "Do you even love me?"

I pushed my chair back. "You know what? I've lost my appetite. I'm over this."

"Don't be so dramatic."

I yanked my arm away when he reached for me.

"Why are you so annoying?" I yelled. My napkin flew from my hand across the room. "You just had to ruin this, didn't you?" I stormed out the door.

I didn't even get to eat a single bite.

I was so angry that I forgot about the missing second tread on his front steps. My foot hit air and I landed face-first on the concrete.

That was us for the rest of senior year. The same fight on repeat. The worst song on the radio playing over and over until I wanted to scream.

And in June, I did.

We both did. Louder than we ever had before.

"I'm done!" I yelled in his bedroom. "It's too much to think about anymore. I've given you enough chances, and I'm done. For good."

Murray threw his arms in the air. "Why did you have to change our plan?"

"We never had a plan!" My voice cracked from the weight of everything. "You just made one up, and when it wasn't what you wanted, you treated me like shit!"

"Well, you still haven't apologized, so I don't need to either."

I let out an empty laugh. "Apologize for what? Getting into college?"

He shook his head, sipping a beer beside his desk. "How can you throw away three good years—"

"Two." I crossed my arms. "I wouldn't count this past one."

He stepped forward and grabbed my shoulders. His fingers squeezed too tight. "I think we can work through this," he pleaded. "We're not like my parents or everyone else at school. We haven't cheated on each other. We don't fight—"

I flinched. "We don't fight?" My lips parted in disbelief. "I wish you cheated. I *wish* we fought worse than we do. It would make this whole decision so much easier."

My words cracked his expression. Something dark flashed across his face. He ripped his hands away and hurled his beer bottle against the wall. Glass exploded, scattering like a broken mirror unable to reflect what we had been anymore. A shard bounced back and sliced my forehead. Blood rushed down my temple.

I staggered forward, thinking maybe he'd help me. Maybe he'd finally feel for me like he used to.

Instead, he shoved me. Hard. I flew backward into the hall. My heel caught on the rug.

"Get out of here!" he yelled, shoving me again. I tumbled down the stairs, head over heels, the world flipping upside down. "I never want to see you again!"

I scrambled to escape without looking back.

Xander clears his throat.

"So that's what happened," I say. The road comes back into focus.

He exhales sharply. "Damn. And you didn't want me to mess with him at the party? I'm pissed I only tied his shoelaces together. I should've done way more. Let's go back."

202

I shake my head. "No, it's fine." I stare at my feet resting on the pedals.

"It's not fine." His voice hardens. "That's abuse, Stetson. That behavior wouldn't even fly when I was kickin' ten years ago."

I wave my hand in dismissal. "It happens to everyone here."

"That doesn't mean it's okay. You didn't deserve that."

My lip trembles.

Someone finally knows. And his reaction, the anger and disbelief, means what happened to me was bad. Which means I was right. The variables finally add up.

Leaving Murray is the right answer.

Xander reaches into his candy bag and hands me a root-beer barrel.

I laugh, wiping the corners of my eyes. "You and this damn candy."

He grins. "What can I say? Remember, health consequences don't apply to me, so I eat whatever I want." He smiles. "See these teeth? Pearl white. Cavity free." He tugs on his cheek. "You see this skin? Pores fresh. No sugar-induced acne."

I laugh harder.

"You sure you don't want this?" He wiggles the root-beer barrel over my lap.

"Yes. It's the most random candy you could offer me."

"Are you a chocolate guy?"

I sniff and wipe snot from my nose. "I guess you could say that."

He rummages through his pockets and pulls out an empty Skittle wrapper, two yellow Starbursts, and a small box of

Nerds. "I got nothing for you, then." He stuffs everything back into his shorts. "The best I can offer you is a big hug."

My throat constricts as I stare at him. A few beats of silence pass before I collapse into his chest.

His warm hands run up and down my back, steady and slow. "Thank you for telling me what happened," he whispers. "I'm sorry he put you through that."

I sob into his shoulder, just as he did into mine the day we met.

Between cries, I mutter, "I think you're cute too."

"What?" he asks, pulling back slightly.

"Back at the party, you said I was cute. I ignored it." I sniff. "You're always so nice and just say what you feel, and I guess I'm not used to that. If you can say you like me so easily, you can just as easily say you don't."

He smiles. "I think I'm coming onto you so fast because I've waited so long to feel like this."

I glance at the roof. "There you go again."

"Fine. No more talking. I'll just stare at you instead."

So I let him.

And for the first time in a long time, I feel fully seen.

33

I stall getting out of bed on the first workday after the holiday weekend.

For the past two mornings, I've slept in, texting Xander until the sun was high and my phone was warm against my palm.

I can't remember the last time I let my alarm wake me. My history with Murray has been bouncing around my head all year like a pinball at the Main Street arcade, every incident another steel sphere ricocheting through my skull, refusing to settle, and keeping me awake most nights.

But sharing my secrets with Xander has reset the game. The flashing images, the buzzing, the keeping score—it's all stopped. At least for now. My mind is quiet and there's a fresh round of waiting to begin.

Xander doesn't text back the way most people do. He sends voice memos and GIFs that are as animated as he is. My earbuds, once reserved for music and podcasts, now play his voice instead. His infectious laugh track cuts through the morning haze like sunlight splitting the clouds.

This morning a memo comes through as he jumps from a steep cliff into the Penango River. His shout echoes before he disappears beneath the surface. Another memo follows where he shares newly acquired dog knowledge while he floats in an inner tube. I picture him grinning at the sky, his wet curls glistening in the sun.

My mattress shakes as I giggle along with him. His day is already full, while mine is slipping away, half wasted.

It's hard to believe it's already July seventh. Even after eighteen years, the speed at which the Fourth of July turns early summer into midsummer always catches me off guard.

July.

July.

I lock my phone and tap my chin.

What was so important about July? A forgotten task hisses for attention like a faulty firework stuck at its launch site. There is something else besides the scholarship essay.

Then it hits me. I sit up and slap my forehead. I speak Kim's words aloud: "The first busload of campers is set to come in early July."

Kim and Sheryl's summer camp begins this week. Rainbow Valley's pool still needs approval. If the campers go in that swampy, green pool, they're bound to get sick. And if I let a group of kids get infected with some weird brain-eating amoeba, there's no way Victor endorses my scholarship.

I throw on my uniform, grab my keys, and drive straight there.

A yellow school bus idles at the entrance when I arrive, unloading kids with colorful backpacks and duffel bags. Kim waves them down the drive toward Sheryl, who sits under a white tent, checking names off a clipboard. Beside her, Mrs.

Pomers hands out name tags and watches the crowd with careful intent.

The presence of Xander's mom means there's no way he's here.

The bus blocks my view of the pool, spiking my nerves, as I imagine campers splashing through algae-thick water. I park and step out, already sweating through my shirt.

"Stetson!" Kim greets me with a bright smile. "You made it for our first day."

"I'm so sorry I didn't get here sooner," I say, rubbing the back of my head. "The days got away from me."

"You're just in time. We're still getting settled. The welcome ceremony is in an hour, then we have a scavenger hunt planned."

I force a laugh. "Actually, I kind of came to check on the pool again."

Kim's smile falters. "Did you get Sheryl's message?"

I shake my head.

"She called the health department and spoke with a man named Victor."

My stomach drops.

"We ended up draining the pool this weekend." She sighs. "Nothing was fixing that stubborn green water. We've got a maintenance team coming to check the filtration system, but for now, no swimming. It's just a shame this first group of kids won't get any pool time."

I exhale relief. "Victor didn't tell me."

She shrugs. "No problem. Sorry you had to make the extra trip."

The bus reverses out of the drive and reveals the empty, cement pool. Middle schoolers, and maybe some high school freshmen, stake claim on the lounge chairs that are Xander's usual spot. I scan the crowd, searching for him and counting the campers.

Two boys in backwards hats sit exactly where he would. But he's nowhere to be found.

"Why don't you stay for a little?" Kim suggests. "You can introduce yourself to some of the kids before the send-off dance."

"Um." I blink. I guess their previous invite wasn't actually optional and I'm being voluntold to help chaperone the dance. "When is that again?"

"Each group stays two weeks. We're throwing a dance every last Friday." She catches me counting days on my fingers and laughs. "You don't have to come to each one. Just the first would be perfect. Bring a friend . . . or a date."

I nod absently, my cheeks warming, unsure if she's teasing.

Kim leads me toward the camp's pavilion, a small wooden structure with a few picnic tables, a mini stage, and a lone mic stand. A rainbow flag flutters from the roof as it catches the warm summer breeze. I slide onto the farthest bench, away from where the welcome ceremony will take place.

A few kids sit nearby. Some wear swimsuits, oblivious to the drained pool behind them.

"Oops," I mutter.

After a few minutes, Sheryl and Kim step up to the microphone and greet the campers with wide smiles. My attention wanes as they discuss activities that I'm not signed up for. This won't be my world for much longer.

But when they call for a guest speaker, my spine stiffens. Mrs. Pomers steps up to the mic. I swallow and shift my position on the hard wooden bench.

She introduces herself, her voice steady but thin. She shares her story—Xander's story. The paper in her hands trembles as her words come out with unspoken weight.

The kids around me barely notice. One boy scrolls through his phone, his thumb flicking loudly against the screen.

I lose my patience.

"Hey," I say, tapping his leg. "Pay attention. This is important." I nod toward the stage. He flinches before tucking his phone between his thighs.

"I want this camp to be a safe space for you all," Mrs. Pomers continues. "A place where you know you're not alone. No one should ever feel the way Xander did."

Sheryl steps closer and rubs her hand along her back.

"As you go about your activities, try to forget what's happening back home. Don't worry about school bullies or confused parents who don't accept you for who you are. These next two weeks are yours. They don't belong to the people who take up space in your mind out of fear."

I fold my hands and squeeze them together until my fingers are white.

"Xander loved coming here." Her voice drops to a whisper. "And I hope you do too. Let this be the first of many communities you can call home."

The microphone squeals as she steps off the stage. The campers sit frozen, their gazes unfocused, their thoughts unreadable. Kim and Sheryl lower their heads in quiet reflection. The seconds stretch on, and the silence never breaks. There's just the cracking of the rainbow flag rippling in the breeze.

It's so quiet, I can only hope Xander heard his mom's words from wherever he is hiding.

34

I run into Victor at the entrance of the health department the next day.

"Hey, kid," he calls, lifting a half-empty coffee cup in greeting. "I forgot to tell you, I got a message from—"

"Sheryl," I finish for him. "Yeah. I went to Rainbow Valley yesterday."

"Attaboy," he says with a smile, seemingly unaware that the message was meant to tell me not to go. "You're always getting things done. How is the pool looking?"

"It's closed, actually. They drained it over the weekend. Something is wrong with the pipes and filter system."

He slaps my back, hard. "Lucky you. That makes it easy. No pool means no inspections. You can sit back and relax for a couple weeks."

We step into the elevator, and I resist the urge to rub my stinging shoulder.

Honestly, I'm glad I missed the message. Going to the club yesterday wasn't just about checking on the pool; it gave me another chance to see Mrs. Pomers and hear her speak about Xander.

What started as a routine health inspection has become so much more than just making sure the pool is safe for swimmers. It's about money, my scholarship, breaking a curse, and being the next gay icon for those kids at camp.

Okay. Maybe not an icon. The jury is still out on my iconography. But visibility counts for something, even if it's not inspiring.

It's probably for the best Victor remains oblivious to it all. This situation is way beyond the expertise of a guy whose primary skill set consists of poop jokes and overly aggressive back pats.

I clear my throat. "So, does this mean you can start writing my letter?"

He frowns as he fumbles with the keys clipped to his belt. "What letter?"

I bite back a groan.

Not that oblivious.

The elevator dings. Before I can protest, Victor strides out the doors and I'm left to follow him like a dog with its tail between its legs.

Across the sea of gray cubicles, Whitley's blond hair sticks out among the bald heads.

"Can we talk?" she asks as I take my seat.

"Yeah?" I raise an eyebrow. "What's up?"

She glances around to scan the nearby desks, exhaling after finding each one unoccupied.

"I'm kind of worried about your situation." She frowns.

I let out a dry laugh. "Which one?"

"The one with Xander."

I jerk my head back. "What? Why?"

She hooks the heel of her shoe around the base of her chair and pulls herself closer. "I couldn't sleep this weekend with the fireworks, so I did a lot of research."

"What kind of research?"

She holds up her phone. "I found some court notes from Louise and Abigail's trial. They were in this book I found on the internet called the *Pennsylvania Provincial Council's History*. It says they lived and practiced spectral witchcraft in the woods by the Ardor Tree."

"I know." I shift in my chair. "So, you're saying everything checks out? They put a curse on the tree?"

She tilts her head. "Kind of. The thing is, spectral witchcraft means they appeared to people as ghosts."

I narrow my eyes. "Okay?"

"They also tried to bring other people back as ghosts too."

"What are you saying?"

She pauses. "I'm afraid Xander might be a ghost brought back from the dead by Louise and Abigail."

I run a hand down my face. "Xander isn't a ghost. He's not dead. He's just cursed by the tree like me. He's like a ghost because no one can see him, but that's not the same thing."

She bites her lip. "Just listen."

Scrolling through her phone, she pulls up a page. "There are five main types of spectral ghosts. The first is an orb. You know, those glowing balls of light people catch in photos."

I shake my head. "That's obviously not him."

"Right," she continues. "Then there's a funnel ghost, but they're basically swirling vortices that make a place cold."

I scoff. "It's been ninety degrees every day around him. You can scratch that one."

She lifts a brow. "I already scratched it. I did a lot of research, and I want to walk you through it."

212

I nod, folding my arms. "Sorry. Go ahead."

"We always talk about how boring this place is," she adds. "Might as well embrace something exciting when it comes along."

"I don't know if I would call it exciting." I take a deep breath, thinking about the possibility of permanent invisibility. I don't think I've wrapped my head around what might happen if we don't break this curse.

"The third one is an ectoplasm or ectomist."

I peer over her phone. "That sounds like something we learned about in biology class."

"It's basically just a fast-moving cloud of mist."

"Like that Stephen King movie *The Mist*? Where everyone goes insane in a grocery store?"

"Exactly like that. We're lucky Xander isn't the mist. If Penango got trapped in a supermarket together, half the town wouldn't make it out."

"Fair point."

She takes a breath. "That leaves us with two options. He's either a poltergeist or an interactive spirit."

I sit up straighter. "Like the *Poltergeist* movie?" My fingers shake. "I hate that movie more than *The Mist*."

"You're safe. I don't think he's a poltergeist." She waves it off. "They're destructive. They slam doors, break dishes, and throw furniture around. Has Xander tossed any pool chairs?"

"No. He's so friendly."

She nods. "Which means . . ." She hands me her phone. "He fits this."

I read:

An interactive ghost is usually of a deceased person, someone you know, a family member, or local figure. These ghosts can make themselves known to you in a variety of ways

*through speech, touch, and scent. Experts say this type of ghost
retains its personality and can feel emotion.*

I swallow. "I mean . . . there are some similarities here,
but he's not dead."

"Keep reading." she scrolls down.

I read aloud this time:

*"Interactive ghosts remain tied to their site for a number of
reasons including being killed through a traumatic event such
as a murder. The spirit may have died suddenly and not
realized he/she died."* I pause and make eye contact with
Whitley. *"Or the spirit cannot rest due to unfinished business.
These spirits can interact with the living world and cast curses
on those around—"*

I stop. The words blur together as I lock the phone and
slam it face down on the desk. "Okay. I've read enough." My
voice is tight.

"I'm not trying to upset you," Whitley says. "This might
be why he disappeared at the pool."

"There's so much more going on," I say. "What about me?
The Ardor Tree? And Dara?"

Whitley swallows. "There's something else."

I lift my head slowly. "What?"

"I asked Amanda for Robbie's last name and did some
digging on Dara's case."

"And?" I grip my chair's armrests. "How long has she
been missing?"

Whitley hesitates. "That's the thing." She twirls a finger
through her hair and avoids eye contact. "Dara isn't missing."
My heart stops. "What?"

"She works at a women's shelter outside Fairmont, West
Virginia. I found a video of her online from March. She was

talking about the services they offer. There's another guy in the video with her."

I stand so fast my chair wheels back into the cubicle wall. "That doesn't make any sense."

She shrugs. "Robbie probably didn't understand what you were asking. Or he lied. Either way, he seemed like a dick. If I were Dara, I'd run away from him too."

"So, what are you saying?" I throw up my hands.

She sighs. "I trust that you see Xander. But maybe—and I know you don't want to hear this—he's the one who cursed you, not those witches from hundreds of years ago. He might be using you for something."

"Like what?"

"To get back at who killed him."

"Stop, Whitley." I pace, shaking my head.

I just opened up to Xander, told him the secret I couldn't tell anyone. And now Whitley is saying he's manipulating me? That he's just another Murray? How many times can I be fooled by a boy before I finally break?

"The Ardor Tree has been around forever," Whitley goes on. "Don't you think someone would've noticed something strange about it by now?"

I clench my fists. "I disagree."

"I just don't want to see you getting hurt. Again."

"I need to talk to Dara." I grind my teeth. "If she's cursed like us, then that will disprove your theory."

Whitley crosses her arms. "Dara's not going to have the answer. She's just going to share normal Penango family drama."

No.

Nothing about this town is normal.

35

I wish I wasn't splitting up with Whitley.

Xander and I plan to drive to Fairmont, West Virginia, today after work to find Dara and figure out once and for all if there really is another cursed heart.

Whitley, on the other hand, isn't coming. She's spending the rest of the day doing more interviews for her research study, then coyote hunting at dusk. She isn't interested in hearing what Dara has to say. When I drop her off at home, she makes me promise I'll be back to help with the hunt.

I get where she's coming from with her theory. She doesn't trust Xander, not because he's done anything wrong, but because she can't witness how he takes care of me, hear his jokes, or see that he's just hoping for a second chance. He's a ghost to her, and we're taught to fear them.

But I don't think she totally understands the intricacies of our curse. I checked that video of Dara online. It's true there's another man in the footage, but they're never in the same scene together.

It was edited—spliced—like he wasn't really there.

I forge ahead acting like Xander doesn't want to hurt me, he simply wants my help, just like I want his. I need to find

Dara as quickly as possible, to prove to Whitley that I'm on the right track, that Xander isn't lying to me, and that I'm not lying to myself.

The heat is relentless today, thick like a wool blanket thrown over the town. My truck's black leather seats are practically sizzling. I crank the air conditioning and hold my fingers over the vent to dry the sticky film of sweat on my skin.

Xander sits in the passenger seat with his backpack at his ankles. He unloads two cans of lime sparkling water, slick with condensation, and places them into the cupholders. Then he flashes me the rest of his bag's contents—an entire stash of candy.

"Road trip ready!" he announces.

"It's barely an hour away," I say with a light laugh.

"We're crossing state lines. That absolutely qualifies as a road trip."

I shrug. "Fair point."

"Look what I brought you." He digs through his backpack and pulls out a sandwich bag full of fun-sized Hershey Bars, KitKats, Snickers, M&M's, and Twix. "Chocolate!"

I blush. "You didn't have to do that, Xander. You like the sweet stuff."

"Yeah, but you don't."

My body becomes weightless in the seat. "Well, thank you." I tear open a Twix with my teeth and pop half into my mouth.

He buckles his seatbelt. "Do you have the directions? Where are we going exactly?" His fingers graze his damp neck before he flicks some moisture off his forehead. The heat doesn't make him look gross, it makes him look edible, like a glazed donut.

I wave my phone in the air and swallow a ball of creamy, caramel chocolate.

"Lead us to our cursed sister, then."

I can't help but grin as he excitedly looks onward. This hot mess of a summer has provided me with many reasons not to smile, but Xander sure isn't one of them. My cheeks ache whenever I'm with him.

We cruise southward on the two-lane road, bordered by familiar green trees, scattered single-story homes, and the occasional white church. The light coming in the passenger window catches Xander's eyes in a way that makes this drive seem new.

He taps his fingers along his thigh. "Would you rather have a Lab or a poodle for a pet?" he asks, watching the hills roll by his window.

"Huh?"

"Which would you rather get as a pet?" He turns to me. "It's a road trip game. Would you rather."

"I know the game. Are you bored already?"

"Far from bored. I'm curious."

I think for a moment. "Definitely a Lab. Whitley has one."

His mouth drops open. "Your best friend has a dog, and you haven't introduced me?"

I grimace. "Sorry."

"Turn the truck around."

"Are you serious?" I check the rearview mirror. It's a vacant road.

"No, of course not. But I would like to meet . . ." He raises his eyebrows.

"Bennie."

218

"Aww. Yeah, Bennie."

"He's a chocolate Lab."

"Fitting." He flicks an empty M&M wrapper onto my lap. "Did you know that the national dog show is in Pennsylvania? I go every year and get front row seats since no one can see me. Invisibility perks."

"I had no idea."

"You should come with me this year. It's around Thanksgiving. Maybe you'll be home from school."

"Yeah, maybe."

"Okay. Your turn," he says after a beat.

"Hmm." I drum my fingers along the steering wheel "Would you rather only eat Skittles for the rest of your life, or never have fruity candy again but eat any chocolate?"

He scoffs. "Easy. Skittles."

"Really? That was quick."

"No need for contemplation. The heart knows what it wants."

I let out a breathy laugh. "Does it? I feel like the heart gives mixed signals."

"Of course." He stretches his legs. "It's the only thing that knows what's best for you. If I listened to my heart years ago and came out, I might not be going on ten lonely years of invisibility and driving down a backroad toward West Virginia to find a strange girl I never met before."

I grip the wheel tighter. "Yeah. I guess you're right."

"I always do what my heart tells me to now." He wipes his hand down his face, resetting his expression. "Would you rather have Dara be like us or not like us?"

I huff. "That's a serious one."

"It doesn't have to be." He takes a sip of sparkling water. The bubbles fizzle against his lips.

"I'd rather have her be like us. Because then we'll have more people on our side to help break this curse and move on with our lives once and for all."

The sip of water catches in his throat, sending him into a fit of coughs and chest pats. "That sounds so final." His voice is hoarse. "What does moving on mean to you?"

"Getting out of Penango."

"And never coming back?" His grip tightens around the can.

"Hopefully not for a long while."

We cross beneath the *Welcome to West Virginia: Wild and Wonderful* sign. The only thing that changes across the border are the roadside weeds. They're unrulier, attempting to overtake the pavement like slush after a snowstorm.

Xander shifts in his seat. "If you had to—" He clears his throat. "Would you rather kiss me or your ex-boyfriend, Murray?"

My grip on the wheel falters. I turn to him, my pulse hammering. We meet eyes, but I quickly get distracted by his plump lips chomping on a Starburst; the juices exploding from the red candy coat his mouth with an extra layer of sweetness. Those lips have taunted me all summer. Now they're right there, waiting for me to try them like a freshly picked summer peach.

I adjust my shorts. "Is this a serious one or a joke?"

He shrugs. "It's however you think of it."

The hum of the highway vibrates beneath us. My knees begin to bounce.

"I'd never kiss Murray again."

"So . . ."

"So, then . . . you."

A slow, satisfied smile spreads across his face. He zeroes in on my lips and ignites a fire beneath my cheeks.

"Do you want to go again?" he asks, leaning across the center console.

I scratch my head. "Would you . . ."

I want to ask, *Would you rather kiss me now or later?* But our unknown future dams the words from leaving my mouth. What if he is tricking me like Whitley said? What if we kiss and the curse becomes permanent? I can't risk that.

The uncertainty turns my words around.

"Actually, let's just listen to music," I say flatly.

Xander exhales and deflates into his seat. "Sure," he says, his voice softer. "I can play you my favorite music from 2015."

I nod. "I'd like that."

He takes my phone and queues a playlist. "Do you like 'Wildest Dreams' by Taylor Swift?"

His words fade as I remember what he said earlier about his heart. And I wonder—if he always listens to what his heart tells him to do, why isn't he kissing me right now?

36

The road rises and falls in lazy waves before dipping into the valley known as Fairmont. The roller-coaster ride mimics my emotions, high, low, and uncertain, and my stomach doesn't seem to want to settle anytime soon.

We're getting closer to answers. I can feel it. But what happens after we break the curse? Is there still a *we* when the magic is gone?

I've spent all year set on leaving behind this town and everyone in it. But the thought of driving off without Xander riding shotgun guts me. Right now, we're bound by this weird in-between, this need to escape. But I'd be lying if I said I didn't want it to be more—or if I said I wasn't scared Whitley might be right about him.

When the curse lifts, I'll finally know if Xander is different or just another name I have to leave behind.

"You've arrived," my phone says. But we're parked outside a brick building that's split into a pawn shop and a home improvement store. Both have *Closed* signs pressed against their glass doors.

I check the time again. The women's center should be open for another hour, according to their website. It also says they provide free, anonymous counseling, legal support, and education for the women of West Virginia. Dara is listed as their program coordinator.

"Do you think it's upstairs?" Xander asks, tilting his head toward the second floor.

"Only one way to find out." I kill the engine, rip the keys from the ignition, and step outside.

The hot air hits me like a wall. It clings to my skin, dragging beads of sweat down my spine. The street is deserted. Most of the parking meters flash red. No one strolls the sidewalk. No doors swing open. It's like we've stepped into a ghost town, a perfect setting for a boy no one else can see.

"Over here," Xander says, waving me down a narrow alley. I follow him between the buildings and onto a path littered with overturned trash cans and warped wooden planks. Tucked behind the storefronts is a smaller, blue-brick building. A white sign above the door reads *Fairmont Women's Center*.

We pause.

"Do you think she'll believe us?" Xander asks.

I shrug. "When she realizes we can see her, we won't have to do any convincing. That's the easy part about this curse."

He smiles. "I never expected to make so many new friends so quickly."

"Hopefully she's nothing like her stepbrother."

His smile flattens and his gaze falls to the fly-infested puddle at our feet. "Let's keep our fingers crossed."

"You first," I say, opening the door. Its hinges cry out like a dying rabbit in the middle of the night.

The waiting area is sterile and quiet, boxed in by white cinder block walls. A row of faded blue plastic chairs lines the perimeter. They're all empty. No people to count. No music.

A receptionist sits behind a plexiglass barrier with thick-rimmed glasses perched on her nose. She sizes us up.

"Can I help you?" she asks.

It's not Dara. The woman on the website had long hair as black as mine, and hollow, sunken brown eyes. This woman has cropped hair and round, watchful eyes.

"Hey, yeah," I say, stepping toward the desk. "We're looking for someone."

"We?" she asks. "Who's we?" She leans to the side, searching the empty lobby. The tap of her pen against a notepad quickens.

I turn to Xander, who is standing just beside me. He spins his thumbs in his hands and pulls in his lips.

I forgot. Again.

It's just me.

I take a deep breath to steady myself. "My friend is waiting in the car. We're—"

"The identity of our clients is confidential," she cuts in, folding her hands over the desk.

"We're not looking for a client," I say. "We are hoping to speak with Dara. She works here."

The woman raises an eyebrow. "Do you have an appointment?"

"No."

The moment the word leaves my lips, I regret it.

She points her pen at the door. "Then you'll have to come back tomorrow. We're closing soon."

Xander huffs. "This is stupid," he says. "I'm going back there to find her."

"What?" I whisper.

He doesn't answer. He strides forward, ignoring the *Please wait to be called* sign, and disappears through a side door.

"Dara is wrapping up with another client right now," the receptionist says, misunderstanding my alarm meant for Xander.

"But . . . we . . ."

I search the lobby for an excuse to stay, something to buy us a little time. But there's nothing. It's all motivational posters and pictures of the Appalachians—the mountain range I can't seem to escape. The images remind me of their permanence in my life.

"But my friend . . ." My voice softens.

The receptionist stands, adjusting her glasses. "Who's in the car? Is this an emergency, young man?"

"Yes!" I shout. The word comes out sharp. I step forward and grip the edge of her desk. The woman presses a hand to her heart. "It is an emergency," I insist. "Can we be seen?"

She pulls open a drawer and retrieves a clipboard stacked with intake forms. "Fill this out. And then—"

A scream tears through the air. A raw, guttural scream.

It ricochets off the cinder block walls and rattles my rib cage. The receptionist gasps and drops the clipboard from her hands. It clatters against the desk, then tumbles to the floor, landing on my foot.

But I don't feel it.

I don't feel anything except the satisfaction of that scream.

"Dara!" the receptionist cries, scrambling from her chair. "What's wrong? What is it?"

But I already know.

37

I throw open the door beside reception and sprint toward the endless screams. The sound cuts through the silence of the hall like a blade.

In the farthest office, Dara is keeled over beside her desk, dry heaving. The choking gasps soon stop her cries. Xander crouches beside her, squeezing her hand and rubbing small circles on her back.

The receptionist rushes in behind me. "Dara!" she shouts. "Have you fallen?"

She steps through Xander to reach her and he bursts apart. A cloud of purple-tinged dust explodes around the office. The particles of his body swirl in the dim light.

A wave of vomit rises in my throat as pieces of his face, arms, and legs scatter into the air, hovering above Dara's head. I swallow it down before it escapes across the office.

The sight of someone popping like a water balloon is something I will never get used to.

"This boy," Dara wails, clutching her chest. "Who is he?"

The receptionist lifts Dara to her feet. "Are you talking about the boy who just came in?" she asks. "He's a new client. I can ask him to leave if you'd like."

Xander re-forms beside me. He shakes it off like a dog after a bath.

"She can see me," he says coolly. "She's one of us."

Dara's breath stutters. She looks up at me, eyes wide and unblinking.

I wave.

"Two boys can see me!" she yells, then throws her head back. Her knees buckle and she nearly crumbles to the floor again. Her limbs go slack in the receptionist's arms like a rag doll.

I lower my hand, wincing.

"Oh, for the love of Christ," the receptionist moans. "I can't help you if you don't tell me what's going on."

After several panicked minutes, Dara finally comes to terms with the fact that we can see her.

Two boys can see her for the first time in years.

Her breath evens, and her tears dry up. She waves the receptionist away and asks for privacy. The woman agrees, with reluctance, questioning Dara's lucidness on the way out as she repeatedly tries to convince her there's only one boy in the center of this room. When the office door clicks closed, Dara lunges at us.

She wraps her arms tightly around our necks, knocking our heads together. I stumble, catching a whiff of musty couch fabric in her hair.

She pulls back, giving me a clear sight of her hollow eyes, with the type of half-closed eyelids that make her look tired even in shock. Her clothes are all black, her skin pale like mine, and her face frozen in time. It's identical to the pictures I saw online, unchanged after so many years, stuck in its early twenties.

"I can't believe this," she says, wiping dried tears from her cheeks. Her voice is raspy, unfitting of someone this young. "How did you find me? How can you see me? I have so many questions. All these years . . . boys, men . . . they haven't been able to see me. I thought I'd lost my mind." Her head falls into her hands.

"You haven't," Xander says. "I know exactly how you feel. Everyone lost their ability to see me in 2015. I didn't understand what was happening. I thought I was dead."

"You poor thing." Her voice breaks. She pulls Xander into another tight hug. Their bodies deflate, sharing an exhaustion only they can understand. "I was a college student in 2017 when it happened. Everyone says your late twenties are better than your early twenties. Well, I'm stuck at twenty-one years old and feel like I might as well be in hell."

She turns to me. "How long has it been for you?"

My throat tightens. All those years of confusion for them. They've been stuck like this for so long. My few short weeks of being invisible to Murray are laughable in comparison.

I swallow. "Since last month," I say.

She blinks.

"That's what started this whole thing," Xander says. "He found me at Pinehurst Swim Club. He was the first person to see me since I disappeared. We think we've been cursed by an old pair of Penango witches!"

The color drains from her face. "So, because we've all been cursed, we can see each other? The rules don't apply to us like they do for everyone else?"

I nod. "We think it works like that."

"We're in this weird limbo that freezes us in time," Xander continues. "It's like a secret club."

"The worst kind of club ever." She wavers on her feet. "Hold on . . . you boys are from Penango?" Her body sways.

I reach for her before she collapses for a third time.

She raises a shaky hand. "Wait . . . wait." She walks across the room along creaky floorboards. "I need to sit down for this conversation. I haven't talked about that forsaken place in a long while." She perches herself on a windowsill and slides open the glass. Hot pavement air curls through the open window.

My thoughts whizz by as fast as I run the one-hundred-meter dash. Where do I start with my questioning? The pool. The tree. The boys. We came all this way. What do I want to learn?

Dara tucks her long black hair behind her ear.

"What's the last thing you remember?" Xander asks before I can. "Before boys stopped being able to see you."

"I was at that damn pool," she says.

Xander and I exchange a glance.

"I was a lifeguard at Pinehurst in the summer of—"

"We met your brother, Robbie," I interrupt. "He told us that you worked at Pinehurst. That's what led us here."

She sniffs. "I'm sorry to hear that. He wasn't the brother I always dreamed of, that's for sure." She laughs. "What else did he say about me?"

"That you ran away. And your mom lost her mind."

She rolls her eyes. "Of course he did. And did you believe him?"

"No way. That's why we're here."

"Good." She takes a deep breath, then leans back against the frame. "My stepdad just used the whole thing as an excuse to leave my mom. She was the only one who tried to help me."

"Where is your mom now?" Xander asks.

She shrugs. "No clue. We lost touch. My stepdad and Robbie eventually convinced her that I wasn't real . . . visible . . . alive . . . whatever you want to call it. She had a nun come by the house to 'rid my spirit.'" Dara puts her words in air quotes. "The old woman nearly drowned me with holy water. That's when I ran away for real. I never saw my mom again."

"I'm so sorry," Xander says.

"Why? You didn't do anything."

"It's still sad. I know what it's like to lose your mom."

"Yeah, I guess both your parents can't see you." Dara flicks a hair from her shirt to the floor.

"My dad died before I was born," Xander says. "So my mom has had to deal with my disappearance alone, which makes it all worse."

Dara sighs. "Well, now I'm sorry."

He plays with the chains around his neck. "What happened to you at the pool?"

Her fingers tighten around the windowsill. "There was this kid . . . I remember him so clearly. Blond bowl cut. Race-car bathing suit. Blue goggles. I saw him flailing in the water all by himself, like he was drowning." I lean forward. She squints as she recalls the story. "So I dove in to save him." She sighs.

The desk phone rings. My heart skips a beat. Dara doesn't flinch. She stays fixed on the story. The screeching sound and flashing red light on the phone's keypad tighten my neck muscles. I force a dry swallow that tastes like ash.

"But as soon as I went in for the rescue, everything hurt. That's where my memory gets fuzzy. The kid went wild, scratching and kicking me. His hands felt like a metal rake

230

across my skin. No one ever did that before. It was almost like he didn't want to be helped."

Silence thickens between us.

"Did you save him?" Xander asks.

She nods. "He was the last boy to ever see me. We made eye contact underwater. I remember him staring at me through the blue goggles. Then things went black for a little, but when I broke the surface, everything changed." She runs her fingers along the window screen, making a melodic scratch. "Where were you boys when it happened? The change?"

"I was at Pinehurst too," Xander says. "Swimming. Then black. Then change."

"But I was in the woods by the Ardor Tree when it all went black," I say.

"So, who cursed us, then?" Dara asks.

We tell her about the witches.

"But we don't know exactly how it works," I continue. "Or why we've been cursed."

My response is somehow funny to Dara. She laughs, then coughs as a breeze blows dust down her throat. "The Ardor Tree? I hate that thing," she says, tapping her neck. "It should be cut down."

"Right?" Xander asks with a smile. "I carved a heart on it filled with my name and a blank line for a future boyfriend."

Dara straightens her back. "That's the sweetest thing I've ever heard."

"And I destroyed my heart with my ex-boyfriend," I say.

"Ouch." Dara grimaces. "Sweet and sour." She crosses her legs and bounces her foot in casual confidence. "Do people still go there after school dances and carve their names? I never had anyone to go with. It made me feel like crap about myself." She takes a long, deep breath. "I wrote *boys suck* after graduation to stick it to them all. And I still stand by those words all these years later."

Xander laughs. "I agree," he says. "Even when you make it clear that you like them, they just don't—"

"Wait," I cut in, waving my hands through the air. "You wrote *boys suck* on the Ardor Tree?"

"Damn right," Dara says.

My insides quiver as everything comes crashing into place.

Xander put no one in his heart—and no one can see him.

I destroyed Murray's name—and now he can't see me.

Dara defamed all boys—and they vanished from her life.

This is an equation that makes perfect sense. It all adds up.

The curse isn't at Pinehurst. It's on the Ardor Tree. And we invoked its powers by breaking the rules.

38

Dara doesn't hesitate to return to Penango with us tonight.

The idea of being seen again by half the population, and sticking it to Robbie and her stepdad, is too thrilling for her to sleep on what we've told her and delay breaking the curse. We're going to fix the tree—like vandals cleaning graffiti under the threat of being caught, we're going to erase our mistakes. Because that's the only thing we have in common—our mistakes.

Our connection to the tree isn't a coincidence.

We're not missing or crazy or dead.

We're linked by love gone wrong.

We were just bitter.

No. Not bitter. Different.

We didn't play Penango's game of love. Our chances of success were calculated, and they weren't good or fair. There was nothing we could do to make it work. High school dreams sometimes emerge at life's lowest point. They shouldn't be binding.

And while high school didn't prepare me for love, it did teach me about inverse functions, which undo another function. When the function f turns the apple into a banana, the inverse function f^{-1} turns the banana back into an apple.

I'm banking on applying this theory to the Ardor Tree's curse.

We return to Pennsylvania under a dying sun. The sky is still lit, but not for long.

We park at the Gregor Preserve's entrance and step out of my truck in formation, a small army ready to face its oldest enemy. A hot wind rolls in and carries the sour tang of asphalt. The trees bend with it, taunting and watching us like a pack of wolves circling their prey.

"Never thought I'd be back here," Dara says, gulping.

"You probably never thought you'd get cursed by a tree either," Xander says.

"Ha. Ha." Dara frowns.

"It's actually not a bad place when no one can see you," Xander adds. "There's good swimming, hiking, and clean air. It's a nature lover's paradise." He nudges her.

Dara laughs. "It's not nearly as pleasant when half of town can't see you. It's just confusing. So speak for yourself."

"Oh, I am speaking for myself." Xander smirks. "And if we're keeping score, I can confidently claim that I got the worst of this curse."

"Because you didn't put anyone in the heart," I remind him.

"There was no one for me to love." He throws up his hand. "I was just trying to have a moment with the tree like everyone else in town. Sue me."

I sigh as I dig through the back of my truck. "Here." I toss him an ice scraper. "Take this."

He frowns. "What's this for?"

"To carve a name into the tree."

"Hmm." He twirls it in his hands for an inspection.

Dara steps forward. "Got anything else?"

I pull out a crowbar from my tire-changing kit. "This should do." I place it in her palm. She weighs it in her grip. "I'll use one of those tools when you guys are done."

Dara marches into the woods. Xander follows, practically skipping. I let them get ahead. I prefer to trail Xander. Even on the darkest paths, the bounce of his tight curls eases the tension in my muscles like jingle bells at Christmas.

But this time I'm met with a winter sadness. When Xander has all the boys in the world to fill the blank space in his heart, who will he choose?

The tree stands just as we left it. Its crowned branches are black against the sunset sky. Its roots curl along the ground like witch hands hunting for their next victim. The graffiti-covered drainage pipe oozes a fluorescent liquid from a love potion gone wrong.

Dara steps over the gnarled roots, continuing to lead our charge. "I don't remember where I carved my *boys suck* message." She flips her hair. The crowbar dangles at her side like a murder weapon.

"I don't think it matters," I say. "Maybe just write something new. Destroying my old message didn't work for me."

She nods, narrowing her lips. "What'll it be, boys? *Boys rule? Dara loves boys? Boys don't suck?* What works best with your fragile egos?"

Xander scoffs. "Let's remember who the real enemy is here. We aren't like those high school boys who rejected you."

Dara laughs. "Who said I was rejected?" She leans back, grips the crowbar, and strikes the tree. "Maybe I just couldn't find any boys up to my standards."

A shiver runs down my spine as bark splinters through the air. One shard lands on my cheek, sparking the memory of my own fatal mistake, the one that set this all in motion.

I touch the healing wound on my forehead. The pink skin is smooth.

I grab Xander's hand and pull him toward the center trunk, away from Dara's relentless carving.

"Hurry." I nudge him up the tree. "I don't want to be out here when it gets dark."

Xander hesitates to climb toward his heart, gripping the ice scraper. "Who should I write?" he asks, voice uneven. "In my new heart."

I shrug. "I don't know. Who was your high school crush?"

He scratches his head. "Does it have to be someone from then?"

"Well, yeah," I say. "Don't just write Timothée Chalamet or someone random."

He sighs.

"Make it someone from Penango who you went to school with. It's your best shot."

He bites the inside of his cheek. "I wish I had some candy right now."

I touch his shoulders. "What's wrong?"

"I'm afraid. The last time I did this—"

"This time is different," I insist. "It's going to work. It's like an inverse function. Math has never failed me before."

His breath shudders. "But what if it doesn't? What if things get worse?"

My hands slide up from his shoulders to cup his face. "They won't. Trust me. The only thing to fear is things staying the same."

236

His throat bobs. His eyes shine gold in the dimming light. "That's my worst case." His voice cracks. "The sameness, with the hope of change completely gone." He bows his head.

I pull him into a hug. "We have to try," I say softly. My gaze flickers to the carved hearts full of couples and futures behind him. "I want you to meet people. There's so much to experience after you come out. It all gets better from here. But to get to better, we have to be brave."

His warm tears drop onto my shoulder.

"Help me up," he murmurs. He takes ahold of the trunk and digs his foot against the coarse bark. I lace my hands together and give him a boost toward the upper branches. He faulters for a moment but quickly finds his footing and vanishes into the leaves.

Dara appears, out of breath. "The deed is done," she says. I take the crowbar from her. It's warm from her grip.

"What did you write?"

"I went with the classic *boys rule*."

I nod in affirmation. "The Ardor Tree appreciates tradition."

"Your turn."

I don't hesitate. My carving requires no thought. I don't need to rephrase or rethink, just redo. I go to the smooth, untouched bark where my old heart used to be. An open canvas.

Stetson + Murray.

I wish I could write someone new. That's who I want to gift my heart—a boy far from Penango. But I'm scared that writing a new name might make that person lose their ability to see me too. I don't want to ruin my chances with any boys before we even meet. So I close my eyes and carve Murray's name again, hoping the tree forgives me.

Once we're all finished, we step back, gawking at the tree like it's a windmill about to spin.

But the tree never moves.

"Do you think it worked?" Dara asks.

"It might take time," I say. "Maybe a day or two. You were at Pinehurst when things changed the first time around. When was that? A few days after you wrote on the tree?"

"Hopefully it forgives faster than it curses," Xander says.

"Who did you write?" I ask him.

"Andrew," he says with a shrug. "I don't even think he was gay. But he was cute."

I cross my fingers.

Xander looks away.

"Y'all want to go to the Bean?" Dara says flatly. "I might as well enjoy the food while I'm back in town. We can watch Xander materialize over burgers."

Xander sighs. "Can we stop at the pharmacy for candy first though?" he asks. "I need something sweet."

They turn toward my truck. I track them through the trees, and the ice scraper in Xander's hand reflects rays from the setting sun back at my eyes. They quickly shrink in the distance. I look over my shoulder one last time at the thick branches, searching, waiting for movements.

Then I spot something. A blackened mark on the bark, as if a lightning bolt pierced the leaves above us to strike one lone spot. I brush away the soot from the trunk and peel back hidden layers of time. I read the carving:

Louise and Abigail.

I freeze. Droning bees enter the air around me, their buzz a warning sent from the tree to get moving or I might be stung.

Just like before when I couldn't tell if there were other boy couples on the tree, this could be any Louise and Abigail from Penango.

But I can be certain this is Louise and Abigail the witches, because this marking isn't inside a heart.

Their names are at the center of the familiar pentacle.

39

I wake the next morning with no news from Dara or Xander about a broken curse. Xander doesn't even send his usual video vlogs. Not even a selfie of him covered in Starburst wrappers.

The lack of notifications presses against my chest like a weight, deflating me back into my mattress. Another day floating aimlessly through the throes of a Penango summer without a light guiding me to shore.

Even my aging earbuds refuse to reach a full charge, and a fresh crack in their case forecasts their impending expiration.

Last night, we dragged out dinner as long as possible, keeping Xander and Dara in public, testing fate. We hoped the waitress would eventually acknowledge Xander, or the chef would give a nod to Dara. Some proof that the tree forgave us.

But they were ignored. Nothing happened.

We left the Bean preaching patience. It's my least favorite word these days. More waiting. More built-up anxiety. Everything is relying on patience. I guess if a decades-old curse was going to break, it wasn't going to happen in the time it takes to eat a burger.

I roll over and check my phone again. There's still nothing from Xander. But there is a new email from my counselor. I sit up, rubbing my eyes as I read:

I've prepared your transcript and my recommendation letter for the scholarship committee. Please send me your second letter and essay as soon as possible.

The message shoots me out of bed like a lightning bolt.

The essay.

My limbs go cold. I've been so occupied with Xander and Murray that I forgot to start my essay.

I open my laptop and log in to the Tennessee housing portal to get myself back on track.

I can already hear Murray's voice in my head, the same one that haunted my entire college application process last fall. It didn't exactly cheer me on. No proud hugs. No *"I'm happy for you."* Just him yelling at me for even thinking about leaving Penango, like it was some personal attack.

I swore I wouldn't let a boy ruin this last chance at escape.

I'm starting to learn my lesson.

Kind of.

A red dollar amount flashes on the screen, bold and blinking, beneath a warning:

Last day to pay your housing deposit to reserve your spot in fall housing. Nonrefundable.

I run the numbers in my head. The deposit is basically the entire amount of money I made so far this summer.

But the bigger problem is that I need both the deposit and the scholarship to make Tennessee happen. If I pay the deposit right now and don't get the scholarship, I'm screwed. If I don't pay and get the scholarship, I'm still screwed. These decisions aren't mutually exclusive. I need both.

I stare at the blinking price until my vision fuzzes over, then click Submit Payment with an aggressive track-pad slam. The confirmation message pops up immediately:

Payment received. Expect communication about your housing soon. Applications are processed in the order they are received.

In summary, more patience required.

I take a deep breath and do a quick balance check in my head. How much money do I have left? I open my banking app.

$6.51.

Not even enough for a burger at the Bean. Certainly not enough money to drive to Tennessee. And definitely not enough to tour half the country with Whitley.

My hands go slack in my lap. The number stares back at me. My ticket out of Penango is paid for. I just don't know if I'll ever get to use it.

At work, I can't wait to tell Whitley what's gone down in the last twenty-four hours. Nothing about what Dara shared was normal, like she swore it would be. The tree is what cursed me, not Xander. She was wrong about him.

But Whitley never shows up at the health department. She doesn't answer my calls either. Maybe she caught the coyote last night and is out celebrating. If that's the case, I need in on the party, anything to distract myself from the fact that Xander, Dara, and I are still invisible to parts of the world.

I reach Whitley's house at twilight. My tires bob over the curb at the uneven driveway. The heat wave that's suffocated Penango since the Fourth of July finally retreats south, leaving behind cool air and flickering lightning bugs.

242

I knock on the front door.

No answer.

I knock again. Still nothing.

After a few more moments of silence, I let myself inside.

Bennie lies on the living room sofa with white bandages wrapped tightly around his hind legs. His ears perk up when he sees me, and he lets out a few soft whimpers.

"Hey, Bennie," I say, patting his head. His warm tongue licks my palm. "Where is Whitley?" The ceiling fan spins aggressively overhead. An empty plate with specks of breadcrumbs rests on the coffee table. The kitchen counters are stacked with dirty dishes.

It's no sign of a celebration.

"Whitley?" I yell. "It's me. Stetson."

A mattress creaks down the hall, followed by a faint whisper. I follow the sound.

Whitley sits on her bed with her ankle propped up on a stack of pillows. The skin around her foot is purple, swollen, and twice its normal size. My stomach drops.

"You let yourself in?" she asks. Her voice is flat.

"What happened?"

She doesn't answer right away.

"I fell out of a tree while I was coyote hunting last night," she says, wincing as she rolls on her side to face the wall.

"Oh my god. Are you okay? Why didn't you say anything?" I step closer.

"You were busy." She sniffs.

My head jerks back. "So? When has that mattered before? I would've come and helped." I scan her body, checking for more bruises, but there's nothing else visible.

"When have you ever lied to me before? Or broken a promise?" She talks to the wall.

Her words hit hard like they've inflicted their own injury on me.

I blink rapidly. My cheeks flush. "Huh? Whitley, what's going on?"

She's quiet for a moment, then she spins around. I brace myself because the look she gives me is one I've never seen before. At least, never seen her give to me.

"I can tell you about yesterday and—" I start.

She rolls her eyes. "I don't care about yesterday." She swings her legs off the bed and forces herself up.

"Whitley—"

She limps past me, clipping my shoulder as she goes.

"You shouldn't be walking. Your ankle is bigger than a basketball."

"Don't tell me what I can or can't do."

She barely makes it to the kitchen before losing her breath, leaning against the wall for support.

"Chill for a second." I place my hand on her lower back. "What can I do to help?"

She shoves me away. "I'm fine. Just get me some water."

I nod and jog to the sink. I fill a glass with water, then open the freezer to find an ice pack for her ankle. It's empty. The ice tray holds mold instead of cubes. The fridge is also bare except for a few soda cans. I grab one, feeling the cold in my palm, and head back to the living room.

Whitley is on the couch with her legs stretched out. Bennie places his head in her lap.

"Here," I say, handing her the glass of water. "And this is for your ankle." I hold up the cold soda. "It was all you had."

She guzzles the glass of water in a few seconds, then swipes the soda from my hand and presses it against her injury.

244

"Thanks," she mutters. Her face is stuck in a grimace. "Where were you last night?"

"I went to West Virginia to find Dara, remember?"

She nods slowly. "Yeah, but do you remember promising to come back to help coyote hunt?" Her words slice through me. "Maybe I wouldn't have fallen if I wasn't alone."

I forgot. Our conversation was only yesterday, but with everything going on, it feels like months ago. The details are blurred. But not enough so that I can't recognize I'm wrong.

I drop my head. "I'm so sorry, Whitley. I totally forgot. When we realized Dara was like us, we—"

"It doesn't matter." She pushes off the couch and hurls the soda can into the kitchen sink. It explodes on impact and sprays fizz into the air.

"Where are you going?"

"For a walk."

I frown. "Why don't we relax?"

"We?" she asks. "I want to be on my own." She exits through the rear storm door. Its metal spring whips the screen back into my face.

"It's going to be dark soon!" I call after her. "What if we went coyote hunting instead? We could sit in a tree somewhere. It'll be easier."

She spins.

"Don't pretend like you care about that now." Her voice shakes. "You were late for our dawn hunts and skipped the dusk ones." She grabs Bennie's wagon from under a bush. "C'mon, boy." She pats her thigh. Bennie hobbles past me and jumps into the red wagon. He spins three times before curling up into a ball. Whitley grips the handle and marches toward the woods.

My shaky hands move through the air without purpose. "Wh . . . Wh . . . Whitley." I jog after her.

"Why can't I do this like you're trying to help Xander, huh? You got me researching witches, for shit's sake. I'm allowed to go for a walk with my own dog."

I flip my hands. "I never said you weren't allowed. It's just a weird time to—"

She karate chops the space between us. "Do you want to know the real reason we're not going coyote hunting anymore?" Spit flies off her lips.

My feet falter. "Why?"

"The coyote has a family." Her voice cracks.

I freeze.

"I went to shoot it, but then three pups came out from behind a tree," she continues. "I couldn't do it. I didn't want to take a parent from them." Her breath hitches. "So I jerked my gun up to miss my shot. That's when I fell."

My throat tightens.

"Bennie is all I got."

I step forward. "You got me too."

"Not at home. You have your family. And all your boyfriends." Her voice wobbles. "But me?" She wipes her nose. "At the end of the day, it's just me and Bennie. I don't have a single parent that cares. Even the damn coyote has more than me."

"That's not—"

"I'm alone." She stares through me. "And for some reason, that's what my family thinks I deserve."

"A lot of people care."

She scoffs. "Yeah, like how you've cared enough about these hunts . . . and to plan anything for our college road trip."

My insides twist.

I squeeze my arm because I can't think of any words to say. I want to keep telling her that I care. That I'm here. But I've already failed her once.

She yanks the wagon forward.

The next few seconds pass by in silence because I'm speechless. Heat swells behind my eyelids. Whitley disappears into the near darkness. I stare until the last thing I see is Bennie's white bandages, glowing against the tree shadows.

"Whitley," I whisper. But she doesn't come back.

I sigh, then lurch back to my truck with my shoulders dipped.

She's right. I should've been here at the agreed-upon time to help her hunt. But I also had to go after Dara to help Xander. How was I supposed to choose? I kick my front driver's side tire until my toe throbs.

Life has tossed me into its deep end, and I can barely keep myself afloat for much longer. I'm drowning in the pressure from all my responsibilities.

Maybe this is Penango's final test for me. If I can make it through this summer, then the county will finally release me from its clutches.

We promise to serve and pledge our love. That's what the Stillwell Trail High School alma mater says. *To always look out for thy neighbor and put Penango above*. That's what I'm doing. I just wish, sometimes, I could get a little love in return.

It's like the Ardor Tree has its own rifle, and it's pointed right at my heart.

40

The next four days drone as slowly as the cargo train crawling past the Bean at five miles per hour. And I'm carrying all the weight.

Dara is holed up in a hotel on Main Street. Xander is hiding in the woods. Whitley won't speak to me. And I've been dodging my counselor so she doesn't press me about my impending deadlines.

That leaves me with one person to talk to, or at least try to talk to, to see if the curse is broken.

Murray.

I text, email, and call. They get no response, bounce back, and go straight to voicemail. I even write a letter and drop it in my mailbox, but I know it burst into nothing the moment it left my hands, just like Xander and I dissolve into dust when the wrong person walks through us.

My hopes that the curse will break anytime soon are dissolving too.

I come home from work drenched in sweat, with my jaw clenched so tight it aches. Dad sits out front in a beach chair, drinking a beer, face tilted toward the sun. My earbuds are back in most hours of the day. They play a podcast I've never

248

listened to before. I thought something fresh could help fill the silence, but nothing compares to Xander's voice.

"Someone is here to see you," Dad grumbles as I walk across the lawn.

I remove one of my earbuds. "What?"

"You have a guest."

My brow furrows. "Who?"

He shrugs with a smirk, like it's a joke I don't get.

My heart rate spikes, equal to the pace of a stampede of deer running through Penango's fields. I picture Murray in my dad's armchair, holding a response to my letter, waiting for me.

I barrel through the front door and trip over a laundry basket in the foyer, my eyes locked on the living room. When I pass the threshold, I freeze. Every muscle contracts. My breath catches in my throat.

Murray stands under the archway between the kitchen and dining room.

Has he finally received my texts?

He holds a brown box with two milkshakes and a basket of curly fries from the Bean. His nails are covered in dirt, and his fingers are taped fresh from football practice. I focus on the food before meeting his eyes. His buzz cut is so overgrown that his hair is nearly slicked back against the sides of his head. Sunburned, pink skin peels across the bridge of his nose.

For the first time in a long time, I'm happy to see him. I know he misses seeing me. I wonder if he can right now.

He stares up at the chandelier with a blank face. I steady my feet and release the breath I was holding. I almost don't want to speak. Because once I do, I'll know for sure.

"Murray," I say, digging my fingernails into my palm.

He tilts his head and looks at me like a dog hearing a new sound. His lips part as if he's about to say something.

He coughs. I jump.

"Murray," I repeat, stepping closer. His body odor covers me in nostalgia, thick as a morning fog.

Then, "Hi, Stetson," he says. "I haven't heard from you and wanted to check if you're all right."

I clap my hand over my mouth. Warmth spreads down my legs and up into my head. My whole body shakes with a sob. His image blurs.

The curse is broken.

He smiles. "I applied for that off-campus apartment by Penango College," he says. "I told Whitley. I don't know if the message reached you. We can live there if you don't go to Tennessee. It's basically free since I'm on the football team. It's not that far, but it could still be something different." The box of food trembles in his hands. "I can show you I'm not the person you think I am."

"Murray." I sigh. "We don't have to talk about that."

"And I think you have a point about getting away from here and seeing new places. My family's been in Penango for a hundred years and I don't think it's done us any favors." He licks his lips. "We could transfer together after two years at the community college."

"Please." I step toward him. "You're never going to believe what's happened to me."

He frowns. His shoulders slump and for the first time maybe ever, his lean muscles appear weak and deflated.

"Two years?" He scratches his head. "Or just one year?"

"Huh?" I question, dropping my chin.

"We could transfer after one year." He nods to himself. "Yeah, that sounds better." He beats his chest. "I got this."

"Murray," I say firmly.

I stop breathing. Not this again. I know this conversation, how it goes and how it ends. My tears dry up faster than they came.

"God, where is he?" Murray huffs. He looks past me out the bay window.

"Stop!" I yell. "I'm here." My voice breaks. "I'm here. I'm here." I try to drown out his words. "Please stop talking."

There's no recognition on his face. I skip across the room with my arms extended. A final rush of hope. Words aren't enough. The ultimate test is touch. If I can just touch him . . .

I launch myself forward for a jump hug, as I did when he asked me to senior prom and when he won his first playoff game after our training.

But this time, rather than being caught, I slip through his arms—and his body.

I land like scattered marbles on the dining room floor. My breathing hastens until I'm seconds away from hyperventilating. Light blots color my vision. My ribs squeeze my lungs like a constricting snake.

Murray is still talking. But not to me. He's practicing for a conversation that will never happen.

The curse never broke.

There are no second chances.

Not for Xander.

Not for Dara.

Not for me.

Not for anyone from within these county lines.

41

"Xander!" I yell, trudging through the woods of the Gregor Preserve.

I haven't seen him since dinner at the Bean. It's okay if he's hiding from me. But it's not okay if he's mad at me. I've never seen an angry Xander. It might be the final sight that'll turn me to stone, a remnant of Penango trapped in the mountains until the end of time.

"Xander, please!"

The farther I go, the thicker the heat becomes, the denser the bushes, the more the trees blend together like a mirror maze. I don't know how I'll find my way back to my truck.

But lucky for me, Xander doesn't believe in blending in.

Then something bright in the distance—white shoes, high white socks, yellow-and-white striped shorts, and a red tank top. A strawberry banana milkshake of a boy. I cross my fingers that his mood is as sweet as he looks.

I slow my jog to a walk as I approach him. He sits on a moss bed, back against a tree trunk, knees curled up to his chin. His skin is slick with sweat as usual, but his expression isn't normal. His sullen face is wrung out like a damp sponge, empty and unsettled.

"Hey, Stetson," he says softly.

"Hi."

"I'm sorry I've been MIA." He sniffs.

I exhale for what feels like longer than the time it took to walk here.

"You have nothing to be sorry about. It's been a weird few days." I drop down beside him. Our shoulders touch. "I should be sorry for letting you down."

"It didn't work, right?" He flips his hands in confusion. "How did it not work?"

I shake my head. "It didn't work." I don't even try to sugarcoat it. Not everything can be sweetened.

"What options do we have left?"

I shrug. "We tried to get the tree to wake up. We tried to fix our hearts on the trunk. I don't know if the curse is—"

"Permanent."

I swallow. "Yeah."

He picks up a dry leaf and crushes it between his fingers. "That seems like a really harsh sentence for a boy who just wanted to go to prom with someone he actually liked." His voice cracks.

I stare at him. I don't know what to say.

His curse is so much worse than mine. The Ardor Tree used the mathematical process of canceling out. He wanted more, but the tree removed all his mores from the equation.

Out of nowhere, a speaker squeals on in the distance, a sharp electronic hum that breaks through the stillness of the woods.

I sit straight up.

At first it seems random. But then the sound clicks into place in my mind. Rainbow Valley Swim Club is nearby. It's

Thursday. Tomorrow is the last day of camp for the first group of kids. They're setting up for the send-off dance.

I jump to my feet.

"What's wrong?" Xander asks, looking up at me through wet eyes.

"Wait here," I say.

"Where are you going?"

I walk away, searching for something sharp, like a rock or pointy stick. A triangular stone catches the sunlight. I lift it from a pile of brown leaves, the surface warm in my palm.

I quickly find a thick tree trunk and start hacking at the bark, using the stone to write a message.

A different kind of invitation.

"What are you doing?" Xander calls. I look over my shoulder and he's standing now.

"Don't look yet!" I shield my work with my body.

"I don't think carving another random tree is going to help us."

"Mic check, one two, one two." A man's voice echoes from the far-off speaker.

I keep carving. Sweat drips down my forehead and across the bridge of my nose. My shoulder burns. The rock slips in my sweaty grip, but I keep going.

Finally, I step back from the tree, dizzy, and read over the words to make sure everything is spelled correctly. My heart pounds against the inside of my chest. I drop the rock and grab Xander's hand. His skin is cool and dry. Mine is hot and slick.

"Are you okay?" he asks with a raised eyebrow.

"Come here." I pull him forward, placing him in front of the tree. He steps in the wrong direction, and I twist his hips so what I wrote can't be missed.

"I've never seen you like this," he mumbles. "I'm usually the chaotic one."

I smile. "Read it. Read the tree."

He clears his throat. "Xander, will you go to the . . ." He stops.

I tilt my head. "What's wrong? Keep going."

His lips tremble. ". . . will you . . . will you," he tries again, but he can't finish the sentence.

"Is it too hard to read?" I ask, suddenly embarrassed. "I tried to make it special on the tree."

His face crumbles. "I see what it says. But I can't . . . I can't."

I wrap my arms around his waist and rest my chin on his shoulder. "Xander," I whisper in his ear. "Will you go to the send-off dance with me?" I read the message for him.

His body shakes in my embrace. "Is this real?" he asks.

"Of course." I grin. "The dance is tomorrow. I hope it's not too short of notice."

"Please." He waves his hand. "I've been trying on prom tuxedos for a decade, waiting for this day to come."

"Is that a yes?"

He spins around and grabs my head. "Yes!"

Xander may never get the chance to live out his firsts—his first prom, first boyfriend, first kiss, or first love.

But as long as we have this summer, I'll give him everything I can.

42

The next day, Xander insists I pick him up for the dance like I would if it were real-life prom.

I wish I had a stretch Hummer with disco lights or a vintage convertible. I would steal one for him in a heartbeat if I were fully invisible. Instead, he gets my beat-up truck and a fraying aux cord.

If he really wanted the full Penango prom experience, I'd show up on a tractor. But I draw the line at smelling like diesel and showing up with greasy fingers.

He instructs me to meet him at the gas station about a mile from Rainbow Valley.

His formalities make me laugh, but after my actual prom night was overshadowed by Murray reminding me it would be our last event ever as a couple, I'm enjoying the redo.

It's almost like I get to turn back a few pages in my choose-your-own-adventure story and pick a different path. I wonder what chapter this choice will take me to.

This night has to be special for Xander. Partly because I feel bad for being wrong about how to break the curse, but mostly because this is his first date to a dance *ever*. He's been waiting for this moment for over ten years.

No stores in Penango have boutonnieres available overnight, so I make my own with flowers from Mom's garden. I pick a few pink roses from a bush, cut off the thorns, and tie them together with pieces of rope. It looks decent, but I have no clue if it will match his outfit.

He says to dress nice but won't tell me what he's wearing.

I'm not sure how fancy to be. I figure it's going to be pretty casual since it's a summer camp dance. I settle on white sneakers, navy pants, a white short-sleeved button-up, and a floral skinny tie. It's too hot for any more layers. It's a happy medium.

Or so I think.

When I get to the gas station, Xander stands beside the ice machine waiting for me. And suddenly, my outfit feels like a mistake.

He's wearing an orange tuxedo with white lapels, a white shirt, white shoes, and an orange bow tie. He's a walking Creamsicle pop.

I can't put my truck in park fast enough. He's like a teddy bear hanging at the county fair—impossible not to want. I jump from the driver's seat, race around the hood, and stop about a foot away from him. He opens his mouth, then snaps it shut.

We just stand there. I smile, breathless.

"Hello," he says.

"Hi."

"You look so handsome!" he exclaims.

I examine him closer. His face is clean-shaven. The sideburns are gone. His curls are shiny, like they've been scrunched and styled with cream. In his right hand, he grips a bottle of Froot Loops–flavored vodka and two red plastic cups.

"You look so cute," I say. "I'm sorry I'm not in a tuxedo." I tug on my tie.

"Don't be." He grins. "We're each in our own unique styles. It's perfect. And plus, no one can see me. I can be a bit outrageous." He mimics an evil laugh.

I pull him into a hug. An overpowering cloud of cologne, a blend of fresh-cut trees and citrus, floods my nostrils.

"I got you something," I say.

He sighs, placing a hand on his hip. "You don't have to do anything more."

"It's nothing extra. This is part of the night." I grab the boutonniere from the passenger seat, hide it behind my back, then spin around for the reveal. "Ta-daaaa!"

He does a double take. "Oh my gosh! I totally forgot about these. Is that the thing that goes on my jacket?"

I nod. "It's homemade too. I'm not sure if pink clashes with the orange, but I think brightening your ensemble is what you're going for." I laugh.

He takes a deep breath. "You're incredible, Stetson."

We stare at each other again. His golden eyes flash like the strike of a match. He bites his bottom lip, then his tongue slips out, slicking the surface. My hand flies to my neck, my pulse pounding beneath my fingertips.

"Let me put this on you," I say.

"Yeah, for sure."

We both move at the same time. Our heads knock together "Oh no, sorry," I say. The tips of our noses brush as we correct ourselves.

His cheeks flush. "No, that was my bad. I went the wrong way."

I hold up the flower and safety pin once we're still. "Can I?"

"Yeah, I'm ready." He turns his head to the side.

I focus on his lapel with my tongue poking through the corner of my mouth. The safety pin slips through my fingers a few times, but I eventually secure the flowers on his chest.

I don't step back. I stay there beneath his chin, pressed against him. Close enough to count the freckles along his jawline and the patches of stubble he missed shaving. I want to reach out and run my fingertips from his chin to his ear, then slide it through his curls.

But I don't. Instead, I just breathe him in.

"Everything okay down there?" he teases. His Adam's apple bounces inches from my face. "I'm not bleeding out, am I?"

I snap out of it. "No," I say, stepping back. "It looks great." I give the flower a final tug to make sure it's straight. Somehow it makes him look even better, an impossible thought.

He inspects my work. "It's perfect."

I thought Xander was the only one getting surprised tonight. I knew I'd feel good doing this for him. But what I didn't know was that he'd make me feel everything I was missing from this past year, just like he promised in the river.

All the boys who keep promises must be invisible. No wonder everyone has a hard time dating.

He hooks his arm around my shoulder. "Ready for the dance?" he asks, raising the vodka with a grin.

Before I can respond, a woman exits the food mart with a gallon of milk. She looks our way and smiles. "You must be headed somewhere nice," she says.

"Let's ask her to take our picture," I say to Xander.

Xander flinches. "No," he says quickly. "She's just talking to you. Remember our first picture?"

"Oh yeah, right." I frown.

He knows the photo will turn up empty. Last time that happened, he shrank into nothing. We just have to do our best to remember the night.

I know I'll never forget it.

43

When we arrive to Rainbow Valley, Xander asks that I check if his mom is here before he gets out of the truck. I complete a full inspection of every camp area, just like I do with pools at work.

She's nowhere to be found.

Xander peers through my windshield, waiting for the all-clear signal, and I wave him forward while Sheryl and Kim recruit me to help finish setting up for the dance. They don't know I'm here with a date, so I can't exactly refuse without seeming rude. But in the end, I don't mind. After all, I'm making the place nice for Xander too.

We hang twinkle lights across the camp pavilion. Every picnic table gets covered with a blue plastic tablecloth and a fake white candle as a centerpiece. Kim inflates two giant unicorns that flank the DJ booth. There's not really a theme to the dance, but it's fun and gay and that's all that matters.

The drained pool is blocked off by caution tape strung between orange traffic cones, giving it a Halloween vibe by accident. I'm off the health department's clock, so I don't stare for too long. But I make a mental note to tell Victor that it's still closed even after all this time. Hopefully it's enough to get him to finish my letter.

The DJ kicks off the night with an upbeat song, and suddenly, a stampede of campers comes rushing from the woods.

No one else is dressed up. They're in shorts, T-shirts, and bare feet, some even in bathing suits. Xander and I are swans among ducks. The only problem is that I'm the only one they can see. I want to proclaim that I'm not from the local church. But tonight's not about me or them. It's about Xander. And he dazzles beneath the yellow twinkle lights, emitting an auburn cotton-candy-like haze that nearly makes the other campers disappear.

The two shots of Froot-Loops vodka we threw back in the truck make my solo dancing seem less awkward, even if it's not. Xander bobs his head and gently sways his hips, with his hands in his pockets, eyeing the growing mosh pit. I'm technically chaperoning this dance, so I keep us off to the side on our own private dance floor.

A rap song takes over the speakers and the new beat gets my feet moving. The campers form a circle around a boy killing a break dance. With all the eyes off us, or me, I lean into Xander's ear.

"Do you want to, like, dance together?" I ask.

"Yes, yes, yes," he replies. "I didn't know if you would feel weird or not."

"I'm all yours."

He smiles. "Let me take my jacket off." He slips out of his orange tuxedo and tosses it onto the nearest picnic table. Underneath, orange suspenders clip to his waistband.

We take each other's hands and spin, twirl, jump, and twist through a dozen songs. Sweat stains appear along our backs and under our armpits, but we don't stop.

"Stetson, do you want a partner?" Sheryl asks, jigging her way over to me from the other side of the pavilion. "Or are you going to dance out here alone all night?" She laughs.

"I'm okay," I shout over the song, releasing Xander so my grip on the air doesn't look so odd. "Just enjoying the music."

She nods. "Thanks so much for coming." Her fingers snap along to the beat. "The kids had a really special couple of weeks."

"I bet. I'd love to help next summer. I don't think I'll do the pool job again, so I'll probably be free."

Xander notices my words mid-arm-wave. He raises his brow and shoots me a smile. "Next summer?" he mouths.

"Oh." Sheryl raises her finger. "By the way, the technician came and looked at the pipes."

My eyes twitch. "What did he find?"

She shakes her head with pursed lips. "Most of them need replacing."

"What? Why?"

"Too much time has passed. They were clogged with mud and debris from the woods. There were even tree roots growing in a few of 'em."

My feet freeze mid-step. "Tree roots? In the pipes?"

"Mm-hmm." She nods. "They went after the moisture. Squeezed them until they collapsed."

"I didn't know that could happen."

"Me neither." She stops dancing too and rests her hand on my shoulder, breathing deep. "All that to say . . . the pool won't be open until next year."

"I can come back soon and close your site out."

"We'll be here." She pats my back. "I'm going to go see if we need more ice for the drinks."

Xander drifts back toward me as Sheryl leaves the pavilion. He presses his shoulder into my chest.

"Did you hear that?" I ask.

"What?" He wipes sweat from his forehead.

"She said there were tree roots in the pool's pipes." I glance at the caution tape. It glows under the strobe lights.

He puts his moist palm over my mouth. "Shhh. I don't want to talk about that."

I inhale through my nose, then gently pull his hand away. "You're right," I say. "But it's still a weird coincidence."

The music slows to a melancholy tune. It's soft enough to hear the nearby cicada screams.

"First and last slow song of the night, y'all," the DJ announces. "Time to grab your new summer crush."

Half the dance floor ceases to exist. Red-faced kids line the edge of the pavilion, whispering and waiting to see who couples up.

Xander squeezes my hand and tugs me forward.

"Wait!" I yell in a hushed whisper. "I can't slow dance in the center of the crowd. It's just me, remember?"

He drags his fancy white shoes to a stop. They're scuffed on the sides from tonight's heel twists and kicks. "Will you dance with me back here, then?"

"Anywhere except directly in front of the DJ."

He laughs, then places his hands on my hips. I drape mine around his shoulders and move us to the shadows. We sway between the picnic tables pushed toward the back of the pavilion, while four other couples dance in the front, soaking up the spotlight.

"I like dancing with you," I say.

264

He cocks his head, looking down. "Even if no one can see me?"

"If everyone could see you, then I'd have to compete with *everyone*."

He grins. "Compete for what?"

My eyes flicker across the pavilion behind him. "Compete to be your dance partner," I say. "Like, that boy in the black T-shirt has been eyeing you up all night."

Xander turns and looks at the crowd. A boy in black with bushy eyebrows sits on a picnic table watching us, elbow on his knee.

Xander snorts. "Uhh, Stetson. He can't see me. So that means he's eyeing *you* up. Probably because your arms are around air right now."

My spine straightens. I release him, then tug on my shirt collar.

"Right, right," I mutter.

"Are you okay?"

I swallow. "Yeah, I'm just . . . sorry, a little distracted after hearing about the pipes."

He studies me. "Do you want to get out of here?" he asks.

I raise my eyebrows. "Are you not having fun?"

"I am. It's just one of those things. You know?"

I shake my head. "I don't know. Tell me."

He sighs, dipping his shoulders. "After a while, when I'm out, and no one can see me, it's as if I'm playing pretend. It makes me feel worthless, like a hole in the ground everyone just steps over. I'm there, but I'm really not." He drags his fingers along my belt.

"Oh." I frown. "Do you want me to go?"

"No." He pulls me back to him. "I want us to leave together. To only be with you, so everything is real." He looks at me with an earnest, puppylike expression, a dog waiting for a treat.

His sweet words tighten my cheeks, as if I've swallowed a sour Jolly Rancher. "I can do an after-party. Where to?"

"My tree house. It's a short walk through the woods. I can finally show it to you." He glances at the drink table. "We can sneak out before Sheryl and Kim force you into cleanup duty."

The slow song ends. The campers clap and catcall at the other dancing couples. "Kiss!" someone yells.

"Quick, then," I say to Xander, pushing him toward the woods. "This could be the end."

Xander giggles and pulls me off the pavilion's concrete slab and into the trees. We scamper across a dirt path. Mud quickly cakes my white shoes.

Without the light from camp, the woods are pitch-black. But Xander knows exactly where he's going. I struggle to keep up with his confident pace as I fight the urge to stop and get my bearings. The trees are like street signs to him. The stars are reference points. And the moon is a compass.

Right. Left. Right. Right.

Soon, we round a thick tree and come upon a ladder.

"Here," Xander says, stopping abruptly.

My neck cranes toward the structure hidden in the branches. It's barely visible in the darkness.

"You don't leave a light on for when you get home?" I joke.

"Hell no," he says. "I don't want someone else finding this place." He pats the camouflaged wood. "I wasn't sure if the curse would break randomly and someone would spot me. You learn a few things after ten years." I think he winks, but in the darkness, I can't see his face.

He takes ahold of the pegs and ascends the tree. I follow.

266

At the top, he pushes on the trapdoor with both hands. It swings open and lands with a thud, sending a drizzle of dust particles down from the wooden planks above. Xander digs around inside, his upper body disappearing while his legs dangle over the ladder.

Then there's a click. Light bursts through the opening, beaming down on me like we've opened the gates of heaven. I shield my eyes with my forearm as the brightness nearly knocks me off-balance.

"Welcome," he says, hoisting himself inside. He spins around and extends his hand. I clasp it and am pulled through the threshold.

Inside, I brush off my knees before looking up.

"Whoa," I say. I bump my head on a hanging plant.

Xander scratches his neck. "You're my first ever guest. Is it weird in here? I've never really thought about entertaining."

"No." I shake my head with a smile. "It's so cozy."

Vintage Edison bulbs hang across the maroon-painted ceiling. Bookshelves line an entire wall with the spines organized in a gradient of colors. A twin mattress, draped with a plaid comforter, is pushed into a corner. A round wooden table sits near a mock sink, set with two place settings.

My breath catches.

"You built this?" I ask, rubbing a hand down my cheek.

"Yeah, but again, over the course of ten years," he says with a light laugh. "It started off as a plywood platform."

I walk to the table and grip the backrest of a chair. "Who is this other seat for?"

He shrugs. "Someone. Eventually. It's kind of like my blank space on the Ardor Tree." His gaze flickers to me. "Maybe . . . you."

A shiver runs down my spine. Every one of his phrases is kinder than the last. All summer, it's been about getting over Murray and getting to Tennessee. Xander was never part of the equation. How do I factor in this new variable? I can't be at this table because I'm not supposed to be in Penango. Hurting a boy by telling him I was leaving town is how I ended spring. It's not how I want to end summer.

"What should we do?" I ask.

He lets out a long yawn. "I'm kind of tired. Do you just want to relax?"

I nod enthusiastically. My legs ache from our dance marathon.

"Those chairs aren't very comfortable," he continues. "I have the bed. We could probably both fit. Or you could have the bed, and I'll take the window seat."

Ten years.

The words echo in my mind. Ten years since he was last held. Who am I to deny him that? I won't let Murray get in the way of us.

"The bed looks perfect," I say.

His whole face smiles—not just his lips but his cheeks, eyes, nose, brows, and even his ears all rise. He quickly drops his tuxedo pants and pulls off his shirt until he's only in his briefs and socks.

I look away, forgetting to connect the dots. I obviously can't sleep in my outfit. Slowly, I peel off my layers. When I glance back, Xander is fluffing the pillows and brushing dust off the comforter.

I haven't seen him this bare since the first time we met, when he was tanning at the pool in his tiny yellow bathing suit. But this time his briefs fit tighter around his legs. I see more. I should have never looked away.

We slide under the cover. His muscular frame fits perfectly against mine. No adjustments needed. His hand rests on my stomach. Mine cups his shoulder. His breath slows as my heart rate quickens so fast I think I might be sick.

We stare up at the Edison lights, silent for minutes. I count them. There are three strands, each with eight bulbs.

Xander draws circles on my skin. I sense his gaze and dip my head. His finger strokes my bottom lip.

My pulse jumps again. The pressure lands like an unexpected shove. Not like a sneak attack in the cafeteria when someone pushes me over with a tray full of food. It's a push from a friend, a nudge in the right direction when I'm standing in front of a crush beside their locker, afraid to make the first move.

My next kiss after Murray was supposed to be a boy from Tennessee. A new chapter. Not here. Not now. But I'm starting to get used to the idea of that plan changing.

"I guess I can finally leave this place now that I know the curse won't break," Xander says.

I stroke his arm. "Where will you go?"

"I have a list of places." He exhales. "Will you join me? After college? Or in ten . . . twenty years when forever is left to us?"

"Of course."

"Even if it's somewhere crazy like the edge of the Arctic Circle?"

I smile. "If that's where you are, then that's where I'll be."

A beat of silence passes. Xander goes still.

"Are you comfortable?" I ask.

"Mm-hmm." He nuzzles deeper into my chest. "This was the best night I've ever had."

Sleep takes him in seconds. His body heavies in my arms. A soft whistle leaves his nose with each breath, a flutelike lullaby blending with the crickets, cicadas, and crackling trees. I finally let my heartbeat slow.

If there's one thing I learned from Murray, it's that when I don't want to, I shouldn't have to. But that's what makes this situation with Xander so different. With him, I want to. I just don't know when.

Maybe this whole thing with the Ardor Tree isn't a curse at all.

Maybe it's a blessing.

44

Checking in again.

It's the subject line of the first email I receive on the morning of July 28th. My counselor wants to know the status of my letter and essay.

Somehow, the world keeps moving, even though everything feels frozen in time since my sleepover with Xander, like morning dew clinging to summer's greenest grass.

We didn't kiss that night, but I know he wants to. Whenever we're together, he watches my hands and stares at my mouth, even when I'm not speaking. Sometimes I feel the phantom pressure of his finger on my lips.

He's waiting for me to be ready.

His eagerness hangs over us like the minutes before a summer storm when the clouds roll in and the town falls still, and everyone waits to see if the rain will break or pass. I'm not sure when the moment will be right for the first kiss. But I bet, like most things this summer, it will sneak up on me when I least expect it.

I quickly type a response to my counselor:
Almost done.
Then I hit send.

Later that morning at work, I sit in my desk chair drafting my scholarship essay instead of doing anything remotely related to swimming pools.

Whitley's not here, and the cubicle is quiet. She could be out on an inspection, but it's more likely that she's still avoiding me. Her absence fuels my focus. I want to fulfill our pact, our promise, and be by her side this August when we leave Penango.

I messed up bad. And this is a love letter in disguise. It's a way to fix what I broke.

My toes curl rereading the corny intro paragraph I wrote days ago. It's some nonsense that talks about my love of counting and numbers like I'm *Sesame Street's* biggest fan.

The truth is, I don't know what kind of career I want to have with math. I just like it. Numbers make sense. Unlike English class or feelings, there's always a right answer.

At Stillwell Trail, the mathletes slogan is *Make our math mean something*. Maybe I need a real-life example to add some depth. But right now, everything meaningful in my life is also making it miserable.

How can I build a career when I'll be stuck looking like a teenager forever?

The cursor blinks on the blank page like it's judging me. I blink back. We're in a standoff.

I wonder how long I'll have to wait for a response from this scholarship committee and if their criteria are as elusive as the financial aid process. It's all like trying to catch a firefly. I see the light, but as soon as I reach for it, it blinks out of existence.

Then an idea elbows its way to the front of my brain. I love math because there's always a right answer built from a consistent set of variables. It's fair.

My first financial aid decision was a math problem where the correct answer was five hundred, but the teacher insisted it was twenty. A spreadsheet was crashing out somewhere behind the scenes.

It doesn't add up that a kid like me is this close to not going to college. It doesn't check out that asking for help is like playing the lottery. And there's nothing that explains why a year of college costs more than my mom and dad earn in a year.

The numbers should speak for themselves. But since they don't, I will. I've listened to enough podcasts to know how to complain about something over a beat.

No one should be stuck in places like Penango if they are working with the right set of variables. Just like my favorite podcasts, I want to explain how stuff works using math. I'm going to explain how we can fix life's broken equations so at the end of each episode, everyone's jars are full of fireflies, and maybe more hope than I've had all summer.

Five hundred words isn't much space to pitch a whole season of my new podcast, but I come up with a name and outline for the first episode. It's going to feature real students, real numbers, and real talk about financial aid. Because someone needs to pull back the curtain and say what we're all thinking: WTF.

It'll be a career behind the scenes, where thirty and forty years from now, my voice can take center stage while my face stays hidden, just in case anyone starts asking questions. Maybe it'll be the longest-running podcast in history. I guess it's time I start looking for the perks of my own invisibility, the way Xander learned to do.

I proofread the essay a few times, then attach it to a blank email draft. But before I hit send, I need to secure my second attachment.

The recommendation letter.

I turn to Victor's office, but my heart sinks like a stone in the river when I see the lights off. I run to the window in his door, keeping my fingers crossed that he's just napping, but my worst suspicions are confirmed. The chair is empty.

He's gone.

Hours pass and he never returns to the department. I sit with my head in my hands, pulling at my hair for most of the afternoon. My phone calls, texts, and emails to him go unanswered.

With the day nearly over, I decide to just send the essay to my counselor on its own, with hopes of reaching Victor tomorrow. But within a minute, she responds to my email.

Thanks, Stetson! I already received your second letter of recommendation, so we're all good there. I am going to send in your essay ASAP. I will let you know of the committee's decision soon.

My eyes widen. I reread the message.

There's no way Victor sent her a letter. I never gave him her email address. I didn't even tell him that Rainbow Valley's pool is staying closed until next year. He had no reason to get a head start.

From who? I reply.

A moment later, the response comes:

Mr. Wyomen. It's a glowing recommendation.

45

Why the hell would Mr. Wyomen write me a letter of recommendation?

I turn the thought over in my mind on the drive home from work. Victor must have told him about it, probably to show off, but then Mr. Wyomen took it one step further, writing the letter himself to win bonus points and snag Whitley's attention. It's the only logical explanation.

And honestly? I don't really care why he did it.

If it's convincing and already submitted to the scholarship committee like my counselor said, then that's good enough for me. But I'm afraid Whitley will care. She'll see it as a betrayal, as me conspiring against her with her dad. And if she thinks that, it will only push us further apart.

At night, I spread out at the kitchen table to research our road trip. If I can't turn back time to coyote hunt, I can at least prove that I'm still committed to our plan. That our escape from Penango is still one of my top priorities.

I devour online videos, skim best-of lists for every state on our itinerary, and queue up podcasts about the Shenandoah, New River Gorge, Mammoth Cave, and Great Smoky

Mountains National Parks as if I'm writing a history paper on the American south.

My Appalachian podcasts might not have helped break the curse, but they definitely made me aware of obscure mountain sites no one would visit except for two kids who don't have a clue what they're doing.

Every few moments, my mind drifts back to Whitley. Alone for the past two weeks. In pain, walking around with a broken ankle. It makes my head spin.

She's the one who ended up as the lonely scarecrow, left in a field, picked at, prodded, and abandoned by everyone she trusts, while I had Xander. I should have been the one facing summer alone with the way I acted, not her. This won't erase what happened, but it's a starting point. I want to show her that she's not forgotten.

By the time my vision blurs from staring at the screen, I have enough of a plan to share. So the next morning I do what I should have done days ago.

I call Whitley.

"What?" she answers quickly. There's a rush of background noise on her end, wind, static, and a distant blare of a car horn.

Sounds of a highway.

My stomach flips. What if she's already left for school and she's doing the road trip solo?

"Hey," I say. "Where are you?"

"Driving. Why?"

"It sounds loud."

"I'm on the freeway."

"Where are you going?" I bite my fingernails.

"Why all the questions? Since when do you care what I'm doing?"

276

I rub my brow. "I'm calling to apologize." She mumbles something I can't understand. "Whitley?"

"Okay, good." She sniffs. Her voice uneven. "Because otherwise I was sending you to voicemail. And I don't listen to those."

I let out a weak laugh, then exhale. "I don't know where to start, but everything was a mess this summer," I continue. "I've never broken up with someone before. I've never gone to college or worked full-time. I've never been . . . kind of invisible." I pause. "It's not an excuse, but that's why I slipped up. I didn't know what I was doing. I was in too deep. I'm sorry."

I suck in a breath.

"Yup," Whitley finally speaks. "Go on."

"I should've been there for Bennie. But most importantly, I should've been there for you."

A turn signal clicks through my phone.

"We both had a lot going on." Her voice cracks. "I was in a terrible mood when you came over that day and lashed out. I regret what I said."

"Don't. You were right."

"Definitely on a few points." She sniffs. "But I am sorry for what I said about Xander."

"How come?"

"Because I should've trusted you too." She clears her throat. "Do you know why I didn't ask a million questions about you and Murray when you first told me you broke up? Even though I really, really wanted to?"

I swallow. "Why?"

"Because you didn't tell me you were thinking about breaking up. You didn't ask me what I thought. You just told me it was done. And I knew that meant you were sure."

I nod even though she can't see me.

"And after my grandma died and I told you I didn't want to move in with my dad in Pittsburgh, you were the only one who didn't second-guess me. Instead, you helped me change the locks so he couldn't make a surprise visit to drag me there."

I chuckle.

"We've always been so sure of ourselves."

"I guess."

"Stetson, you are the bravest, most intense person. You came out in tenth grade in Penango of all places. You like math like a weirdo and you're not ashamed of it. You got a crush on a boy, fell in love with him, and then fell out of love. Now you like another boy who might be make-believe."

"Okay, you're being corny."

"Only honest." She inhales. "Xander means a lot to you. And I shouldn't have doubted. I might've just been jealous."

I shake my head. "You'll always be the mountain to my field."

"Who's corny now?"

I smile. "So, where are you actually driving to? I hope it's not to Florida. Because I made an itinerary for our road trip and want to show you."

"Wow, so this isn't an empty apology? I'm driving to Main Street to set up my clarinet for a performance during our lunch break. This is a big moneymaking day."

"Can I come by and see you?"

"Why would you do that?"

"Because I miss you."

Silence falls over our conversation like a cloud blocking the sun.

"Whitley?" I ask. "Whitley, are you there?"

"I'm here."

"Can I visit?" My breath catches.

"Yes."

I exhale.

"But only if you apologize again."

I laugh. "I'm so, so sorry. It will never happen again."

"Apology accepted. And then you need to give me twenty dollars for pain and suffering."

"Are you serious?"

"No. I make more money than you do."

I shake my head. "Where are you posting up?"

"Outside the salon. The old ladies are always very generous because they knew Grandma."

"Okay. See you soon."

"Don't take too long."

I shift in my seat. "Actually, Whitley, before we meet, I have something to tell you."

I need to be up-front about her dad's letter. Otherwise, my apology is meaningless, like watering a dead flower.

Be up-front. Be honest.

She groans. "Are we seriously only going to be friends again for five seconds?"

I sigh. "I hope not." I scratch the back of my head. "For some reason, your dad wrote my second letter of recommendation. I never asked him to! I swear. I don't know why he did it and I—"

"Stetson, you idiot. I wrote that."

My jaw drops. "You . . . what?"

"I wasn't going to let Victor ruin our road trip. There are only so many people who will look after you besides yourself. My dad is not one. Neither is Murray. And neither is Victor. I knew that the moment we met him. If we don't have each other in this town, then we have no one."

My fingers tighten around the phone. "Whitley, I don't deserve you."

"Yeah, I know. But you sure as hell need me."

The salon is about half a podcast episode away from home. I park along an alley, then sprint toward Main, my shoes stumbling over the bumpy brick sidewalk. The summer grass has conquered the century-old path, forcing its way through every cracked joint. By the time I turn the corner, I'm sweating.

Then I trip over an empty clarinet case. My arms flail as I lurch forward, barely catching myself before my face meets a brick wall.

"Stetson!"

I turn.

Whitley stands behind a white mop bucket full of change and crumpled dollar bills. Her clarinet is pressed to her lips. Her eyes widen before she cuts her song short with a sharp, awkward note.

"You scared me," she says, clutching her instrument. "I thought you were a thief coming for my money."

I don't say anything. Instead, I pull her into the tightest hug I can muster. And I don't let go.

Her shoulders shake beneath my hands, and her whole body is solid, real, and grounding like a life preserver, because that's what she is for me. My lifesaver. She kept me afloat all summer, hell, my whole time on earth.

If Louise Gregor and Abigail Mattson came to me in a dream and offered me a spell to start new anywhere in the world, I'd decline. Because I wouldn't risk missing the exceptionalism of Whitley Wyomen.

"Stetson, I can't breathe," she chokes. "Let go of me."

I loosen my grip, my chin still resting on her bony shoulder. For a time, everything on Main Street looks normal. Two boys lick ice-cream cones on a nearby bench. A man in a hard hat and orange vest leans against a lamppost. An elderly woman disappears into the antique store.

And Whitley and I stand here, just a girl and a boy who want more, who want to reach the next intersection beyond Penango's single stoplight.

"Thank you, Whitley," I whisper.

"You can thank me by stepping aside." She nods toward the bucket. "You're blocking people's access to my bucket."

I jump over her earnings with a laugh. Then I raise a finger. "Wait. Did you send the letter from your dad's email? I can't believe the counselor didn't suspect anything."

She smirks. "Yeah. He uses the same password for all his log-ins. He's not hard to hack. I've been eyeing his bank account too. Just in case." She winks.

"What did he think of your research? Did it help fix things a little?"

She lowers her chin. "It did nothing."

"Really?"

She shrugs, shifting her clarinet to her other hand. "I mean, I didn't think it was going to magically fix our relationship. I just wanted to show off a bit." She holds out her phone. "But he was beyond unimpressed."

I take her phone and read:

Dad: *Whitly. Thanks for sending thiss. Your paper looks okay. I found an old researchj paper of mine that received a lot of praise. I jst emailad it to you for reviewe.*

Whitley: *Okay*

Dad: *Youy should take a look at the research methodas section in my papper. Perhaps you could incorporater some of the theories from there iinto your work to make it better.*

Whitley: *I sent my paper to you because it was finished.*

Dad: *I think it's a good first draftt. Let me know if you want me to provide editds.*

"Ouch," I say with a grimace, handing back her phone. "Why are there so many typos? Was he—"

"Drunk," she says. "Yeah, probably."

I hang my head. "I'm sorry, Whitley."

She smiles. "You don't have anything to worry about. I actually like the response."

I blink. "Really?"

She exhales. "Yeah. I mean, if he'd been nice, what was I supposed to do then? Have him in my life?" Her arms hang at her sides. "I've basically made it through half my life without him. This just proves that's how it's meant to be."

"You're sure?"

She turns back to me, eyes sharp. "Bennie is worth seeking revenge. You're worth a lie. My dad is not. See how it works? You have to drop some weight to make it out of Penango."

I nod slowly.

"When you reach out to people and they don't respond, that's their response. Life really isn't all that complicated."

I see it playing out, but I'm not sure I understand *why* life works the way it does.

Some people are meant to be in our lives for brief moments, others forever. But time doesn't always equal impact. Some creeks run shallow for decades, trickling along the banks, steady but insignificant. Others rage after a storm, rushing in for a day, shifting shorelines, uprooting trees, flooding everything in their wakes, then they vanish.

The hardest part is knowing when to leave the shallow creek that's always been there but no longer serves me, and when to dive into something deeper, even if I don't know where it leads.

Whitley and I are choosing to dive in. Our river is flowing somewhere new. And we're about to explore the unfamiliar landscape together.

A hiccup from Whitley catches my attention. I turn to her, and she's sobbing.

"Whitley, oh my gosh." I pull her into a hug. "It's okay."

"He spelled my name wrong," she says. "Like, who does that?" She blows snot on my shirt.

"No one worth your time." I comb her hair with my fingers.

"What kind of dad can't spell their daughter's name?"

"We're almost out of here."

"Did you get the scholarship?" Whitley asks, voice shaking. "Please say yes."

I exhale. "I don't know yet. But I'm leaving regardless. I want to be with you. If it's not school, I'll find something else to do outside Penango. Maybe I'll serve smoothies on the beach somewhere in Florida."

She smiles through a cry, then sets her clarinet down to hold me closer. "Where's our first stop on the trip?"

"New River Gorge National Park in West Virginia."

She raises a finger. "Remember we have a dog in recovery, so we can't do any intense hikes."

"Got it."

"When do you want to leave?"

"Maybe next week. School starts August twentieth or something. That gives us two weeks on the road."

She dabs tears from her cheeks. "What are you going to tell Xander?"

I press my lips together.

I'm still figuring that part out.

46

I meet Xander at the Bean for dinner, my mind crowded with the conversation we need to have.

I'm going to tell him about the scholarship, my road trip, and moving on. I don't want to leave him behind, but it's the only choice I have left. I can't bring an imaginary friend to college and risk making no new real ones.

And I can't invite him on the road trip. That wouldn't be fair to Whitley. The whole way would be me translating conversations and talking to someone she can't hear.

I remind myself I've only known Xander for a couple months. No matter how much he means to me, how linked we are by this curse, he can't come between Whitley and me.

I hear my counselor's voice in my head: *Do not let another boy make you miss this deadline like the last one.*

But Xander isn't just a boy. The whole situation reminds me of walking barefoot on the blacktop in the middle of summer, stuck between two choices. I can keep moving forward and explore the unknown, or I can retreat to avoid getting burned.

I don't know what to say to him. All I know is I don't want to hurt him.

My earbuds are in again, just in case someone sees me talking to thin air and I need to play it off like I'm on the phone. But this time, I almost want to actually use them, to blast music loud enough to drown out Xander's inevitable whimpers.

We could plan visits. We can figure something out. I don't want this to be goodbye. It can't be. Because in fifty years, in the end, when we're still teenagers and everyone we know has passed, we'll be all each other has.

I stare at the old black-and-white photo of Penango's Main Street framed on the diner's wall. If we had broken the curse, none of this would be a question. If the spell was gone, I know exactly where I'd be.

By his side. As much as I could.

But before I can say a word, he takes the conversation somewhere else.

"Could you help me out with something before the end of summer?" he asks, pushing his food basket forward, only scattered bits of his burger bun left.

I nod, swallowing a fry. "Yeah, with what?"

"I think I've thought of another way to communicate." He exhales.

I tilt my head. "Communicate?"

"With someone other than you and Dara." He looks out the window where the sun catches his eyes. Brown. "With my mom."

His request gives me full-body chills. My jaw locks.

"I'll write down what you can tell her," he continues. "If you're up for it."

I nod with a tight expression. "I am. But what made you change your mind? The other night, you didn't want to see her."

"That was before our sleepover."

His voice is quiet. I reach across the table for his hand. He takes my index finger and traces the lines along my knuckle.

"I didn't realize how much I needed to be held," he says. "I've learned to cope with being alone, you know? There's always places to go or another book to read. Things to fill the time." He shrugs. "But feeling lonely never goes away. It hits me at random times. Like on the drive to a concert when I have to pull over and cry. Or in the middle of a book chapter when I zone out for who knows how long, only to come back when the pages are soaked with my tears." He squeezes my palm. "You made it go away. That night. With that hug."

I can't sit across from him any longer. I scooch out of my booth and join his side, draping an arm around his shoulders and resting my other on his thigh.

"I want to give my mom a hug with my words," he whispers. "It's all I can do at this point. She's been waiting for that moment for so long, just how I've been waiting for my moment with you."

A lump rises in my throat. I'm grateful I didn't break the news to him about me leaving just now. I want to do this first.

"I'm here for you," I say.

He nods. "I was hoping by the end of the summer I'd be able to hug her in person, but this will have to do." His shoulders sag. He pulls a crumpled piece of paper from his pocket and slides it toward me. "This is what I have to say."

I unfold the letter carefully, my fingers trembling as I read his words.

"How will she know I'm not making this up?" I ask.

"There are a few things I wrote that only she and I would know."

I nod and fold the paper like it's something sacred. "Will you come with me?" I ask.

"I'll take you to my house, but I'd like to stay in the car when you go inside, if that's okay with you."

I rub his thigh. "This is your thing. It's totally okay with me."

He softly pushes his forehead against mine. We share breath, until one too many curious stares from other diners force us out the door.

We arrive at Xander's childhood home just before dusk. His house is pressed up against the sound barrier that separates his neighborhood from the freeway. The view from the back windows must make the house feel like a jail cell, with no view but a gray slab of concrete.

"I'll leave the engine on so you can have the air conditioning," I say.

He nods, avoiding eye contact. "Come back out if she gets weird," he says. "I can always find another way."

I grip his forearm. "I got this. Sit tight."

As soon as I exit the truck, I realize the sound barrier doesn't block much of anything. Honking horns, revving engines, and screeching tires ricochet from the other side of the wall onto the front lawn. The air reeks of engine exhaust, drowning out the usual summer scents of cut grass and barbecue smoke. I steady my breathing and step onto an uneven brick pathway leading to the front porch.

I ring the doorbell.

The white, wooden door swings open instantly, as if she's been waiting.

Maggie Pomers stands behind the screen. Her dark hair flares in all directions, surrounding her head like a black hood. Every feature mourns, from the deep wrinkles on her forehead to the crow's feet carved into her cheeks. Everything except her amber eyes. They glimmer, just slightly, with hope that hasn't fully burned out yet.

I clear my throat. "Hello," I say.

She studies me, then offers a faint smile. "Hello. Do I know you?" she asks.

"I'm Stetson Delancey. We met a few times over at Rainbow Valley Swim Club. I'm the pool inspector."

Her lips part. "Yes, of course. My apologies. I remember now. How are you?"

"I'm fine."

Her eyes wander back to my truck.

Panic rips through me like static electricity. I should've planned this better. I didn't even think about how I would bring up the note or get inside. I don't even know where to start. If I say the wrong thing, I could blow up whatever fragile sense of peace she's built over the years. But I trust Xander's instincts. If he thinks this is the moment, then so do I.

"What can I help you with?" she finally asks.

I straighten my spine. "I was actually . . . I hope this isn't too forward . . . but I was wondering if I could talk to you about your son, Xander."

Her breath hitches. "Ohhh." The sound leaves her mouth through a shudder. "What about?"

"Do you think I could come inside? It might be better if we're sitting."

She tilts her head, hesitating, then gently pushes open the storm door. "Please," she says, gesturing me through the threshold. "Forgive me. It's too hot outside for a conversation anyway."

"Thank you," I say, stepping past her. My fingers press into my pocket where Xander's note waits. "I promise I won't take up too much of your time."

The living room smells like lemon cleaner. Vacuum lines stretch across the beige carpet, and angel figurines stare at me from inside a glass cabinet. A vase of fresh flowers sits on the coffee table, too big for the glass surface yet somehow too small for the room. Above the floral love seat, a painting of Jesus hangs with a prayer card for Xander tucked into the frame.

Maggie moves to the kitchen table and sits, crossing her legs. "Would you like any water?" she asks.

"I'm okay, thank you."

She dusts her lap with her hands. "Is the county keeping the water clean?" She smiles. "Are there any of those toxic chemicals from the news that I should be worried about?" The distant rumble of traffic enters the home through the window over the sink.

I shake my head. "It's all good as far as I know." I pull a chair out from the table and sit.

She hums, nodding.

An image bursts in my mind. A closeted Xander, seventeen, hoodie zipped to his chin, hunched over this same table, eating a bowl of Fruity Pebbles cereal. A lost puppy with nowhere to go.

I'm here to tell her what that boy was feeling.

I shake the thought away.

Maggie folds her hands on the table. "So, is there something going on at Rainbow Valley? I'm afraid your visit is a bit confusing."

290

I bounce my knees. I need to just read the letter.

"Um. I don't know how to say this."

She leans in. "Do you have a tip for Xander's case?" Her voice wavers. "The sheriff has all but stopped communicating with me. If it's a secret, I can keep it."

My stomach tosses my dinner. If I don't talk soon, I might throw up instead.

"It's not that. It's . . . I . . . I've been communicating with Xander." My lips quiver.

She stiffens. "You've what?"

"Talked. Hung out. All summer."

She pushes back from the table and yanks aside the curtains, scanning the front yard. "Where is he?" Her voice rises two octaves. "Why haven't you said anything?"

"It's not like that," I say quickly. "He's . . . I'm the only one who can see him."

She clutches her arms and begins pacing the kitchen. "Excuse me? Is he in hiding?"

I rub my temples. "No, like, he is invisible to everyone except me . . . if that makes sense."

"Of course that doesn't make any sense!" Her voice shakes. "You came here to tell me this? Why? Why would you do this?"

"Because I have a message from him."

I stand. The chair bounces back and topples to the floor. My legs are jelly. She doesn't believe me. I have one shot at changing that. I yank the note from my pocket so fast the paper rips. I start reading.

"*Hi, Mom. I love you.*"

A hiccup leaves the back of her throat.

"*A lot has happened since the day I went missing,*" I continue. "*I've watched you second-guess how you raised me, wondering if you made a mistake somewhere along the way. I want to take that uncertainty away from you. Because I am certain of two things. You knew who I was, and I'm certain you were fine with it."*

Maggie stumbles back.

"I was only taking my time. I knew you'd wait for me because you loved me."

She gasps for breath and trudges to the front door, then throws it open. "This is very disrespectful, Stetson. I'm going to politely ask that you leave my home."

"But I'm not done!" My voice breaks.

She grips the doorknob. "If this were really Xander, he would come here himself."

I flip the note over, searching for something—anything— that only she and Xander would know.

"Please, it's time for you to go." Her voice is steady.

"Thank you for adopting Toby!" I blurt.

Maggie stops cold.

"I'm thankful you gave him a good home to spend his final days."

Her body sags inward as she drifts back to the kitchen table. "How do you know about Toby? Toby is gone. He's been gone. How do you know?"

"I don't. Who is he?"

She sinks into a chair, limbs shaking. "He was . . . an old dog at the Four Paws Animal Hospital. Xander wanted him, but I always said no." She wipes her eyes. "I adopted him after Xander went missing. It was an ugly thing. A mutt. But Xander had a soft spot for him. I felt so bad for never getting that dog." She wheezes. "Toby only lived for about a year after that."

I smile. "Xander loves dogs."

292

"Is there more?" She nods at the note.

"Um." I press my brow and skim the final paragraphs.

"He says he's sorry for how he acted before prom." I raise an eyebrow.

She chokes on a sob, pressing her hands over her mouth.

"You should've been at the prom pictures." The words become harder to read as I fight back my own tears. *"I was upset I didn't have a date and took out my anger on you. I'm sorry we fought. But now I realize you were all I needed."*

She breaks. Her body convulses as she slides from the chair to the floor. I drop the note and lunge for her, catching her in my arms. We melt onto the floor, tight within each other's embrace.

"Where is he?" she wails, her voice breaking into fragments that shatter my ear. "When can he come home to me?"

"I don't know," I whisper. "I don't know."

I look up.

Xander stands in the living room, still as stone, watching us with wide, unblinking eyes like the nearby figurines. His tender face fit to be alongside the angels. My heart splinters for him as if the glass cabinet bursts and sends shards in every direction.

His lips part. He mouths two words. *Thank you.*

His smile is faint, like a flower blooming on winter's darkest day.

What if this is the future I've been searching for, and I'm not meant to leave town? Time has stopped to hold me here, showing me that I have purpose in Penango.

Xander and I aren't trapped in place but connected.

Maybe this past year's impatience was a lesson. If I chase after my future, I'll sprint past the people cheering me on. But

if I pause, if I turn and see them, really see them, I'll find
where I'm meant to run toward.

And the finish line isn't somewhere else.

It's their arms.

47

On the last day of work, Whitley quietly counts a stack of dollar bills at our desk. Her fingers flip through the worn edges while I gather the last remnants of my summer job, like orientation handouts and random doodle pads, and toss them into the recycling bin, clearing my desk for the next temporary worker to take my place.

Victor knocks on our cubicle wall.

"Good morning, Stetson," he says, too chipper for my liking. "Whitley."

"Morning," I reply, my tone flat. A scowl sets deep into my face. He never answered my messages about the recommendation letter.

Whitley doesn't even bother to look up.

"Last day, right?" he asks.

"It is." I rub my hands along my thighs.

"It went fast." He grins.

Not fast enough, I want to say.

"How many inspections do you got left?" he asks.

"None. I just promised Kim and Sheryl at Rainbow Valley Swim Club that someone would help them prepare for next year." I pop in my earbuds, making it very clear I'm not in the mood for small talk.

"See? All that worrying you did at the start of summer, and everything there turned out okay. No one died." He chuckles. "I guess it's not as legendary as they make it out to be."

A bitter taste rises in my throat. No one died there, sure. But two people were never seen again after swimming in their pool. If he only knew what really happened this summer at Rainbow Valley Swim Club. We are the opposite of okay.

I spin my chair away from him, hoping he'll get the hint, when my eyes land on the last piece of paper left on my desk. It's his coffee-stained map that was about as useful this summer as my truck without gas.

"Do you want this back?" I ask, extending the document to him. "I'm cleaning up."

He scrolls through his phone. "Want what?" he asks. His attention doesn't leave the screen.

"This map of Penango you gave me when I first started."

"You can toss it. Or keep it if you want an old sewer map." He smirks as he begins to walk off. "If you think pool inspectors have it rough, try working in the sewage department."

"Sewer map?" I flip to the front page. It's titled *Penango Sewer Service Areas*. I never noticed the name before. I unfold the layers to reveal a tangle of pipes and drainage lines, like a spider sprawled across the county.

My eyes immediately lock onto familiar places like the bend in the river behind Murray's house, the road leading to Whitley's, and the thick woods of the Gregor Preserve, home to the infamous coyote.

And then, a thick red line cuts through the trees. I check the map's legend—*stormwater runoff.*

My fingers trace the pipe's path, following it from the Ardor Tree right to Rainbow Valley. A sharp yelp escapes me. Seeing Penango from above makes everything clear.

"Whitley." My voice shakes.

"Huh?" She barely glances up.

"Come here for a sec."

"What?"

"Just come. Look at this map."

She huffs, evens out her stack of bills with a pat, then shuffles over to my desk.

"What's up?"

I point at the paper. "Where would you say the Ardor Tree is on this map?"

She squints. "Um, somewhere in this area." She taps the tip of the red line.

"And if I said that line is a pipe, what would you say?"

She crosses her arms. "You mean, like, the pipe that the tree grows on top of?"

"I mean exactly that. This map . . . it's like all the puzzle pieces are finally in one place."

Her brows knit together. "I don't follow."

"The pool at Rainbow Valley? It's not a coincidence between Xander, Dara, and me. It's a connection. Like the pipes on this map." My breath shudders. "The Ardor Tree isn't just cursed. Its roots are spreading the curse through these pipes."

She stares at me, the realization setting in.

The Ardor Tree may have cast its curse at its base, but its roots carried out the sentence. I was claimed by them in the woods, their grip swift and unrelenting, maybe because they were starved for a new victim after so many years without one.

But for Xander and Dara, it reached through the sewage system, extending its grasp beneath the pool's surface where the pipes, and the roots' passageways, opened.

It wasn't a lightning strike or drowning child that took them before they blacked out.

It was the Ardor Tree claiming its next victim.

48

Rainbow Valley is eerily quiet when I arrive. The usual hum of music and laughter from campers checking in should be filling the air, but instead, there's only silence.

Sheryl said she'd be here for the close-out inspection, but I count zero people as I look onward from the drive.

Birds chirp overhead, perched safely out of reach, while below, the trees spread across the ground like an unchecked virus. My gaze drifts to the pool, now a crumbling relic of what it once was. Jagged pipes protrude from its decaying cement walls, leading into blackness.

Except for one.

From its opening, roots spill outward in five directions, like gnarled fingers reaching for a ledge. My breath stammers. How many curses have they cast? How many innocent children have fallen into their grips?

It's a small relief knowing we were right about the tree. We weren't just desperate or grasping at straws. We trusted our instincts and now the truth is clear. But the realization doesn't change anything. It won't break the curse.

I search for Xander, eager to tell him what I've learned. Clarity, after ten years, has to be worth something.

"Hey, Stetson," someone says.

My heart jumps. I spin around to find Sheryl walking toward me across the pool deck.

"Hey, Sheryl," I say, exhaling.

"You okay?"

"Yeah," I lie, distracted by the roots. "I was surprised to find the place so empty."

Sheryl thrusts her hands in her pockets. "Oh, yeah. Kim took all the new campers down to the Ardor Tree."

My clipboard slips from my fingers. It clatters against the concrete between my feet. "What?" My voice comes out too loud. "Why?"

"We thought it would be a cute way to start camp. The kids are going to write a word to describe their next school year on the bark. I'm guessing you've heard of it. Most people in Penango have. Queer kids were always left out of the tradition, so we're going to reclaim it as—"

"No!" I shout.

Sheryl steps back.

"It doesn't work like that," I say, my hands flying behind my head. "Oh my god. When did they leave?"

"Not too long ago." Her expression becomes uneasy. "Stetson, what's going on?"

"The tree has rules that can't be broken or else . . . things happen. Bad things!" I motion toward the pool. "Those roots. They're from the Ardor Tree."

She laughs. "Come on. Those rules were made up by old folks in this town."

I suck in a breath through my teeth. "What if I told you the rules weren't made, but cast? Like a curse."

She chuckles again, shaking her head. "When I was in high school at Stillwell Trail, I used to write all these boys' names on the tree, hoping it'd make them like me. It never did. They only ignored me more than before."

"Exactly! So why would you make these kids do that?" I start backing away. "I have to stop them."

"Now, hold on." She raises her hands, signaling me to slow down. "When I met Kim, that all changed. We fell in love, and I carved our names in a heart." She pauses, her face softening with the memory. "Suddenly the boys noticed me. It was like for the first time, they could actually see me. But at that point, I didn't care. It's like the Ardor Tree knew when my carved heart was full of true love."

My whole body stiffens.

True love.

The words slam into me like a punch to the gut. My summer rewinds at warp speed—Xander and me, twirling under twinkle lights, laughing in my truck on the open road, fingers intertwined as we walked through the woods, his body curled against mine in the tree house.

Xander and me, over and over again.

"True love?" I echo, my voice nearly breaking.

"You'll know when you find it." Sheryl nods. "It fixes most things."

A sharp pain shoots across my chest. "I . . ." It's nearly impossible to talk through the knot in my throat. "I really need to go."

Just like all other curses before ours, this one can't withstand true love. The tree allows people to fall out of love, but it rejects lies!

Back in my truck, I grip the wheel, my knuckles white as I speed down the road, swerving between lanes while I call Dara and Xander.

"Meet me at the Ardor Tree now," I instruct.

I don't have time for explanations.

We carved the wrong names into the tree to break the curse. I wrote Murray's when it should've been Xander's. All along, I've been too afraid to admit my feelings for Xander, terrified that letting myself love again would trap me here, just like before. But now it's clear that loving him isn't what's keeping me stuck, it's the only way to escape.

My truck crashes into the road's shoulder for an uneven park job. I exit with my crowbar in hand, my palms slick with sweat.

I take the shortest path through the woods and reach the tree first, but the sound of laughter and high-pitched shrieks echoes behind me.

Twigs snap. Leaves crunch.

The campers are close.

We don't have much time.

I scramble down the rounded hill, following the thick, clawing roots into the sewer pipe. It yawns open before me, a six-foot-high tunnel covered in graffiti. My pulse pounds so hard it feels like it's lifting me off the ground with every step.

I switch on my phone's flashlight to cut through the darkness. A root, twisted like a Twizzler, stretches infinitely along the top of the pipe. I reach for it. A shock zaps through my fingers.

I gasp, then break into a sprint, heading deeper into the shadows. My feet slam into shallow water and send waves crashing against the curved iron walls like a hurtling log flume.

The roots never stop. They aren't searching for moisture, like the pool guy at Rainbow Valley assumed. They're searching for people. People who live and lie for love.

The Ardor Tree's magic isn't just an old Penango legend. It's alive. And it's spreading.

"Stetson! We're here!"

Xander's voice reverberates through the tunnel, stopping my heart as fast as it stops my feet. I turn back. A sliver of sunlight remains in my vision.

"Xander!" I yell, sprinting toward the opening. "I know how to fix it! We can break the curse!"

I leap through the tunnel's mouth and collide into Xander. He groans. Dara stands beside him, dressed in all black, looking unimpressed as usual.

I grip Xander's forearms. "Stetson, what's going on?" he asks, breathless. "Why are all these people here?"

"Please tell me this was worth sticking around Penango," Dara says, folding her arms.

Above us, the campers crowd the tree's base, chatting and giggling as they press their hands to the bark. Their bright outfits form a rainbow before the storm.

I lick my lips. "It all clicked today. We were right. The tree cursed us. It punishes rule breakers, and its roots run through the sewer system so no one can escape. The curse spreads across the whole county!" I point into the tunnel's darkness. "This pipe leads straight to Rainbow Valley."

Xander and Dara trace the roots with their eyes as their expressions darken.

"Well, now that we got the backstory," Dara quips, "what do we do? Tear up these roots? We already tried rewriting our names." She reaches for a root, but it zaps her before she can touch it. "Ouch!" She sucks on her finger. "Damn, I hate this thing."

"That's where we were wrong," I say.

I pull Xander up the hill, pushing aside campers who block our path to the trunk. Dara follows.

"Excuse you!" a camper squeals.

"Hello, hot camp counselor," one boy says under his breath.

"What are we going to write now?" Xander asks as we reach the tree.

At my feet lies the same jagged rock I used to destroy my heart with Murray's name. I pick it up and place it in Dara's hands.

"Take this and carve someone's name in a heart. Someone you truly love."

Her lips part. "Even if it's not a boy?"

I nod. "As long as it's honest."

With a deep breath, she vanishes behind the trunk.

I turn to Xander, searching his face. "Back in your tree house," I say, my voice shaking, "you told me I could be the name for your blank space. Did you mean it?"

He raises his eyebrows. "What?"

"You said you had an extra chair for someone to sit." I swallow. "The same person who could fill the blank space in your heart. Can it be me?"

His face flushes. "Well, yeah. I was hoping it would be all summer."

"Then trust me on this."

I nod before starting to carve my newest heart.

One that's true.

"Stetson!" Kim yells. She steps in front of the onlooking campers. "What are you doing here?"

"These. Kids. Can't. Touch. This. Tree." I etch each letter of my name with my crowbar. "It. Is. Cursed." I gasp for breath. "Only. People. In. Love. Belong. Here."

The heart comes together faster than any before. I drop the crowbar to admire my work, my chest heaving, fixing the curse for both of us.

304

"*Xander and Stetson,*" Xander reads.

"Xander and Stetson," I repeat.

He stares. "You're in love with me?"

Suddenly, the tree moans to life.

A sonic boom erupts from its core and sends shock waves through the ground, rattling our knees. Everyone shudders. Campers shriek and grab on to each other. Xander jumps into my arms.

I find Louise and Abigail's pentacle on the bark, and it glows bright like the sun.

"Stetson!" Dara yells. She crawls toward me on the shifting earth.

I reach for her, but hundreds of leaves break free from their stems and plunge like nose-diving planes. My hand recoils. They spiral into a tornado. The suction lifts Xander's curls and wraps his shark-tooth chain tight around his neck. Dara's shirt flaps like a flag.

I hold on to Xander with everything I have.

"Is it working?" he shouts over the storm.

"I think so!" I respond.

Then—silence.

As quickly as they started, the tree's movements stop. The whirlwind dies.

I'm the first to face the consequences of our actions. The leaves rain to the ground and pile up to our knees. My clothes are nearly inside out, my hair sticks in all directions.

We gasp for breath.

"Xander, it's done," I whisper, shaking him. "You can open your eyes."

His body trembles. Slowly, he opens one eye, then the other.

"I'm ready now," I say, cupping his cheeks.

He exhales. "You still haven't said—"

Before he can finish, I kiss him.

A rush of sweetness floods my mouth like biting into a Starburst. At first, he's stiff, then he melts into me. He grabs my neck and kisses me back, forcefully, with pressure, like he's thought about this for ten years.

The campers applaud and whistle.

"Is this a theatre camp?" one girl asks. "Because I love this show."

"Right?" a boy echoes. "The special effects are slaying. Where did the other guy and girl appear from?"

"God, I'm jealous," another boy groans. "I thought this camp was supposed to make me feel better about myself."

We separate, laughing.

"You are late," Xander says.

"And you are right on time," I say.

"Maybe that's by design." He looks to the tree.

"I'm sorry I took so long," I say.

Xander presses his forehead to mine. "Stetson, I've waited my whole life," he says. "I'd give up another decade just for one more day with you."

He turns. His face flushes as the dozens of campers stare directly at him. "I can't believe it." He pats his chest, testing his new reality. "I get to start over."

"No." I shake my head. "You get a second chance to keep going."

Dara clears her throat. "I didn't know I was third wheeling this whole time," she says, brushing leaves from her arms.

I smile. "We kind of just figured it out ourselves," I say.

"Speak for yourself," Xander says. "I knew the day I saw you."

I gasp.

"Who did you write?" I ask Dara.

She exhales. "Ra-Ra." Her heels bounce. "I gave that girl too hard of a time when I was younger. Learned to love her over the years."

My gaze drifts upward and gets lost in the Ardor Tree's vast crown. Its leaves glow in the sunlight, translucent and trembling like thousands of tiny, beating hearts. Thick branches stretch wide, their shadows cast like protective arms over every couple.

Maybe it is a good matchmaker after all.

For the first time, I notice just how high the trunk reaches. It towers above every tree in the forest, rising above the rest of Penango.

I've spent too long looking down, trying to cover dust from broken hearts and tear out my roots. That's how I thought I'd escape.

But now I realize all I had to do was stand on them and lift my head.

The names covering the bark blur together. There's too many to count. I no longer see them as ghosts of the past or couples to envy. They morph into an ascending map—every couple, or individual, a guide along the journey—not to what has been, but to everything that still could be.

49

Later, Xander walks out of the pharmacy with two tote bags stuffed with candy.

I thought we'd head straight to his mom after breaking the curse, but nope, we had to stop for sweets first. He figured once he reunited with her, she wouldn't let him stockpile sugar like this. Apparently, she hated his sweet tooth. But I have a feeling that after ten years apart, she'll let him do whatever he wants. I lean across the center console and push open the passenger door as his beaming smile nears my truck.

"That was insane!" he squeals, tossing the bags on the floor and hopping in. "The moment I stepped inside, a worker said *hi* to me. Then I bumped into a woman in the candy aisle, and she apologized. She looked at me. They saw me!" He's breathless. "When I checked out, the cashier handed me the receipt and our fingers brushed. I felt his finger! Can you believe that?"

"I don't want to," I say. "Not if other guys are out there holding your hand."

He grins and hands me a chocolate bar. "Don't worry. No one else's touch makes my heart stop like yours." His nose wrinkles.

"Barf," Dara says from the back seat. "Can I have my credit card back?"

"Yeah." Xander flips it into her lap. "Thanks for the treat. I'll try to start making my own money soon."

"You better," she says. "I thought you were getting a candy bar, not the whole Halloween aisle."

"Oh, his addiction is real," I say.

"I hope Stetson still likes you when your teeth fall out," Dara says, swiping a pack of M&M's from Xander's lap.

His face falls. "I hadn't thought of that. I'm going to get cavities now. And stomach aches. And sunburn. And wrinkles. And under-eye bags. We need to change me back."

I laugh. "I think once you see your mom, all this will feel worth it. Should we take you home?"

Dara clears her throat. "Can you drop me at the bus station first? I need to get back to Fairmont."

I glance at her. "You don't want to see your family?"

"I do," she says softly. "But just my mom. And she's not in Penango. She's the only one who never gave up on me."

"Where is she?"

"I don't know." She hums and looks out the window. "But I've got a feeling the winding roads will take me to her. Just like they took you to me."

We drive without a word. Xander munches on Sour Patch Kids while Dara stares out at the passing fields, her black hair swirling in the wind.

I won't miss the cursed life, but I'll miss cruising around town with two people who understood me instantly, when the rest of town couldn't figure me out in eighteen years.

At the bus station, only one other person is waiting to leave Penango. Most are still choosing to stay.

Dara hops out just as the bus rolls into the lot.

She leans through Xander's open window. "Hey, you two. Don't let anyone tell you your love doesn't belong on the Ardor Tree."

My cheeks warm. "When will we see you again?"

She looks to the sky. "Let's meet at the Ardor Tree next summer. We'll make it our annual reunion."

"Deal," I say. "We can make sure no other kids repeat our mistake."

She shrugs. "Or maybe we let them learn their lesson."

"No!" Xander blurts. "Some lessons don't need to be taught twice."

Dara and I laugh.

"Take this," Xander says, tossing her a pack of gum. "I've got a feeling there's going to be a lot of kissing in your future. The boys haven't seen a face that pretty in years."

She rolls her eyes and walks backward toward the bus. "Good luck at college, Stetson!" She waves. "Good luck at life, Xander! Don't blow your second chance! I know I won't."

I glance over and catch Xander wiping a tear. "Are you crying?" I ask.

"Maybe," he says. "I forgot how much it hurts when people leave."

"That's what makes reunions so special." I place my hand on his knee. "Let's bring you home."

A few minutes later, we pull up to his house. The white front door is shut tight. The sun glints off the freeway sound barrier, casting a shimmer on the pavement.

"Will you come in with me?" Xander asks.

I exhale. "This is a moment between you and your mom."

"Maybe you can knock like last time," he says. "Tell her that you've been talking to me in secret, and I'll pop out from the bushes."

310

I shake my head, smiling. "I think that was traumatic for her. Just walk inside."

He scratches his neck. "Well, what if I write her another letter and you read it to her first?"

"Hey." I take his hand and squeeze it. "It's going to be okay."

His lips tremble. "How do you know that?"

I swallow and lean a little closer. "You know what I realized this summer?" He lifts his gaze, eyes glossy. "That the universe really doesn't factor enough time into our lives. Not for me. Not for you. Not for anyone. And deep down, we all feel it. We wish for more time. We try to freeze the best moments, stretch them out, hold them tighter." I pause. "When time stopped for me, I started to see why the people around me might've hurt me. They weren't trying to. They were just reacting to a world that's fleeting. Maybe your mom stayed quiet back then not because she didn't care but because she didn't want to ruin what time you had together. Maybe she was trying to protect that moment the only way she knew how." Xander looks toward his house. "Even now, she waits in silence, doing her best to freeze time in case it brings you back, just like how it took you."

He doesn't speak for a long second.

I take his chin in my hand. "Her face is going to light up," I say. "The curse is broken. You don't have to worry."

He finally exhales. "She won't look past me?"

"I bet she won't be able to look away from you."

He nods, flicking a tear from his nose. "I love you," he says.

"I love you too."

"I'll see you later?"

"You'll see me later, tomorrow, and every day after that."

He steps out, walks slowly down the uneven brick path, and knocks.

As I drive down the street, I hear a joyous shriek, like someone unwrapping a puppy on Christmas morning.

Dara and Xander aren't the only ones with big reunions ahead. Mine might not be as happy, but it's necessary. I need to finish what I started this summer. I need to end things with Murray once and for all—so that this time, he understands.

I take a sharp right toward Penango College.

As soon as I pull into campus, I spot him, Murray's unmistakable sulk moving through the chain-link gate behind the football stadium. I shift into park before the truck fully stops, gears grinding as my body jerks forward.

The sound catches his attention. His head snaps up, eyes locking on mine. He doesn't hesitate. He starts toward me.

I step out, rolling my neck.

The distance between us feels endless, even though it's barely a dozen yards. We meet in the shadow of the bleachers, standing inches apart, where he thought we'd spend the next four years. I scuff the toe of my sneaker against the pavement.

"Hey, Murray." My voice is steady. "Long time."

He lets out a dry laugh. "Yeah. It feels like forever."

"How is football camp?" I press the back of my hand against my forehead to block the sun glare.

"Hot. Brutal." He scans me from head to toe. "You look different."

I smirk. "I look the same."

He glances over his shoulder. "Do you have time for a walk?"

I frown. "I can't. I just wanted to stop by before leaving for college."

His fingers clamp tighter around the helmet at his side.

"Look," he says, rubbing the back of his neck. "I'm sorry for how everything went down between us. After graduation. But even before that too."

I keep my face neutral. "I appreciate that."

His jaw tightens. "I'm sorry for not being what you needed." He looks to the ground, shaking his head. "For not saying the right things. Or doing the right things. For pushing you." His voice cracks. "I don't know."

The late summer air thickens between us.

There's so much I could say. I could tell him how much he hurt me, how confused I've been all year, how I spent my summer nights going over our conversations like a record stuck on repeat. But there's also so much I've already let go. Standing here now, it all seems different, like a memory that doesn't feel so heavy anymore.

"You tried," I say finally. "You just weren't ready." His eyes flick back to mine. "And you weren't supposed to be."

He shifts on his feet. "All summer during practice, I kept looking for you in the bleachers here. I thought maybe, one day, you'd show up. Just like before." I stare at the sweat beading across his forehead. "I wish I could remember the last time I saw you up there. You always looked so cute." A shaky smile tugs at his cheek.

I know the exact Friday night he stopped looking for me. If only it had mattered to him then as much as it does now.

"I miss you," he admits. "You were my best friend." A lone tear slips down his cheek. He reaches out to me but quickly snaps his hands back to his sides.

My heart skips a beat.

"I miss what we had," I say, and I mean it. He was part of my story. The chapter that led me to Xander. How can I not be grateful for that?

"I understand." He nods, exhaling hard, then wipes his nose with his forearm. "So, we're good?"

"Yeah, Murray. We can be good." I drop my arm, and the sun burns my nose. "We're not the same people we were when we were sophomores."

"I wish we were," he says. "I'd do anything to go back to sophomore year."

I could tell Murray that's the last thing I'd ever want, to go back in time and relive high school, but I'll give him the past, now that I have my future.

"Have a good football season," I say instead, retreating.

"Thanks." His voice is quieter now. He clears his throat. "Have fun in Tennessee. I'm glad you made it."

I pause, letting my brow furrow. "Are you actually?"

But my words get lost to the air between us. He's already walking away, still avoiding the questions that scare him most.

In the silence that follows, all mine are answered.

50

Next week, the sky is as blue as a brand-new pool.

Whitley finishes packing the last of her things into my truck bed while Bennie, injected with a fresh rabies booster vaccine and finally able to move at a near-normal pace, sniffs through the boxes.

"Is that everything?" I ask.

Whitley nods, then slams the hatch closed. "Whatever we don't have, we can buy on the road."

"This isn't fair," Xander says from the curb, his arms crossed. He wears an orange bucket hat that shades his frown and big, round sunglasses. "I finally appear, and everyone has to leave."

I reach for his hand. "Are you sure you don't want to come? I know we planned our visits, but we can still change it."

He rubs slow circles into my palm with his thumb. "Yeah, I'm sure. I'm just messing with you. You've worked so hard for this. This is your and Whitley's dream. And . . . I need to be here to spend time with my mom."

I smile. "You're right. That'll be so great."

Maggie Pomers stands a few yards behind us, her eyes never straying from her son. She hasn't let him out of her sight since his unexpected return, hovering like a protective force, just like the news cameras clicking in the distance.

Dad placed lawn chairs at both ends of the block to keep the reporters from getting too close, but they don't seem to be giving up anytime soon. After ten years of chasing Xander's mystery, they're obsessed with tracking him now, desperate to know where he's been, what happened, and where he's going.

We talked about whether telling the truth or spinning a lie would attract less attention. Xander knows from his years of reading true-crime cases that staying silent makes the story die faster. I know from my podcasts that the news cycle moves quickly. Another case, mystery, or person will replace him soon.

We're committed to playing the long game, something Xander has perfected over the last decade.

Mom storms out of the house with two bags of groceries. "These are just snacks to hold you over," she says as she stomps across the yard. "You can't live off what's in these bags for your whole trip. You hear me?" She drops the bags next to my truck. "You need to stop for meat, vegetables, and fruit every now and then. Do not arrive at college skinnier than you are now." She whacks my arm.

"Don't forget this," Dad shouts. He emerges from the garage, balancing a case of beer on his shoulder. Mom crosses her arms with a huff. "Don't drink this while driving," he mumbles.

I laugh, shaking my head.

County precedent excluded me from its traditions. I wasn't supposed to leave. My broken promise on the Ardor Tree was meant to trap me here. My grades were supposed to go unnoticed, and my cross-country achievements were meant to be forgotten. But my parents helped rewrite the rules.

"Also," Mom says, lifting a finger. "Can we keep this one?" She grabs Xander's shoulders, shaking him with a growl. "He's so mature for his age." Then pulls him closer. "And so stinking cute."

I laugh. "I plan to."

Xander blushes.

"Good," Mom says. "Don't fall for those college temptations."

Maggie crosses her arms. "He's all mine for the time being."

Whitley loads the food into my truck before climbing into the passenger seat. Bennie hops in the back, panting. I move toward the driver's side but skip to Xander instead for a final goodbye.

Every kiss with him is unlike the last. I don't know his body movements as well as I know Murray's. I hesitate, sometimes unsure if I'm pleasing him or doing something wrong. His legs move more than Murray's when we kiss, maybe because they tingle like mine. He touches my face more too, and I'm learning I like that. I usually trace his jawline in return. His curls are fun to grab, so different from the close buzz I'm used to.

I memorize these things like our own secret language. Because kissing someone without regret makes me never stop wanting more.

His hugs are different too. His hands press against the center of my back, while Murray's were always near my hips. I have to hunch my shoulders when I nuzzle into him, whereas with Murray, I had to rise onto my tiptoes.

But I like it all. It's new and promising, and something to hold on to rather than push away.

When our lips separate, Xander digs through his backpack. "A few more things," he says.

"What is it?"

He unpacks a green Polaroid camera and holds it out in front of us. He quickly removes his bucket hat and sunglasses.

"Smile," he instructs. We look at the camera, but right before he takes the picture, he turns and kisses me on the cheek.

I giggle. "Hey!"

The camera clicks and instantly prints out the photograph. Xander shakes the film in the air before handing it to me. "The first picture for your bulletin board in Tennessee."

I glance at the photo, and it captures both of us.

Xander is there. Clear, colorful, and present.

I swallow hard. "I'll need more than one."

Xander grins. "If you insist."

We take a dozen more photos, all while making silly faces, sticking out our tongues, throwing up peace signs, and landing more stolen kisses.

"Guys, it's cute," Whitley says from the truck. "But I'd like to get on the road before dark."

Xander laughs. "Sorry, Whitley! One more thing."

She sighs.

"More?" I ask.

He reaches for the shark-tooth chain around his neck and unhooks it. "I want to give this to you." He dangles it between us. "So you can have something of mine. It's not much, but I wore it all summer, when it was just the two of us, when time stood still."

I take it from him, my fingers shaking. "It's everything." I fasten it around my neck. It falls against my chest, warm, like the weight of one of his tightest hugs.

"It suits you," he says softly.

A small, closed-lip smile spreads across my face. I take in his fire-emblem eyes one last time. He winks before lifting his sunglasses back onto the bridge of his nose, then blows me a kiss.

"Watch the truck, Xander!" Maggie calls from the yard as Whitley starts the engine.

"I'm about to run y'all over just to wrap up this goodbye party!" she shouts from the passenger seat.

Maggie tugs Xander back toward the grass.

I climb into my truck. The engine rumbles beneath me. As I begin the long drive to Tennessee, I glance in the rearview mirror one last time.

Mom, Dad, and Xander don't stop waving, even as Whitley and I descend the hill and disappear.

I never thought I'd look back when I left. But just like Penango's mountains are ever present and unchanging, I know my friends and family will be too.

EPILOGUE

I won the Keystone Rural Youth Mathematician scholarship on the second day of our road trip.

For the first time in as long as I could remember, I felt pure relief.

When I got into college, I had to figure out which choice would disappoint my parents the least. Once I broke up with Murray, every conversation afterward felt like a never-ending sad song trying to define what we were. After I enrolled at the University of Tennessee, I had to wait for financial aid, unsure if I could even afford to go.

There was always something else to do, another hurdle to moving on.

But not with the scholarship. The money was mine. No conditions. The weight was gone.

As the fall semester in Tennessee wrapped up, my anticipation turned toward the day I could drive back down Main Street again with Xander and Whitley by my side. It was like waiting for the leaves to change color: knowing it was coming, but unable to do anything to make it happen faster.

Now, I pull into the hardware store's parking lot as the first snow of December begins to fall, soft and steady, from the night sky. I left Penango when the trees were green and lush from the summer heat, and now I've returned to find them brittle and dead, stripped bare by the cold. And yet, here I am, after so much life has happened.

I'm home from Tennessee a day early. My favorite person doesn't finish their shift until eight p.m., but I don't have the patience to wait a few more hours just to hug them.

Inside, I'm greeted by inflatable snowmen, glowing plastic reindeer, and the sharp scent of sawdust and metal. "I'll Be Home for Christmas" plays from the speakers. A quick scan of the registers doesn't reveal who I'm looking for. Neither does the paint area.

The long aisles and towering shelves remind me of the endless days I spent searching the woods of the Gregor Preserve last summer.

Then the garden center doors slide open, sending a swirl of flurries around my head.

And there they are.

Even with their back to me, I spot them instantly by the Christmas trees, donned with an orange apron and a black-and-white Pittsburgh Penguins hat pulled over their hair.

My pace quickens. Wet snow lands on my warm cheeks.

People move all around me, but I don't count them anymore. I've left the small numbers behind. I've crossed state lines and seen how big the world is. It's more comforting to think of myself as one of eight billion than to feel like one of only six.

They're mid-conversation with a customer, some guy who has no idea how lucky he is just to be speaking with them, shaking their hand. He has no clue that I've waited months for this moment.

He'll have to pardon my interruption.

I tap their shoulder. "Excuse me," I say. "I need help finding a six-foot Fraser fir Christmas tree."

Whitley Wyomen turns, brows pressed. "Give me one second. I am—"

Her eyes soften the second she sees me.

"Stetson!" she shrieks.

The man beside her stumbles backward, startled, as she throws herself into my arms. We crash into the stack of Christmas trees, laughing as pine needles rain down on us.

"What are you doing here? What day is it?" she asks, breathless.

"I'm early," I answer, grinning.

"I'm sorry," the man interrupts. "Should I find someone else to help me with my tree?"

Whitley spins, already untying her apron. "Yeah. I'm clocking out. Nathan can help you." She points to another worker one aisle over. The man hesitates, then trudges away.

"I can't believe it," she says.

"Believe what?"

"That we're back together. We have so much to catch up on. I need to tell you how I fought off an alligator in the Everglades a couple weeks ago."

My earbuds are packed deep in my duffel bag, far out of reach, so I can hear every word she speaks.

"Let's get out of here," she says. "Are you hungry? I haven't been to the Bean since I got home."

"Starving."

In the parking lot, I snap a selfie with the mountains behind me, the familiar rolling peaks standing tall against the early evening sky. *Guess who's back a day early?* I caption the photo before sending it to Xander.

Even though we've talked nearly every day since I left for school in August, distance has a way of hiding life's little details. I wonder how time has shaped him since the curse was broken. Have the lines around his mouth deepened from more frequent smiles? Has the skin under his eyes darkened from sleepless nights?

How has time carved its mark?

His response comes immediately with a selfie of his own. His golden-orange eyes burn bright. They're the perfect color to keep me warm through the break.

Then I notice he's holding something in his hand. I pinch the screen and zoom in with my fingers. My breath catches. It's two tickets to Pittsburgh's pop radio station's holiday ball—our first concert.

I squeal.

I don't even know who's playing this year, but it doesn't matter. There're always a dozen artists, enough live music to scream until my throat burns and to dance like the whole arena is my stage. I'm sure people will look at me funny, but that's my dream—to be a dot in the crowd, among the thousands who wanted to be a part of something bigger.

I lower my phone and glance past the garden center fence, taking in the town I once dreamed of escaping. But now everything beyond it feels new again, like entering the woods after the snow has melted.

Murray is out there somewhere. I hope that he's better, doing okay.

Whitley grabs my hand, grounding me before I can float too far into my thoughts. She tugs me toward Main Street, beneath the glow of old streetlights with brighter bulbs, laughing as flurries catch in her hair.

I always thought leaving Penango would be the greatest feeling in the world. But coming back, after promising myself I never would, hits just as hard.

Turns out, life isn't simple math. Two things can be true at once.

County lines are meant to be crossed, in both directions.

Hometowns are places we outgrow yet somehow always belong to.

And there's no spot more magical to fall in love—or have my heart broken—than beneath the Penango sky.

Brian Zepka is an award-winning author and environmental scientist born and raised outside Philadelphia, Pennsylvania. His debut young adult novel, *The Temperature of Me and You*, was a Brazilian bestseller and honored as the best translated young adult stand-alone novel of 2022 at the Tres Cantos International Festival of Children's and Youth Literature. Outside of writing, Brian works in global sustainability research, while pursuing his doctorate in public health at Johns Hopkins University. Learn more at www.brianzepka.com.